8-89

1695

W9-BFP-067

Lutz

TIME
EXPOSURE

TIME EXPOSURE

JOHN LUTZ

ST. MARTIN'S PRESS
NEW YORK

DESIGN BY CLAUDIA CARLSON

Library of Congress Cataloging-in-Publication Data

Lutz, John.
    Time exposure / John Lutz.
       p.   cm.
    "A Thomas Dunne book."
    ISBN 0-312-02990-X
    I. Title.
  PS3562.U854T5   1989
  813'.54—dc19   89-4180
                                  CIP

First Edition

10 9 8 7 6 5 4 3 2 1

Time, the avenger! unto thee I lift
My hands, and eyes, and heart, and crave of
Thee a gift.

> —BYRON, *Childe Harold*

Who knows what may be slumbering in the
background of time!

> —SCHILLER, *Don Carlos*

TIME
EXPOSURE

At first they thought she was crossing the street to buy doughnuts. Nudger was seated at the stainless steel counter in Danny's Donuts, just passing the time, when he noticed the sad-eyed Danny gazing beyond him out the wide, grease-spotted window at Manchester Avenue. Swiveling on his stool, Nudger saw a slender blond woman pause for a bus to pass, then, with a cautious glance for eastbound traffic, run the rest of the way across the rain-glistening street. She had on high heels but still moved gracefully and with surprising speed. A treat to watch.

"Ain't she a cute little bit of pastry?" Danny said. He related everything to his baking. The ultimate compliment would have been to call the woman a Dunker Delite—Danny's specialty. No doubt he needed a closer look at her before granting her that culinary honor.

He wasn't going to get a closer look. The woman squinted up at the low gray sky, as if to assure herself that it was still raining, then veered slightly and opened the door next to that of the doughnut shop. Nudger heard the metallic scrape of the latch and the vacuum swish of the door closing. The door that led to a narrow stairwell, that led to a door on the second-floor landing, that led to the center of the web: Nudger's office.

Danny grinned. "A client, Nudge!"

Nudger sort of resented his tone of voice, which suggested that clients were so infrequent they rated amazement. It wasn't like that at all. Surprise, maybe, but not amazement.

Nudger listened to the ascending *tap tap tap* of high heels on the steep wooden stairs on the other side of the west wall. Then silence. She'd reached the landing. He listened for a knock on his office door but couldn't hear it. Too far away. Wall too thick.

He said, "What if she's here to serve a subpoena?" His former wife, Eileen, was after him with rare vengeance to pay back alimony into her already swollen bank account.

Danny flicked the counter with the frayed gray towel he always kept tucked in his belt. Crumbs flew like shrapnel. "Naw, not her, Nudge. She don't look like no subpoena server."

"They're tricky sometimes."

"Not *that* tricky."

"Remember the time I thought I was accepting literature to get rid of a Jehovah's Witness?"

"This one's different."

Nudger wasn't so sure about that. He was more cynical than the simple and trusting Danny. Everyone was more cynical than Danny, who said, "Only one way to find out, Nudge."

True enough. Nudger left the uneaten half of his Dunker Delite on its white paper napkin. It reminded him of something wounded lying on a stretcher. He nodded good-bye to Danny, got down off his stool, and carried his foam cup of acidic coffee out of the doughnut shop.

It was still miserably close and hot outside, though twenty degrees cooler than it had been an hour ago. September in St. Louis, the unpredictable month in the schizophrenic city. The weather could swing to any extreme this time of year, sometimes within hours. Drizzle that was almost mist still rode the air. Wavering moisture was rising like restless spirits from the pavement. The concrete remained warm from the afternoon sun that had taken cover behind leaden clouds.

Nudger swiveled on his heel and made a sharp U-turn to the left, opened the street door, and climbed the narrow, steep stairs toward his office door. The landing was empty. Since he'd only run downstairs for an early, doughy supper at Danny's Donuts, he'd left the office unlocked. There was no way anyone could go upstairs without him or Danny noticing. The woman would be inside waiting for him. He was glad he hadn't switched off the air conditioner.

He left the heat of the landing and entered the coolness of his office.

The office wasn't exactly a rat-hole. Not exactly. Sparsely but rather neatly furnished, it had a desk, typewriter, file cabinets, a window, a door to a cramped half-bath. Didn't have an anteroom. The blond woman was standing hipshot near his desk, staring at him.

He said, "I'm Nudger."

She said, "It smells like doughnuts in here."

"From downstairs," Nudger said. "Danny's Donuts. You should try one. You should try everything once."

"Then I'm on the right track. This is the first time I've attempted to hire a private investigator."

Okay, no subpoena. She *was* a client. Prospective one, anyway. She might want Nudger to do something he didn't want to do. Something dangerous. He was particular about the cases he accepted. Kept him poor but alive. And kept his nervous stomach—the reason he'd resigned from the St. Louis police department twelve years ago—from getting out of control and digesting itself.

He flashed the old sweet smile and motioned with his arm for the woman to sit in the wooden chair in front of the desk. She smiled back and sat. He walked around behind his desk and lowered himself into his swivel chair. It squealed as it always did when he sat down. The woman winced at the piercing sound. He noticed her hair and clothes were damp from the rain. Wondered if she'd forgotten her umbrella.

—— 3 ——

She said, "My name's Adelaide Lacy, Mr. Nudger. Do you . . . er, have a first name?"

"I do, but I never use it unless I have to. Keeps things simpler and less laughable. Just Nudger will do fine." He swiveled slightly in the chair, this way and that. *Eeek eeek.* "You have a problem you need help with, Miss Lacy?"

"I'm afraid so."

He looked at her more closely. She was upset about something, all right. All mussed by external and internal stormy weather, all wild blond hair and wild blue eyes, haunted by the lightning. That was what had driven her to Nudger's office. She made Nudger, who was used to dumpy divorcees and pilfered cash registers, feel a little like Sam Spade. It was an inflating sensation.

He waited for her to get to her problem. Didn't push. Patience was essential in his business. She shifted position nervously in the chair. The action allowed a glimpse of startlingly pale legs with slender ankles. The word "thoroughbred" came to mind.

"First off, are you busy now? I mean, can you take on a new case?"

Nudger nodded to the ankles. He could handle six new cases and still have time to make a quilt, but he wouldn't tell Adelaide Lacy that. All of a sudden a sheet of rain hit the window hard enough to rattle the glass, as if out of malice. It was getting gusty outside. Nastier. Maybe blowing in another drastic change in the weather.

He sized up Adelaide Lacy for potential to pay. She was wearing a plain navy blue dress. Her clothes were medium-price and made no pretense of high fashion. She was about thirty-five, neatly groomed except for the muss from the rain, and wore no wedding ring. She didn't appear to be the sort you'd run to with the notion of financing a business venture, but she looked as if she could afford Nudger's piddling fee. All things being equal, he'd take her case. The alternative was another round of conversation with Danny, another Dunker

Delite. And another and another. Until he was swimming in grease and bitter coffee.

"What exactly's your problem, Miss Lacy? When I know that, I'll be able to tell you if the job and I are compatible." The old hard-to-get act.

It worked; she got to the point. "These," she said, and removed a square brown envelope from her purse and leaned forward to place it on his desk. "You better look, then I'll explain."

He opened the damp envelope and withdrew an eight-by-ten black and white photograph of a downtown St. Louis street. He recognized the street. Locust Avenue, a north-south thoroughfare in the heart of the city. The photograph was sharp. There were no people or traffic in it, only buildings.

Beneath the first photo was a second, a blowup of one of the buildings, the Arcade Building. It was an old but refurbished office building Nudger had been in more than once.

There was a curious thing about that photograph. All the windows in the building seemed to reveal empty rooms. All except one. In that window was a heavyset, balding man seated at a desk. A pen in his hand was plainly visible. His head was bowed and cocked to the side slightly, a bit awkwardly, as if he might have been considering what he was about to write. He was in perfect focus; Nudger could count the buttons on his shirt. He looked familiar, but Nudger couldn't place him. A ghost from a dream.

Something about the photographs made Nudger uneasy. He placed them on his desk, squared them carefully with his fingertips. Looked up at Adelaide Lacy, who was staring at him with her intent blue eyes.

"Can I get you something to drink, Miss Lacy?" Nudger asked. He wanted to slow the pace of this encounter. He was experiencing unpleasant intimations and needed time to think. He didn't want to take on anything that might get him hurt or killed, but he knew he probably would. He had no choice, really. His unpaid bills were piling up. And Eileen's lawyer, a

—— 5 ——

snappy dresser with a dorsal fin, was getting serious about dragging Nudger back into court, where there would be a feeding frenzy around his meager assets. "I could run downstairs and get you a soda or cup of coffee."

"Call me Adelaide," she said, forcing a smile. "And no thanks, I'm not thirsty. Last week a free-lance photographer named Paul Dobbs came to see me at my apartment with those." She nodded toward the photographs on the desk. "He said he'd been commissioned by an architectural firm to take photos of certain downtown streets. His employer was interested in the buildings, nothing else. So Dobbs used special film and took forty-five-minute time exposures during the evenings, when it was still light but the streets were virtually deserted."

"Very long exposure time," Nudger said.

"And for good reason," Adelaide told him. "As Dobbs explained it, at that slow exposure rate, occasional passing vehicles, or pedestrians, wouldn't show up in the photo; they'd be moving too fast for their images to form on film. There could be a bank holdup on those streets and it wouldn't appear in the photograph."

Nudger understood. The same held true of any movement inside the windows of the photographed buildings. That was why all the rooms in the Arcade Building appeared empty. All but one. Nudger felt a cold weight in his stomach. He liked the drift of this conversation less and less. Soon his insides would be forcibly reminding him that he was ill-suited by temperament for his work.

He rummaged around in the top desk drawer until he found a roll of antacid tablets. Peeled back the aluminum foil and popped one of the chalky white disks into his mouth. Chewed lustily.

Adelaide confirmed what he was thinking. "Dobbs told me the only way that man could appear so sharply focused in the window would be if he was as still as the building itself. If he was dead."

Nudger's stomach kicked. Dead. Gee, he disliked that word.

Felt uneasy about this case. Didn't want this conversation to go any further.

He knew he was at the balance point—one way or the other, in or out. Fish or cut bait, whatever that meant.

More rain. A sudden, noisy downpour. Lightning flashed like a warning. Thunder rumbled like the threat of a collection agency.

Nudger sighed. "What else did Paul Dobbs say?"

2

Adelaide shifted in her chair, obviously made uncomfortable by the thought of what she was about to tell Nudger. Nylon swished as she crossed her elegant legs the other way. Nudger drew a deep breath. She drew an even deeper one and began.

"Dobbs noticed the man in the window in one of his photographs, blew up the scene, and took it to a friend who's a reporter on the *Post-Dispatch*. Said he thought the man was dead. The reporter told him he was crazy, that the city leased that floor of the Arcade Building, and that the man in the photo was Virgil Hiller, the assistant city comptroller."

Oh-oh! Face and name suddenly connected in Nudger's mind. And in a manner that caused anxiety. He popped another antacid tablet into his mouth and rolled it across his tongue to waiting molars.

"The next day Hiller and his secretary disappeared," Adelaide said, "along with half a million dollars in city funds."

Nudger watched a gray and white pigeon flap awkwardly to perch on the ledge outside the window. It wanted to get out of the rain. If pigeons had that much sense. It defecated on the ledge. Jesus, he hated pigeons! Winged rats!

He said, "I read in the papers about the disappearance of Hiller and his secretary. And the money. That kind of thing happens. Maybe they're on the beach somewhere in Bimini in the Bahamas."

"No," Adelaide said firmly, and pursed her red, red lips. "They're not anyplace like that." She sounded certain.

Nudger considered the Arcade Building photograph. "Hiller's disappearance made Dobbs all the more suspicious of murder?" he ventured.

"Yes. But the comptroller, and even Mayor Faherty, claimed they saw Hiller alive the morning *after* Dobbs's photograph was taken."

"Dobbs buy their story?"

Adelaide shrugged. "He had no choice. I mean, contradicting the mayor . . ."

"Right. City Hall and all that." Nudger wadded up last month's telephone bill and hurled it at the window. It bounced off the glass near the upper right corner and the startled pigeon flapped away into the gloomy sky. "So what did Dobbs do?"

Adelaide widened her luminous blue eyes in surprise, not at Nudger's assault on the pigeon, but at his question about Dobbs. "Why, he came to me. He told me everything." She seemed to realize suddenly that she'd gotten ahead of herself, and of Nudger. Smiled a nervous, shadowy smile and sat back. "Virgil Hiller's secretary, the woman he supposedly ran away with, is my sister, Mary, Mr. Nudger. And I know what she really thought of her boss. She told me often enough he was a tyrannical creep. Slothful, repulsive, and incompetent. She despised him."

So did Nudger, and he'd never met the man. If Mary was Adelaide's sister, and if she thought that way about Hiller, well, Nudger had chosen sides.

"He'd maneuver Mary into a corner and try to feel her up every once in a while," Adelaide said. "Mary was raped when she was nineteen. Violently. She never really got over it, never could trust any man completely. When Hiller made advances it drove her almost wild with revulsion. That struck him funny, and it was only because she'd threaten to file a sex discrimination suit that he'd stop harassing her. Then, when a week or so had passed, he'd begin again."

"You're telling me she hates the man everybody thinks she ran away with."

"If she didn't actually hate him, she was building up to it. I'm sure she'd have gotten another job eventually, when the pressure built high enough. Men don't understand sexual harassment, Mr. Nudger."

Nudger couldn't remember ever being sexually harassed. He supposed it could happen.

"And because of how the rape . . . left her, it was especially rough for Mary," Adelaide said.

"Why didn't she actually file charges against Hiller?"

Adelaide shook her head. When she turned away from the window her eyes were gray in the dim light, crystal blue again when she faced the brightness. "Mary didn't want to testify in court about that kind of thing again. Not ever."

"Yeah, I can understand that." He remembered a few rape cases he'd testified in as a cop. The bruised bodies, the haunted eyes. Things were easier now for rape victims, but not easy enough.

"Mary would never have run away with Virgil Hiller, Mr. Nudger. Not in five million years."

"Guess not," Nudger said. "This photographer, Dobbs, where is he now?"

"He's disappeared."

Conversing with Adelaide Lacy was like a stroll into quicksand, Nudger thought bitterly.

"No one knows where he is," Adelaide reiterated.

"That's disappeared, all right." Nudger longed for a nice dull divorce case, a punch in the nose from an irate adulterer. "You told the police all this?"

"No. The night after he gave me the photographs, Dobbs

came by my apartment again and cautioned me not to go to the police. So did Mr. Kyle. Finally it occurred to me to see someone like you. You're not exactly the police."

Nudger's stomach fluttered. Like pigeon wings. "Not Arnie Kyle the gambler?"

"Why, yes," Adelaide said. "You know him?"

"Only well enough to avoid him like bubonic plague."

Adelaide nodded and brushed back an errant strand of blond hair that was still damp from the rain. She had the high, broad cheekbones of a movie star, but somehow there was a daintiness to her bone structure. Something about her said quality. Something else said stay away. She appealed like honey in a hive of bees. She said, "I can understand that, considering your profession. Kyle came to my apartment the second time Paul Dobbs was there, but he didn't pay much attention to Dobbs. He demanded an envelope Mary had left with me for safekeeping. He was so insistent, so quietly menacing, that I was frightened. So was Dobbs. When I looked on the top shelf of my bedroom closet, where I'd put the envelope, it was gone."

"Is this *another* envelope?" Nudger asked. He wanted to keep things straight. "What envelope are we talking about now?"

"Another envelope—not the one on your desk. Three weeks ago Mary came to me with the envelope. She was kind of shook up, though trying not to act it. She left it with me and made me swear I'd open it only if something happened to her. I tried to get her to explain, to tell me what that something might be, but she wouldn't say. My sister's high-strung, maybe even a little paranoid."

"And did you open the envelope when you found out she'd disappeared along with Hiller?"

"No. I would have, but there wasn't enough time. As it turns out, it wasn't where I left it on the shelf anyway. And to tell you the truth, I only remembered the envelope when Kyle asked about it; Mary often gets upset over things that don't amount to much. He was curious about whether I'd opened it."

"What did you tell him?"

"That I hadn't, of course. That's the truth."

"He believed you?"

"Of course. He had no reason *not* to believe me. At that time it wasn't known for sure that Mary hadn't simply gone to visit a friend for a few days, so I had no compelling reason to rush to the envelope and examine its contents. By the time it dawned on me that something was really wrong, and that Mary was somehow involved, it was too late."

"What do you think happened to the envelope?"

She hunched her shoulders and shivered slightly. "I don't know, but I've changed my apartment locks."

"When you accepted the envelope, you were sort of humoring your sister, weren't you?"

"Humoring? That's too strong a word. I didn't take her melodrama as seriously as I should have. I guess because, even though she seemed particularly upset, I'd seen her in that kind of mood before and it wasn't based on reality."

Nudger said, "How did Kyle react when you told him there was no envelope?"

"He got mad. Real mad. He warned me, and Dobbs, that his brief visit should be forgotten, especially in regard to the police. He seemed to know who Dobbs was, and Dobbs knew him. After Kyle left, Dobbs told me what kind of man he was. He advised me to do as Kyle had said, not to call the police."

"Then what did Dobbs do?"

"Acted scared, even after Kyle was gone. He stayed for a while, then he said good-bye and left the apartment in a hurry."

"Think he really was scared?"

"If I'm any judge, he was terrified."

"What exactly did you tell Arnie Kyle when you let him know the envelope was missing?"

"I said I'd kept it on my closet's top shelf, but it was gone. That he was welcome to look for himself if he didn't believe me. He didn't look. He got angry, like I said, but in a gentlemanly kind of way that was somehow more frightening than if he'd raved and shouted."

"He was only acting gentlemanly," Nudger assured her. "He's no more a gentleman than Genghis Khan and was probably mad enough to chew steel. Kyle's the dominant force in bookmaking and prostitution in this city. Not a nice man. He's had people roasted in their cars before breakfast, then had an extra piece of toast."

"That's what Dobbs said, more or less."

Nudger grunted. "Before Dobbs disappeared." He rubbed his hand down his face, as if trying to wipe away his features and acquire total anonymity. Disappearances, dead bodies, organized crime, politics. Hoo-boy!

"Mr. Nudger . . ." Adelaide began tentatively.

"Just Nudger, please."

"Fine. Nudger, I need to know what it all means. I need to find Mary, or at least learn what happened to her. I'm a librarian out at the county main library on Lindbergh. That means I'm not rich, but I can pay you. I've got money saved, and if I have to, I'll use it all."

Nudger absently massaged his twisting stomach, rapped a knuckle on the desk. Ah, the corners life forced people into. The luck of the desperate; tainted and leaving so little choice. Luck that might be good or bad, depending on what you got for grabbing the brass ring. And what was the alternative but to grab? Going round and round and nowhere until the ride was over. "Why'd you come to me in particular, Adelaide?"

"I didn't know any private investigators," she said candidly. "Picked you out of the yellow pages."

"The yellow pages is how most of my clients find me. One school of thought is that it's apropos."

Adelaide stared at him without blinking. Her wide blue eyes seemed to mist and her lower lip quivered like a child's. Then she brought herself under control.

"It's possible to read someone wrong," Nudger said. "Even a sister. Mary might not approve of what you're trying to do. Might not want to be found."

"You mean you think she did run away with Hiller? Steal the money?"

"I mean I don't know."

"I know she didn't," Adelaide said. Her certainty hadn't wavered. "I have several thousand dollars in my savings account, and I can't think of a better way to spend it than to hire a professional. That's you, Nudger. Finding people is your business—at least part of it—and this is a business arrangement I'm suggesting."

Nudger chewed on the inside of his cheek and looked at her. Business. If she didn't hire him, she'd hire someone else. Maybe someone more capable but less honest. There were plenty of those in his line of work.

Her voice was steady but pleading. "I need help, and I'm sure Mary needs help."

Those eyes. Nudger gave in completely. He smiled at her. "And I need money. Let's talk fee."

3

Lt. Jack Hammersmith was in his office, Nudger was told by
a cop in the Third District station house parking lot. Over a
decade ago, Nudger and Hammersmith had been partners in a
patrol car, and the bond still held. Nudger had almost killed
Hammersmith one night, though Hammersmith looked on it
differently. During a burglary-in-progress call at a downtown
department store, Nudger had frantically sprayed bullets
around in the dark, and one of them had wounded a man about
to open fire on Hammersmith. The lieutenant had never forgotten. It was a debt he'd always owe and always keep paying.
Sometimes Nudger kicked himself for taking advantage of that.

The station house, a relatively new brick building on the
corner of Chouteau and Lynch, was warm and full of movement
and voices. Sergeant Ellis behind the desk, who was acquainted
with Nudger, nodded to him and then went back to itemizing
a suspect's personal effects before the man was booked and
escorted to the holdover cells. Wallet, change, comb, wrist-
watch were dropped into a standard yellow envelope that was
sealed and dated. A couple of blue uniforms swaggered past

Nudger, barely glancing at him as they argued about baseball. Two plainclothes detectives standing near the bulletin board were sipping coffee from plastic mugs and carrying on a subdued conversation. One of them had his right foot propped up on a chair, and his suitcoat hung open to reveal a belt-holstered automatic with a checkered grip. Something obscene about that.

Hammersmith looked up, saw who'd entered the office, and gave a kind of half smile, half sneer. He'd once been sleek and handsome as a Hollywood screen idol, but in his middle age he'd become a florid, portly man whose bulk strained the seams of his clothes. The sharp blue eyes were the same, but the hair was white and receded now, the firm jawline blurred by fat. Hammersmith's image had finally caught up with the foul-smelling cigars he'd always smoked. The Thin Man had become Sidney Greenstreet.

"What's with Virgil Hiller?" Nudger asked, settling into the straight-backed wooden chair at the side of Hammersmith's desk. It was a tough chair to settle into; Nudger and anyone else who sat in it felt an irresistible urge to stand up after about ten minutes and straighten out spinal kinks. The lieutenant had planned it that way. He was a workaholic and didn't like visitors hanging around his office and distracting him. Took his crime fighting seriously.

He said, "Thing I like about you, Nudge, is you get to the point." He laid down the short yellow pencil he'd been using to mark in the margin of a report, then scooted back slightly in his chair. From outside the office the metallic voice of the dispatcher drifted in, directing cars here and there, plugging the dike against trouble in the big city, usually too late. "Guess you mean Hiller the wayward assistant comptroller."

"The one," Nudger confirmed. He saw two greenish cigars protruding like curious vipers from Hammersmith's shirt pocket and hoped they'd both stay unlighted for a while. Nudger noticed that the cigars were a darker green than the institutional-green walls of the office. He was sure the walls had been gray and the cigar smoke had turned them green.

Hammersmith laced his fingers behind his smooth reddish neck; there were dark crescents of perspiration beneath the arms of his pale blue shirt, though the office was cool. "Tell you, Nudge, Hiller fell victim to two of man's greatest temptations: money and a woman."

"Don't give me wisdom," Nudger said, "give me facts."

"Same thing, Nudge."

"I wish."

"Yeah, facts are easier to come by, aren't they? Well, the facts are, as far as we know, it was indeed money and a woman in this case. The two temptations seem to run together often, have you noticed? Goes all the way back to the Garden of Eden, and Adam and Eve and the apple, I guess, there not being any actual currency in those days."

Nudger said, "Have you found religion?"

"I find it, lose it. Anyway, money and a woman. Hiller saw his chance to get his hands on both on a more or less permanent basis, tucked one under each arm, and fled the city for parts unknown."

"Anything in his background to suggest he'd do that?" Nudger asked.

"Nope. There doesn't have to be. We're talking about opportunity seized. Just think about it. Half a million dollars and the woman he no doubt loves, or thinks he does. Even thee and me, Nudge."

"Me, maybe," Nudger said, "not thee. What about the secretary, Mary Lacy?"

"Her? Thirty-six, straight, hard-working, and kind of homely. But Virgil Hiller was never offered leading roles in the movies either." Hammersmith did it. Fired up one of his abominable cigars, puffing and wheezing like a blacksmith bellows. He squinted at Nudger through the greenish smoke. "You hired to find Hiller?"

"The secretary," Nudger said.

"Same thing. They're a set. You want a cigar?"

"No thanks, I love life. Did a photographer named Paul Dobbs come to see you?"

"Oh, him, sure. With his time-exposure photo that showed Hiller sitting at his desk, maybe asleep."

"Or dead. How do you explain it?"

Hammersmith observed the glowing ember of his cigar closely, as if something minute had appeared there that gripped his interest. He said, "Question is, how do you explain it to a grand jury? The date of the photograph can't be firmly substantiated. Even Mayor Faherty says he saw Hiller *after* Dobbs claimed the photo was taken. And who understands all that photographic technical jargon? I know I don't. Depth of field. Light sensitivity. Apertures. Damned confusing, you ask me. I mean, I wish I had six months to learn about F-stops and sort it all out—"

"But you've got a caseload up to here," Nudger finished, holding his hand rigid across his neck. He'd heard this story before from the police. He understood their point of view, too. They were undermanned and struggling to cope with a backlog of cases they at least *might* solve. This one didn't warrant much time or effort, because it had about it the whiff of lost causes. Dobbs's story was too vague and arcane to prompt department action. And Hiller and Mary Lacy were probably thousands of miles away, basking on foreign sands, standing up and brushing themselves off every once in a while to go spend some city money.

"I'm trying to remember," Nudger said. "Didn't the papers mention Hiller was married?"

"*Is* married," Hammersmith corrected. "Though at the moment the prospects of him spending his old age with his wife are dim."

"Got an address on the wife?"

Hammersmith sighed, then sat forward abruptly in such a way that momentum helped to lift his bulk from his chair. Moving with incredible grace for such a fat man, he glided over to a file cabinet, slid open a drawer, and studied the contents of a file without removing the folder.

He slid the metal drawer shut and said, "Her name's Gina. Lives over off Chippewa with their three kids." He sat back down at his desk, scribbled the address on a piece of paper, folded the paper in half, and handed it to Nudger.

After folding the paper neatly into quarters, Nudger stuck it in his shirt pocket. He noticed the shirt was damp with perspiration and hoped it wouldn't obscure the writing. "Hiller left his kids, too?"

"Sure, Nudge. You don't often take the kids when you run away with the other woman. 'Less you're all going to Disney World, someplace like that."

"What if I told you Mary Lacy hated Hiller?"

Hammersmith smiled around his fat cigar and said something that sounded like "Heehumph!"

A cloud of smoke had been emitted with Hammersmith's reply. Nudger felt his stomach do a few tight turns and loops. God, the office was foul! Why hadn't Hammersmith died of lung cancer years ago? Why hadn't the entire Third District? Nudger opened his mouth slightly in an effort to breathe in more air and less smoke. Didn't work very well.

Hammersmith misinterpreted the gesture. Thought Nudger was preparing to speak. He removed the cigar, propped it just so in an ashtray so that smoke curled up from it like a writhing snake, and said, "I know what you're gonna ask next: What about Dobbs's disappearance?"

"I was getting around to it," Nudger said. "I'd like to get an answer before one of your lungs collapses."

"If I don't smoke these," Hammersmith said, "I put on weight."

"What about Dobbs's disappearance?" Nudger said, still betting on lung failure.

"Well, officially Dobbs hasn't disappeared, despite a phone call we got from a certain young lady named Adelaide Lacy. We checked, Nudge, and Dobbs has dropped out of sight off and on over the last ten years. The kind of work he's in, it's not unusual for him to be gone months at a time. He's probably in Fiji photographing natives for *National Geographic,* or maybe doing some porno work to turn a fast dollar. He's done both those things in his varied career."

"You really believe that? This guy stuffed his camera in a suitcase on short notice and caught a plane to Fiji?"

Hammersmith jammed the cigar back into his mouth, then talked around it in cigarese. "He'sh a proffeshional photographer for Chrishakes, Nudge." Down went the cigar, back into the ashtray. A cloud like a green nuclear mushroom rose toward the ceiling, spreading rapidly. Nudger held his breath. "Yeah, I believe it," Hammersmith went on. "It's his job to jump out of bed when the phone rings and dash off someplace and get salable photos. How a guy like Dobbs lives. Kinda romantic, don't you think. You remember looking at pictures in *Life* magazine when you were a kid?"

"Now and then. Who called Dobbs? Who gave him the assignment?"

"Guy's a free-lance, Nudge. It'd take a year and a half to track down everyone who *might* have given him an assignment but didn't, and then finally find the person who might have and *did*."

While Nudger was trying to sort that out, Hammersmith blew more acrid green smoke.

"Hiller ever have any connection with Dobbs?" Nudger asked.

"Not as I know of, Nudge."

Nudger's back was beginning to ache. His ten minutes in hell chair were almost up. "How's Arnie Kyle fit in with Hiller?" he asked.

Hammersmith wiggled the cigar clamped in his mouth, then balanced it on the edge of the ashtray once more. "I didn't know he did. But I'm not surprised. Kyle's the sort that likes to be seen with any politician. Makes him feel respectable, though I can't imagine why."

There were footsteps outside in the hall. Voices. Nudger recognized the peculiar broken rhythm of the footsteps, the occasional scuffing sound. A prisoner, probably handcuffed, being escorted to the holdover cells in the back of the building. A high-pitched man's voice said, "Not so fast. Take it fuckin' easy!" Two other voices, cops' voices, bantered back and forth good-naturedly, as if the prisoner hadn't spoken. The noise faded down the hall. The sounds of police work would always be familiar, always be a part of Nudger.

He stood up to leave, stretching his cramped back muscles. "Thanks, Jack."

"Nothing, Nudge. Hey, maybe you can tell *me* where Kyle fits in with Hiller," Hammersmith suggested, aiming the cigar at Nudger as if it were a smoking gun.

"When I find out, you'll be the next to know."

"If there is a next," Hammersmith said. "You're in shark waters, Nudger. I hope you realize that. You be careful of Kyle." Purely by accident, he blew a perfect smoke ring. He glared at it, a bit surprised and alarmed. He'd always been skeptical of coincidence. "Shark waters," he repeated.

"*Life* magazine," Nudger said. "Remember that shot of Muhammed Ali screaming with both arms raised after a fight?"

"Sure. How 'bout that one of the sailor in Times Square, kissing his girl just after World War Two?"

"Now you're going way back," Nudger said.

"Kinda magazine *Life* was. A great photograph's forever in the mind."

"Maybe Dobbs's shot of Virgil Hiller will turn out that way."

"Doubt it," Hammersmith said. "Say, you remember that one of Adlai Stevenson with his foot propped up and the hole in the bottom of his shoe?"

"I remember."

Hammersmith puffed on his cigar, leaned back, and closed his eyes, leafing again through the black and white pages of his youth.

Nudger left him like that. Then he walked through the crowded, noisy booking area and out the door. Down the concrete steps to the street.

Into shark-filled waters.

4

Virgil Hiller's home was in St. Louis Hills, a conservative, Germanic, and immaculately clean section of South St. Louis. Most of the houses there were constructed of brick. Many featured pseudo-Gothic architecture, with steeply pitched roofs, ornate eaves, and pointed dormers. It was the sort of neighborhood where you might still see someone wearing a spiked helmet.

The Hiller house was a pale brick building with a red tile roof and a wide picture window with evenly spaced potted plants hanging in it. Along the foundation line were several windows of glass brick, to allow light but not vision into the basement. The house sat on a gently slanted hill; its spacious front yard was covered with zoysia grass, a curiously thick and low-lying type of growth that turned brown in early fall and stayed that way until mid-spring. During the summer months it was like a plush green carpet, a perfect place to display plastic flamingos and miniature Dutch windmills. Someday South St. Louis would be choked to death on zoysia grass. That would be too bad.

Nudger parked his rusty Ford Granada at the curb and strolled up the curved walk toward the front door. Hiller must have employed a lawn care service; the hedges were trimmed with topiary precision and the edged grass stood at rigid attention three inches away from the walk as if repelled by a magnetic field.

Nudger stepped up onto the concrete porch and pressed the bell button. Westminster chimes sounded faintly from deep inside the house. Traffic hummed in the distance. Birds chirped from where they were perched on a telephone line leading to the peak of the house's roof. They weren't perched in a tree because there were no trees in the yard. South St. Louis did not abide trees. Trees dropped leaves. Undesirable. Messy.

The door was answered by an attractively plump woman in her forties, with wise dark eyes and wavy brown hair streaked with gray. She was wearing a short-sleeved blue blouse with a delicate black sequin design on it. Dark slacks. Her upper arms were getting gelatinous and her heavy breasts strained the front of the blouse. A thick black belt cinched tight with a silver buckle showed she still had a waistline. There was something about her. She was appealing in a homebody kind of way, as if she'd be great in bed and could also bake a terrific apple strudel. Nudger cautioned himself about being a male chauvinist and said, "Mrs. Gina Hiller?"

She said she was.

Nudger introduced himself and said he was a detective. He didn't say he was with the police department. Didn't say he wasn't.

"Please come in," Gina said rather hurriedly, somewhat breathlessly. "You mind having a seat and waiting a few minutes? I'm in the middle of an important phone call about my son. With his school."

"I've got plenty of time," Nudger said, and followed her down a short hall and into a large living room with white walls. It was carpeted in a kind of rose color. The furniture was gray-blue and white and looked as if it could be soiled by a dirty look. French provincial. The room was cool and smelled strongly but not unpleasantly of perfume.

On the brocade sofa sat a dainty, attractive blond woman in a yellow summer dress that clashed with the carpet. She had a turned-up nose, pouty red lips, and nifty nyloned calves pressed close together as if Nudger might dive for her legs and try to pry them apart. What was this? Could she read minds?

Gina Hiller said, "Oh," then "Oh," again, flustered, as if she hadn't known the woman was there—a pesky apparition that had appeared uninvited on the sofa. "This is Bonnie Beal, Detective Nudger. Please excuse me. The phone in the kitchen's off the hook." She smiled nervously and jogged out of sight, bouncing in her tight slacks.

Nudger could hear her hard leather heels make contact with a tile floor, then came the soft, indecipherable sound of her voice. He couldn't understand what she was saying, but her tone was conciliatory.

"There's a problem with her youngest son at school," Bonnie Beal said. There was a controlled vibrancy in her voice. Nudger bet she'd been a high school cheerleader. She sure was the type. A freshman's wet dream and a hell-raiser at pep rallies.

"Are you family?" he asked.

Bonnie laughed. Same vibrancy. Perfect little white teeth. Like pearls; like pearls for sure. Her tiny turned-up nose crinkled with her smile. Cute. The woman was cute. She said, "I'm Mrs. Hiller's Nora Dove lady."

"Nora Dove?"

Bonnie's eyebrows rose in mild astonishment. "Nora Dove cosmetics. You've never heard of them."

Where had Nudger been, in a deep hole? "Well, no, I haven't."

Bonnie smiled, putting him at ease in his ignorance. "We don't manufacture or sell men's cosmetics yet," she said, as if that explained Nudger's dearth of knowledge. "But the new Max Hawk line in male cologne and underarm deodorant will be out soon."

Cosmetics. Perfume. Nudger saw the pink vinyl sample case

at Bonnie's feet, its lid open. That explained the sweetness of the room's atmosphere. He wondered, Was there a real Max Hawk someplace? There was a Ralph Lauren. Even an Adolfo. Nudger had seen them on talk shows.

"It must be interesting, being a policeman," Bonnie said. "How long have you been on the force?"

Nudger couldn't lie to those wide, innocent eyes. It was unthinkable. Like Ken lying to Barbie. He said, softly enough not to be overheard by Gina Hiller, "I'm private, actually."

Bonnie's eyes popped open even wider. "My God, a private eye! I didn't know such people really existed."

"It's not easy existing sometimes." He knew what was coming next. It did.

"That must be a tremendously exciting life!"

"It is right now," he said.

"Huh?"

"Never mind." He'd better watch himself. "Is that a full-time job, selling Sally Dove cosmetics?"

"Nora Dove," she corrected. "And I also do temporary office work. None of it's making me rich, but I'm single instead. A real good writer once said that being single's almost as good as being rich."

Nudger wasn't so sure about that. He wondered if the writer was married. Or rich.

Gina Hiller's voice from the doorway said, "Benny kicked some pipes loose and flooded the boys' restroom."

Bonnie smiled, crinkling her pert little nose again, and shook her head briskly so her fluffy blond hair bounced. "Teenage boys," she said. So exasperated. "That kinda thing's to be expected now and again."

Gina returned the smile. As if the two women thoroughly understood how it was with teenage boys. Nudger wondered what his mother would have done if he'd kicked plumbing loose and flooded the restroom at school. Probably not much, because there'd have been very little left of him after his father was finished. The good old days had been something.

"I told the principal not to worry, that I'd take care of the cost of repair," Gina said, as if she were trying to assure Nudger and Bonnie that she could pay, that her life was still in control even without her husband.

"They going to send him home?" Bonnie asked.

"No, I talked them out of that. He's got study hall detention for a week. The school's got a plumber coming out to give them estimates later today. They think the damage is in the hundreds."

"God!" Bonnie said.

Gina shook her head helplessly and said, "Boys!" Then, more firmly and with an edge of pain, "Men!"

Bonnie stood up and smoothed her yellow dress over trim thighs, then held herself erectly, as if trying to appear as tall as possible to compensate for her smallness. For all her daintiness, she had surprisingly full breasts. Nicely flared hips. A vest-pocket-size beauty was Bonnie. She said, "I'll leave you a bottle of Hot Shoulders and you can try it. Pay for it later if you decide you like it. The company thinks it's going to be very popular, one of our really big sellers."

Nudger watched as Gina thanked her and accepted a small fancy bottle with an atomizer on top. Then she escorted Bonnie toward the door.

"Been a pleasure, Mr. Nudger," Bonnie called over her shoulder.

"Same here." *Hot Shoulders?*

Gina talked with Bonnie for a moment at the door. Both women laughed, though Gina's laughter was subdued. Then Gina said good-bye and came back and sat down on the sofa opposite Nudger. Where Bonnie had sat. She glanced down and said, "Oh, she forgot her Nora Dove scent patches!"

"Scent patches?"

Gina held up a stack of glossy papers with labeled, colored squares on them that looked like paint samples. "You just scratch your fingernail over these little squares and sniff," she said, "and you get an exact sample scent of any Nora Dove perfume."

"Clever," Nudger said.

Gina said, "She'll come back for them," and laid the scent patches on the coffee table. She fixed her large, resigned eyes on Nudger. "I guess you think I'm frivolous, thinking about perfume at a time like this in my life. But I need something other than strife to occupy my thoughts."

"That's easy enough to understand," Nudger assured her.

"I won't inquire if there's any news on Virgil. The answer's always the same. There never is."

"I need to ask you a few questions, Mrs. Hiller. Bear with me, please, because I'm sure you've heard some of them before."

She tried a smile, but it didn't quite make it all the way across the rose carpet to Nudger. "Answering questions has become almost a way of life for me since Virgil left. Asking myself questions has, too."

"What kind of questions do you ask yourself, Mrs. Hiller?"

"Well, I have to wonder what part I might have played in whatever caused this . . . situation."

"Did Virgil act peculiar in any way before he disappeared?" Nudger asked.

"No. They say he ran off with that woman, but I don't believe it. Everything was going along the way it always did here at home, with Virgil, me, and the boys. Virgil loved the boys—and me. He'd never leave us. Not for good, anyway. Virgil had a happy home life. I know. A man can't fake that for years on end, Mr. Nudger. It's not possible."

"Ever meet his secretary?"

"Mary Lacy? No, we never met. That wasn't unusual, though. Virgil kept his work separate from his family. Even when something important was bothering him, he'd keep it to himself so as not to make us worry."

Nudger decided on the element of surprise. "Have you heard from him since he disappeared, Mrs. Hiller?"

She smiled sadly and shook her head no. "Wish I had. I wish it so much . . ."

Pity constricted Nudger's throat and made his voice break as he asked his next question. This wasn't the job for him; he should be selling insurance or appliances. Collect his salary and commission and go home at peace with himself. Steady work, steady pay. "Did Virgil ever mention Mary Lacy to you in any context?"

Gina Hiller rubbed her palms over the roundness of her thick knees, staring at them as she thought. Her hands were surprisingly older than the rest of her, reddened and chapped, as if she worked at hard labor with them. "I don't even recall how or when he mentioned her. He must have, though, because I knew her name."

Nudger could see her control slipping. He was losing her. "If you don't believe he stole the money and ran away with Mary Lacy, what *do* you believe, Mrs. Hiller?"

She lifted her gaze and riveted it on Nudger. Twin laser beams. "I believe my husband's gone and I don't know where, why, or how. I believe I have three sons to raise, and not enough money to do it. I believe if this isn't resolved soon, if Virgil doesn't come back, I'll go insane. I can't handle this at my age. Just can't. For years I leaned too much on Virgil, like a tree not in the sun and leaning on the one next to it. I'm not strong anymore." She bowed her head and her shoulders began a gentle, rhythmic lurching as she wept, rocking on the sea of her mistake.

Nudger stood up. He'd heard enough. Done enough. Felt small enough. He said, "I'm sorry I upset you, Mrs. Hiller. Really."

She drew a deep, rasping breath, looked up at him, and actually smiled. Smeared mascara made her face a tragic mask. "Your job isn't easy sometimes, is it?"

Christ! Why would Hiller leave this woman? "No," he said, "it isn't." He moved toward the door. "Thanks for your help."

"I wish I was a help, but I wasn't, was I?"

"Maybe," Nudger said. "There's no way to know for sure about that yet."

He let himself out.

As he was stepping down off the porch, he noticed a blue Chevy station wagon pull to the curb behind the Granada.

Bonnie Beal got out, bustled around the back of the car, and started up the walk to the house. Her golden hair bounced as she strode. The straw purse slung over her shoulder rode jauntily on her hip, and her breasts jounced firmly beneath the yellow dress.

She was preoccupied and didn't notice Nudger until she'd almost run into him. She stopped short and looked beautifully startled, as any life-size doll would, and said, "Mr. Nudger. Didn't see you there. Darn near bumped into you."

"My loss."

She ignored the remark, but in a way that somehow suggested she'd been aware of it and was above replying. She was used to clever repartee and chose not to partake. "I forgot my scent patches," she said.

He nodded. The paint samples. "Mrs. Hiller found them and put them on the coffee table."

"That's a relief," she said. "I was so worried about Niki."

"Niki?"

"Mrs. Hiller's toy poodle. He's a curious little thing and likes to chew, and far as I know, some of that stuff in those scent patches might be poisonous." She crinkled her nose in a smile and started to move around him deftly on the narrow sidewalk, brushing up against him as if it were necessary. One foot off the concrete and the grass would have her.

He surprised himself by saying, "Want to have dinner with me tonight?"

She surprised him by saying yes.

Just like that.

That was how life got complicated.

5

Why did I ask her out? Nudger wondered, as he steered the Granada onto Interstate 44 and headed west toward Lindbergh. A tractor-trailer doing at least seventy forced him to yank the steering wheel to the right and brake, staying in the acceleration lane until the truck had roared past. His heart hammering, he told himself to use one side of his brain to pay attention to his driving, if he was going to ponder with the other.

He checked his rear-view mirror and eased out into the traffic flow more cautiously. Settled the car at a safe and legal fifty-five. He knew nothing about Bonnie Beal other than that she was cute and sold Nora Dove cosmetics. This was quite a detour in Nudger's life. He'd been romantically involved for the past few years with Claudia Bettencourt, a woman he'd talked out of suicide and then come to love.

Still loved.

He thought.

Trouble was, Claudia's psychiatrist, Dr. Oliver, had advised her to follow her instincts and see other men occasionally in order to bring about what he and Claudia called her self-actualization. Nudger wasn't sure what to call it. Or what to do about it. Oliver had assured him that Claudia still loved him and would eventually wend her way back to him on a permanent basis, and the bond between them would be stronger than ever. Meanwhile, Claudia was going out regularly with Biff Archway, who taught sex education at Stowe High School out in the county, where Claudia taught English. Archway was handsome, athletic, a spiffy dresser, and a sportsman. *He* was probably self-actualized twice over. Nudger hated Biff Archway.

And he hated his and Claudia's new arrangement. And maybe he was getting sick of it to the point where other women *were* beginning to tempt him more than they should. Adelaide Lacy, prim librarian, had come on like a young Marlene Dietrich. Bonnie Beal had struck him weak-kneed with her smile, and out had popped his invitation to dinner. Pathetic.

The hell with it, Nudger thought, with grim satisfaction. Claudia deserved this. And he deserved dinner with Bonnie the Nora Dove lady. Their relationship might develop into something worthwhile. Maybe she'd give him a deal on deodorant when the Max Hawk line came out.

The late afternoon was cool, so he had the Granada's air conditioner off and his window cranked down. He turned north on Lindbergh, listening to the whirling air pound drumlike in the back of the car. He'd had to buy a new carburetor for the Granada last month, but now it was running like a champion. Danny had gotten him a deal on the car; it had belonged to an old lady out in Kirkwood who reputedly had given it meticulous care. Although, according to the title Nudger had examined after the sale, she'd only owned it two months before selling it. Her eyes were getting too bad for her to continue driving, she'd told Danny. Nudger had bought the Granada almost as much out of pity as need.

When he'd almost reached Clayton Road, he turned right into the library's parking lot, slowing to avoid three teenage girls lugging stacks of books and yammering at each other. There were plenty of parking spaces in the blacktop lot, although across the street in Plaza Frontenac, an expensive shopping center, the lot was filled. Nudger supposed that for most people shopping was more fun than reading. Not for the three teenagers, apparently. Or maybe they had reports to write for school.

As he climbed out of the Granada he saw the girls, still tirelessly chattering at each other and juggling books, jog across Lindbergh on their way to the mall. Well, maybe they were heading for B. Dalton.

The library was a low and squarish brick structure that looked as if it had been built for easy conversion into a supermarket, just in case. When Nudger opened one of the twin glass front doors a rush of cold air roared out at him; didn't the thermostat know it was cooling off outside? He let the door swing shut behind him and the gale subsided. The library had "in" and "out" turnstiles to herd the public, and one of those electronic gizmos that looked like a metal detector out at the airport. If anyone walked through there with a book that hadn't been checked out, sirens would wail, lights would flash, and Library Security would burst out of the stacks with guns blazing.

It was a spacious and well-organized library, with a large selection of magazines on wooden racks back in one corner. An inviting place to sit and read *Consumer Reports*, find out which was the best toaster you couldn't afford. Nudger made a mental note to do that someday.

Adelaide Lacy was one of three women working behind a long, low desk just inside the turnstiles. Her co-workers looked like librarians. She *did* look a little like Marlene Dietrich!

Nudger walked over to the desk and tried to sound like Cary Grant. "*He*llo. *Got* a min*ute?*"

"Catching cold?" she asked. "It's this weather. Keeps changing." The other two women stared curiously at Nudger, as if he might be here to burn books. Adelaide came out from behind the desk.

No longer Cary Grant, Nudger followed her across the library, weaving among rows of wooden tables and chairs. There were books and magazines spread out on some of the tables, waiting for a meticulous librarian to scoop them up and put them in their proper Dewey Decimal places.

They sat in softly upholstered vinyl chairs, facing a rack that contained a disheveled *New York Times* and various other out-of-town papers. The chairs were the comfortable, promiscuous kind that sighed and embraced anyone who sat down in them. It had been a long day; Nudger wasn't sure if he ever wanted to get up. A heavyset guy in a wrinkled blue business suit sidled up, selected a copy of the *Chicago Tribune*, and drifted toward one of the other chairs. He dropped into it suddenly with all his weight. *Hisss!*

Adelaide looked hard and blue and hopefully at Nudger. "Have you learned anything?"

"I talked to Gina Hiller, the wife of Mary's missing boss. She told me Virgil loves her and the kids, and he wouldn't run out on them."

"Think she believes that?"

"Yeah."

"Then she probably wouldn't believe her husband was a habitual groper."

"I dunno," Nudger said. "Maybe, if you pressed her on the point. Thing is, she loves the guy, and despite his perpetual seven-year itch, he might very well have loved her back. People are nothing if not complicated. There are three sons, and I doubt if they're neglected. Way it looks, Virgil had strong family ties."

"Which suggests he wouldn't have stolen city money and run away with Mary."

"Suggests that," Nudger agreed. "I also talked to somebody I know on the police department. He said Dobbs came to the law with his photographs, but nobody paid much attention to them. Too technical, and they proved nothing. Besides, as you pointed out, the comptroller and the mayor saw Hiller alive *after* Dobbs claimed to have photographed him at his desk. Not dead, only sleeping."

"The man in that photograph wasn't sleeping, Nudger."

"Didn't look like it. Not sitting up at his desk that way with a pen in his hand. Civil servants don't work hard enough to bring on that kind of exhaustion. Of course, there's no way to be positive he was dead; he wasn't spouting blood from bullet holes while somebody held a mirror to his mouth. When you talk to the police, you have to talk proof or you're wasting your time and theirs. It's a job to them, that's all; they have to weigh the probabilities. From where they sit, it looks as if Hiller and Mary and half a million dollars are off somewhere having a hell of a time, and the wayward lovers will turn up again when their luck or money runs out and the merry-go-round quits revolving."

"Mary doesn't go to carnivals."

"Once in her life, maybe. Half a million dollars."

"Mary's not that way about money. She doesn't have a driving desire to be rich."

"Maybe that's because she never really thought it was possible. Until hot-pants Virgil Hiller gave her the opportunity."

"Hiller is dead," Adelaide said. She'd talked herself into believing it thoroughly.

Nudger thought she was right but reserved final judgment until the funeral. He said, "And you think Mary might know something about his death and went into hiding?"

"It's possible."

Nudger knew that worse things were possible, but he kept that to himself.

"What now?" Adelaide asked.

"I need the key to Mary's apartment."

"That's no problem; I have one in my purse. We carried keys for each other's apartments. Wait a minute."

She got up and sashayed among the tables, back toward the checkout desk. He watched her disappear through a doorway to the right, probably into a room where she'd left her purse. He wondered idly if librarians had locker rooms where they suited up in conservative clothes and tucked pencils behind their ears before trotting out to man—or woman—the desk. Laughed and snapped towels at each other before the doors opened. It wasn't likely.

A minute later she came back, stood over him, and pressed a brass key into his hand. Her own hand was warm and moist.

"I'll get this back to you soon as possible," he said.

"No rush. Her apartment's in Richmond Heights, on Hoover."

"I know," Nudger said, "I got the address from the newspaper." He felt real smug, like a genuine detective in one of the books in the mystery section behind him.

Adelaide didn't seem impressed. She was probably always looking up things. "Well, I'd better get back to work."

He thanked her for the key and watched her weave among the tables again on her way to the desk.

The library was quiet and peaceful. He didn't feel like getting up out of the comfortable chair; he'd rather stay and check out those toasters in *Consumer Reports*. But, like Adelaide, his job beckoned. Both of them were victims of the work ethic.

He pushed himself up out of the soft vinyl chair. It hissed as if telling someone to shush, this was the library.

Hoover was a side street that ran east and west off Big Bend near Highway 64. There were a number of four-family flats on it, a few of them rundown but most fairly well maintained. Brick buildings with squarish brick and concrete porches and sun-ravaged lawns. It was a middle-class neighborhood that hadn't changed much in the last twenty years, and just the kind of area where you'd expect a devoted and punctilious female civil servant to live.

The vestibule smelled like most old apartment buildings: a combination of ammonia-based cleaning compounds, greasy enamel, and mingled cooking scents. Muffled classical music was coming from one of the units, a maudlin violin concerto. There were a few pieces of what looked like junk mail in Mary Lacy's locked mailbox. She probably could win a new Buick simply by visiting a lakeside resort.

Nudger trudged up a short flight of wooden steps with tacked-down rubber treads on them. The violin music got louder, then fell silent. He found the door to 1E and used the key Adelaide had given him.

The door swung open on a small but neat living room. The venetian blinds were slanted upward so the early evening light was diffused and bouncing off the white ceiling. It made everything seem dustier than it was. An uncomfortable-looking green modern sofa faced a low, expensive console TV with a vase of dead flowers on top. The space-age remote control for the TV rested on a mahogany coffee table. There were wall hangings of modern museum prints over the sofa. Cubism, they looked like to Nudger, though he was far from an art expert. He used to like those Keene paintings of the kids with the big sad eyes, but you didn't see many of them anymore. Or those paint-by-number kits. Trends in the arts, he supposed. The air was still and stale, telling him the flat was empty and had been for some time.

He nosed around a while, trying to get a feel for the sort of person Mary Lacy was. He figured her for a neat and controlled life. Determinedly neat and controlled. He remembered what Adelaide had told him about her. Undoubtedly Mary Lacy was too tightly wrapped.

The bedroom furniture was black laquered wood. She slept in a very narrow single bed, but Nudger didn't see anything Freudian in that; the bedroom was too small to contain a double bed and the rest of her furniture. The wall hangings were more conventional than in the living room, silver-framed prints of lavish flower arrangements. Somehow they seemed more funereal than cheering.

He shoved open the closet's sliding doors. They caught and rumbled on their runners. A subtle, spicy scent wafted out at him. He saw a sachet dangling from a red string tacked to the edge of the wooden shelf.

The closet was full of modestly priced conservative dresses, several matching skirts and blazers. A wire rack on the floor supported a dozen pairs of sensible, medium-heeled dress shoes. A working woman's wardrobe, apparently complete. If she left of her own accord, Mary hadn't packed for wherever she was going. On the other hand, half a million dollars and a new life were the sorts of things that might make a woman—even a fortyish, spinsterly one like Mary Lacy—decide it was time for a new wardrobe.

Her dresser drawers were also well stocked, all the underwear, socks, even the panty hose neatly folded. A compulsively neat woman, all right. The bottoms of the drawers were lined with newspapers to protect against dust and splinters. Nudger lifted some lingerie and found himself reading about John Hinckley's attempt to assassinate President Reagan. All of the lingerie was white. No bikini panties with angels, devils, or days of the week on them. Nothing from Frederick's of Hollywood.

On top of the dresser was a framed photo of Mary with Adelaide. Though Adelaide was the younger and prettier of the two, it was mostly her plain dress and—even in the photograph—diffident manner that made Mary seem to merge with the background while her little sister glowed. They were standing in front of what looked like an ornate iron gate with trees behind it. Adelaide was smiling, Mary wasn't. Both looked young in the photo. Nudger wondered if it had been taken after Mary was raped and her trust of the opposite sex destroyed.

He stood in the middle of the room and turned in a slow circle. Then he walked down the hall. Glanced into the tiny pink-tiled bathroom. Everything there was neat: folded towels symmetrically hanging from their racks, box of Kleenex with the top tissue puffed up for easy access, bathmat draped over the tub. Cosmetic bottles were precisely aligned, like chess pieces in the game of love, on a wicker shelf above the washbasin. The soap in the porcelain tray was dry and cracked. There was a single red toothbrush angled in the holder next to a water tumbler. A lonely sight.

Nudger walked the rest of the way down the hall and into the living room, took a last, appraising look around, and let himself out.

In one way he hadn't learned anything in the apartment, yet in another he had. It was impossible to spend time in a place where someone lived without getting a more accurate sense of the person. Maybe it wasn't anything the conscious mind could concretely identify, but so what? You never could tell; maybe something was there all the same, lodged in the subconscious and playing a part in the unfolding of everything you thought about that person.

As he crossed Hoover and got into his car, he didn't notice the broad-shouldered man watching him from inside the new black Lincoln parked down the street.

When Nudger drove away, the man didn't follow.

He didn't need to.

He knew where Nudger lived.

6

Nudger drove to his office and parked across Manchester by the broken meter, then checked in with Danny at the doughnut shop.

Surprise. No one had been by to see him.

Clients weren't queued up on the stairs to get to his door.

In his office, he switched his answering machine to Play and kept his finger resting lightly on the button that signaled a jump to the next message.

Beep! "Hi, Mr. Nudger! Arlo Smith here. With Keller Vinyl Gutter and Waterproofing. I understand you own—a fuckin' answering machine! I wish they'd—"

Beep! "Please call Union Electric as soon as possible in regard to the past due amount on your—"

Beep! "This is Eileen, Nudger. About that line of bullshit you gave me instead of my alimony money. My lawyer says to tell you that if you don't—"

Beep! Silence.

He switched off the machine. No important messages.

It was warm in the office, he suddenly noticed. In deference to Union Electric, he pried the window open a few inches instead of using the air conditioner. Sound decision. A cool breeze pressed in, making the office comfortable within seconds. September. Such a whimsical month.

Nudger sat at his desk for a while, catching up on paperwork, typing reminders to clients who owed him past due fees. It was important work, maintaining his link in the daisy chain of people who did things for people who couldn't afford to pay them because the people *they* did things for hadn't paid *them*. This, he'd decided, was pretty much the way society operated. His society anyway. Everything in a sort of nervous and precarious balance. Everything but the ledger books. Economists no doubt had a word for it. And another word that meant exactly the opposite. They were part of the grand design themselves.

When it was almost six o'clock, he scooted his rolling swivel chair away from the desk and stood up. Stretched his arms and cramped back muscles. Time to pull himself away from the job. He was supposed to pick up Bonnie Beal at her place at seven.

It might rain tonight, so he wrestled the stubborn window closed, almost pinching his fingers between it and the sill. Someone had told him that a little cooking oil rubbed in the tracks of old wooden windows made them work more smoothly. He decided he'd try it, next time he had a bottle of cooking oil in the office.

He went downstairs, bringing his weight to bear heavily on the creaking wooden steps. The breeze that had graced the office met him like an old friend as he pushed open the door to the street. He waved to Danny through the doughnut shop window, then crossed Manchester to where he'd left the Granada parked. He was feeling pretty good.

Pigeons had made a mess on the windshield, as if returning Nudger's animosity. Two of the air rats were perched on a nearby second-story ledge, puffing out their feathered chests and chortling at him. God, he wished he had a rock to throw!

He drove to his apartment on Sutton, showered and changed

into gray slacks, brown sportcoat, and a paisley tie with practically invisible gravy stains on it. He still had fifteen minutes to get to Bonnie's house.

As he locked the door behind him, it occurred to him that he'd forgotten to shave. Nobody was perfect.

Bonnie lived on Pleasant Lane out in Rock Hill, on a block of subdivision houses that had been built in the fifties and were almost identical. Low frame ranch houses with garages extended into concrete driveways on the left, architecturally balanced by artificial stone blending to brick chimneys on the right. They all had scraggly oak trees planted in precisely the same spot in their flat front yards. A few of the copycat houses were a color other than white. Some of them had two-car garages instead of singles. It was a good thing they had address numbers.

Nudger found Bonnie's number tacked in brass numerals on one of the houses that weren't white. It was pale blue with darker blue trim. Almost pale enough to be white.

He parked in the driveway behind the Chevy station wagon. As he climbed out of his car, he noticed a magnetic sign stuck flat on the wagon's driver-side door. The sign featured a serene-looking woman smiling and gazing lovingly at a fluttering white bird perched on her finger. Below the woman was lettered NORA DOVE—WITH LOVE. The bird looked to Nudger like a pigeon.

When he was ten feet from the front door, it opened and Bonnie charged outside. She was smiling her dazzling, crinkly-nosed smile, wearing a snappy green dress, and carrying the straw purse she'd had at Gina Hiller's. She looked her same cute self and Nudger was glad he'd asked her to dinner. Never the best at the dating game, he smiled back at her and said inanely, "Hungry?"

"Sure am! Don't *you* look nice?" As if he never had before. She was at his car, opening the door. He guessed maybe she really was hungry and not just making conversation.

She was already fastening her seat belt as he walked around

to the driver's side. He noticed there were a lot of grease and oil stains on the driveway and stepped carefully so he wouldn't get anything on his shoes.

"You know your car's leaking oil?" he said, as he backed the Granada out into the street.

For a second she looked alarmed, her doll's eyes widening. Then she said, "It's okay now. I had it worked on."

"Is it a company car? Nora Dove?"

"No, but most of the mileage is tax deductible. That's fair enough of the company, I think. And if you sell a hundred thousand dollars worth of cosmetics two years in a row, they give you a white Cadillac to drive."

"Sounds like a good outfit to work for." He couldn't imagine anyone selling that much cosmetics, but maybe when they started in with the Max Hawk line.

They had dinner at Stuart Anderson's Steakhouse out on Olive Street Road. Not the most expensive eatery in town, but it had a solid upper franchise atmosphere, with tall upholstered booths to deaden sound. Two people could converse in the place without yowling infants or canned music making the silverware dance on the table. All this and the food was excellent.

Bonnie had never been to the restaurant. She acted as if it were Tony's down on Broadway, with its five-star Michelin Guide rating. She might have been right; the steak might be just as good here. Guy named Stuart figured to be a better chef than a Tony. Better at steaks and sauces, anyway.

Over dessert, Bonnie abandoned coquettishness and said, "I guess you were at Gina Hiller's house to ask about her missing husband."

"That's it," Nudger said, watching her fork cheesecake in between her perfect red lips, chomp it neatly with her precisely aligned little teeth. He was having coffee only; if he'd matched Bonnie in ordering dessert, he might not have enough money left for a tip. And he was way overextended on credit. In fact, MasterCard, Visa, and American Express had teamed up to get him, like the Axis powers.

"Where do you think Virgil Hiller went with that secretary of his?" Bonnie asked.

"I don't know. Where do fugitive lovers run away to these days? Is the Love Boat still afloat?"

"You can be a fugitive lover anywhere," Bonnie said, licking her fork. Flirting?

"Has Gina Hiller talked much to you about Virgil?"

"Some." Bonnie idly twirled her fork, sending bright reflections playing over the table, across her breasts. Cute breasts, Nudger would bet. "My impression is it's—or it *was*—one of those old-fashioned marriages. He goes out and earns the money, she stays home and raises the kids. The way it used to be and maybe still oughta be."

Nudger said, "Would you guess they loved each other?"

"Sure. But Gina guessed that, too, and she was wrong."

"Maybe."

Bonnie's eyes shot cold sparks and she sat forward. Her voice was hushed and curious. "You don't think he really *did* run away with his secretary?"

"Don't know," Nudger said. "Trying to find out." He carefully added more cream to his coffee and stirred. A waiter wandered by and topped his cup, messing up the mixture. Sort of smiled. Bastard do that on purpose?

Bonnie finished her cheesecake, gave the lucky fork another lick, and dabbed at her lips with her napkin. Checked the napkin to make sure too much lipstick wasn't smeared on it. "You have an interesting job," she said, "finding out things."

"Sometimes it's interesting."

"Sometimes scary?"

"That, too."

She leaned back and sighed long and loud. Contentedly. As if she might pat her full belly and comment on the quality or quantity of the food. But she was silent and smiling. She smiled a lot.

Nudger said, "You mentioned you were widowed."

She dragged her coffee cup over to her as if it weighed twenty pounds. Lifted and sipped. "Two years ago Gary died of a heart attack. He was only thirty-nine."

"I'm sorry."

"Well, I am, too, but those things happen. And it's been long enough ago that most of the pain's gone."

"Time's a friend and enemy," Nudger said.

She gazed at him as if he'd just said something that made Socrates seem backward. "Why, that's sure the truth."

"Kids?"

"No thanks." She laughed at her own joke. She sort of squeaked when she laughed, like a rubber squeeze toy. Nudger wasn't surprised.

"I'm divorced," he said. "I pay alimony, but no child support. No children were caught up in the mess we made of our marriage."

"I didn't think anyone paid straight alimony anymore."

"You haven't met Eileen's lawyer. I thought the bastard wore sharkskin shoes, but those were his feet."

Gasp, squeak! Nudger was not only wise, but some bunch of fun.

"So," he said, "luckily, no kids."

She dabbed again at her lips with the napkin, unnecessarily, and said, "This was a wonderful meal, really." As if she was ready to leave.

Okay. They'd been there long enough; Nudger's buttocks felt welded to his chair. He signaled the waiter and paid the check. Left a tip of thirteen percent.

Bonnie was ready to call it a meal, but not a night. Nudger drove north on Lindbergh, and they had a few drinks at the Marriott lounge out near the airport.

Bonnie drank margaritas, possibly so she could lick the salt from the glass rim. Nudger sipped Budweiser, made small talk, and watched her through two drinks. She seemed unaffected by the liquor, while he was beginning to feel the glow. He'd only had the two beers since his before-dinner cocktail at the restaurant; still, maybe he shouldn't drive.

It crossed his mind that they were in a hotel, and there were hundreds of rooms with double beds in the place. But something kept him from sharing that thought with Bonnie.

She indicated that she'd drunk her limit, so he had a cup of black coffee and took her home. It was 10:45. Still early.

There was a twenty-year-old gray Plymouth parked in front of Bonnie's house. It was spotted with rust and red primer paint and had a sticker on the trunk that read WE ARE THE PEOPLE OUR PARENTS WARNED US ABOUT.

As soon as Nudger parked the Granada behind the Plymouth, a gangly teenage boy, who must have been lying out of sight on the front seat, got out and walked back on the sidewalk side. He leaned down so he was close to Bonnie. Nudger didn't know what was going on; he was ready to put the car in reverse and get out of there.

The kid had acne, mussed greasy black hair, and an oversized nose that made him look like Basil Rathbone after a late-night movie experiment gone wild. When he grew up and filled out he might appear normal, but not now. He had intense dark eyes aglow with bewildered hostility. Cops and high school teachers knew that look. It could make their jobs hell.

Pointedly ignoring Nudger, he said, "Mom, Belinda's got something stuck up her nose and can't get it out. I think it might be the battery from your watch."

Bonnie moaned. "This is my son Tad, Nudger. Tad, Nudger."

Nudger said, "Hi, Tad." Tad said nothing. Apparently he was protective of his mother and didn't approve of her dating. Common enough in boys that age without a father. Looking at Bonnie, Nudger said, "Belinda the youngest?"

"Yes," she said, "and there's Janet, Carlotta, and James between Tad and Belinda."

While Nudger was counting, she said, "You might as well come in and meet the rest of the family."

They followed the greyhound-thin, bounding form of Tad into the house that looked like all the other houses.

In the glow of the pole lamp in the small living room, sullen Tad looked even more like a starving Basil Rathbone. Janet was fifteen and pretty like her mother, only she didn't have a turned-up nose and she didn't smile at Nudger. Carlotta was an adopted Mexican girl of ten who herself looked oddly like a dark, calm version of Bonnie and stared with open curiosity at Nudger. James was a four-year-old with wild, straw-colored hair and Huck Finn features. He had on what appeared to be small army-issue combat boots. He turned his face away when Nudger was introduced, then fixed him with the sideways stare of a boxer about to launch a sneak left hook. Janet gazed dispassionately at Nudger. Carlotta and Tad stood silently by, also staring.

Belinda was in another room screaming while the introductions were made. Nudger seemed to be the only one who heard her.

Finally Bonnie smiled hopelessly and said, "'Scuse me," and left the room.

That sure helped to put everyone at ease. James hesitated a tenth of a second, then threw a few windmill punches at an imaginary enemy and scampered after his mother.

Nudger glanced around. The color television was rolling soundlessly, tuned to MTV. Mick Jagger was mugging at the camera, bugging his eyes and sticking out his tongue. There were two potato chip bags crumpled on the coffee table. What looked like crackers were broken and ground into the carpet. A mountain of schoolbooks was stacked on a chair in a corner. A few of them had fallen onto the floor, one of them open to a page kinked in half diagonally. The house smelled like smoldering rubber; there was an incense burner, a little silver elephant, on top of the TV, sending up a tiny dark curl of smoke. Jagger stared insolently at Nudger, then leaped back, wiggled his ass, and stuck out his tongue again. Naughty lad pushing fifty.

A phone in another part of the house jangled. Everyone

except Nudger and Tad raced for it. James screamed. Janet laughed, squeaked like Bonnie, and called him a geek.

Tad shuffled to the center of the living room, glared hostilely at Nudger, and said, "You like that Granada?"

Nudger wasn't quite sure how to deal with teenage boys. "It's okay. Gets me where I need to go. Usually."

"I don't think they're worth shit," Tad said. "They got bad carburetors and they're always needing exhaust work."

I'll be damned! "You're right," Nudger said. "I've had both those things repaired."

Tad snorted with contempt. "I got a slant six engine in that Plymouth of mine. Best engine Detroit ever made. Be running long after that Granada of yours is wheels up in a junkyard."

"That could be true."

"Fuckin' right it's true. How fast you think that pile of crap of yours'll go?"

Nudger was getting tired of this. "Just under two hundred. What are you, Tad, about seventeen?"

"Eighteen."

Belinda had stopped crying. Bonnie came back into the living room carrying her perched on an outthrust hip. She was a two-year-old who looked as if her photo belonged on a cereal box. Could give even her mother lessons in cute. "It was only an ordinary bean stuck in her nose," Bonnie said. "God knows where she got it."

Tad said, "She was crawling around in the kitchen, but she had your watch, too."

Nudger figured the watch story had been a lie to get Bonnie out of the car in a hurry and into the house, away from the lustful groping hands of Nudger the Ripper.

"You and Nudger been talking man talk?" Bonnie asked.

Tad looked uncomfortable. "We been talking about cars."

"That's just about all Tad talks about these days," Bonnie said, pasting on a smile. It slipped a little crooked, but it stuck.

"Listen," Nudger said, not feeling charitable toward Tad,

"maybe Tad and Janet can watch the younger kids and we can go out for a drive."

"Wouldn't get far in your pile of junk," Tad said, staring fiercely at Nudger. "Besides, I can't hang around this place. Gotta go meet somebody."

"I'll be running along, too, then," Nudger said. He edged toward the door. "Mind if I call you tomorrow?" He wasn't sure if he asked because he wanted to, or because it was expected. He *knew* it was expected, but only if all this domesticity hadn't discouraged him.

Now Bonnie's smile was genuine. It lit up the dingy, cluttered living room. "I'd like that. I'm doing temporary office work at a data processing company, but I get home about five."

They touched hands tentatively and parted.

Tad walked out of the house less than a foot behind Nudger, as if to lend intimidation and make sure he was really leaving. If they hadn't been in step, Tad would have kicked Nudger with each stride. Nudger thought they must look like a stray contingent of a military drill team.

When they were halfway down the walk, Tad danced to the side and said, "Nudger, you lay a hand on my mom, I promise you me and my friends'll make sure you're sorry. I fuckin' mean that!"

Nudger said, "Tad, you got a battery cable loose in your head."

Tad said, "Fuck you," and climbed into his dented Plymouth and slammed the door. Made the tires screech as he tore away from the curb.

He was right; the old Plymouth could up and move. Nudger watched its horizontal-slash taillights disappear around the corner. The Plymouth almost ran into a big black Lincoln parked there.

Nudger wondered, Was Tad normal? Was this what Beaver Cleaver had become just a few short years after the TV series?

Then he told himself to go easy on the boy. Only eighteen. Make allowances. Tad's father had died not all that long ago. The kid must still feel the loss. Feel lost himself.

Nudger felt ashamed for having been critical of Tad. Insensitive adult confirms teen's paranoid delusions. Puts another chip on an already overburdened young shoulder.

He got in the Granada and drove away, slower than Tad, wondering what it might be like, really, to be a father.

7

"I dunno, Nudge," Danny said over the doughnut shop counter the next morning. "Teenage kids, who can figure 'em?"

"I know who can't."

"Adolescence, it's a kind of temporary insanity."

"Hmm."

"My cousin Ray's boy, sixteen years old, he went to take the test to get his driver's license when he was stoned on something. Ran over the foot of the state trooper who was gonna ride along and grade him. Poor cop hadn't even got in the car; he was checking to make sure the headlights worked, when Ray's boy accidentally stepped on the accelerator. Car hit the trooper, then hit the side of the State License Bureau building. Lotta damage all the way around. Ray's car."

"I didn't know Ray had a son."

"Oh, yeah. From his first marriage. That's one reason Ray don't like to be employed. Says most of his salary'd go for child support payments. Soon as the kid hits twenty-one, Ray's gonna go to work down at the truck docks on Hall Street."

"I'll bet." Nudger knew Ray. Incredibly lazy Ray, who lived

down Manchester in the St. James apartments on a Section 8 government subsidy program and even resented having to go pick up his food stamps. Wanted them mailed to him.

Danny laid a Dunker Delite on a napkin in front of Nudger. It made a weighty, clunking sound that made Nudger's insides draw up. He reminded himself he was having breakfast on Danny's friendship and generosity, as he watched Danny hold a foam cup beneath the spigot at the base of the big steel coffee urn that looked like some sort of launchable space exploration device. The coffee looked much better than it tasted.

Danny placed the full, steaming cup of acidic brown stuff next to the Dunker Delite on the counter and said, "Ask me, you should appreciate what you got in Claudia." He was a real Claudia Bettencourt fan. Thought she was too good for Nudger. Maybe she thought so, too, Nudger reflected. Maybe they were both right.

He said, "I'm following Claudia's advice. Doing what she's doing. Seeing somebody else. Nothing unfair about that. Maybe it'll get me self-actualized."

"Or living into old age by yourself in a crummy furnished room. Like yours truly here."

Danny had a point, but Nudger didn't like to think about the future. He was beginning to wish he hadn't told Danny about the recent past. Last night with Bonnie and her brood. Five kids, some of them hostile troops. That was sure something Nudger hadn't figured on.

"What's this cosmetic woman got that Claudia ain't, Nudge? I mean, besides all them offspring?"

"Well, she's cute."

"Claudia ain't dog meat. And she's got class besides."

Nudger agreed. That was the problem. Still, there was something about Bonnie. Several things, actually.

"You had to choose between the two, who would you pick?" Danny asked, wiping his hands on the gray towel tucked in his belt.

Hell of a question. Blunt, ill-timed, and from the heart. A Danny question. Nudger didn't reply.

Danny's sad, basset-hound face creased into a grin. He said, "Never mind. You and me both know the answer to that one."

"You don't know Bonnie. Never even seen her."

"Know Claudia. Know you, too."

One of the secretaries from the office building across the street came into the shop. Judy was her name, a tiny, middle-aged attractive woman who was one of Danny's few regular customers. She was wearing a no-nonsense gray business suit. Her short dark hair was engineered in a stiff, tightly coiled hairdo that looked as if it might shatter if she tripped and fell. The door clattered shut behind her and she stalked across the tile floor in noisy, choppy strides in her black high heels, a tight swivel to her hips. As if with each step she were stomping and grinding something into the floor until dead.

Danny's red-rimmed eyes lit up. He liked Judy. Possibly fantasized about her. "Some beautiful morning out there," he said.

"Give me the regular," she snapped. She was mad about something, as usual.

Nudger knew what was bothering her—what was always bothering her—and thought he'd goad her, make himself feel better. Perverse. "When's that boss of yours gonna wise up to the fact it's a new world and come out and buy his own doughnuts?"

Judy aimed her flashing brown eyes at him. "You wanna go back across the street with me and ask him? He can't fire you."

"Not my fight," Nudger said.

"Not your business, either."

She was a fireball, all right. Nudger bit into his Dunker Delite, chewed laboriously for a while, then sipped some coffee. Danny, stuffing a dozen glazed-to-go into a greased-stained white box, was grinning. He got a kick out of Judy.

He handed her the box, took her money, then gave her change in such a way that his hand lingered, touching hers. Said, "It'll be a better society all around when men like your boss finally realize the sexes are equal."

Judy wasn't fooled by this for a moment. She knew Danny.

Knew he was mired in male chauvinism. Exasperated, she thanked him politely and left.

Watching her cross the street, Danny said, "Sure is one snazzy little broad."

Snazzy, Nudger thought. You didn't often hear a woman described that way these days. Might that be good or bad?

Danny stopped staring after Judy and said, "Being your friend, I gotta tell you, Nudge, I don't approve of you stepping out on Claudia."

"I gathered that."

"I mean, sure she's having her problems, but if *you* start seeing somebody else. . . . Thing is, at least one of you has gotta work at keeping the relationship going."

Nudger was getting his fill of this, and of the Dunker Delite. "Who the hell are you, Dear Abby? Claudia's going out with that Biff Archway jerk. What am I supposed to do, go to a drugstore and buy hormone depressants till she gets her act straightened out? Take a cold shower every hour?"

Danny flinched at this flare-up of invective. "Hey, only trying to help, Nudge."

Nudger resolutely took the last bite of the Dunker Delite and swiveled down off his stool. Damn! He always felt like a bloodstained monster after kicking Danny's delicate psyche. "I know, Danny. Sorry."

"S'okay, Nudge."

Was it?

His stomach churning, Nudger carried his cup of coffee out of the shop and upstairs to his office, so as not to further injure Danny.

The beautiful morning Danny had mentioned was warm, so Nudger switched on the air conditioner before going into the half-bath and pouring the remainder of the coffee down the washbasin drain. He stood and watched the brown liquid swirl, then ran cold water for a few seconds so the basin wouldn't be stained. Then he got a fresh roll of antacid tablets out of the medicine cabinet and broke the foil.

As he thumbed off two of the tablets and popped them into

his mouth, he heard a faint noise from the office. An odd kind of double-slap—first a sharp blow, then a more solid one.

Chomping the antacid tablets, he walked back into the office, thinking maybe something had shifted weight and slipped off the desk. A magazine or thick pamphlet might have made that kind of noise, if it had landed not quite flat on the floor.

It was already much cooler in the office. And everything looked the same as when he'd stepped into the half-bath.

Then he noticed the hole and the spiderweb crack in the window, a few inches above the air conditioner, and his stomach lurched. He swallowed the partly chewed tablets, scratching his throat and bringing tears to his eyes.

But his vision wasn't so clouded that when he turned he didn't see the white sprinkling of plaster dust on the floor.

And directly above it a small round hole high on the wall opposite the window.

A bullet hole.

8

The uniform gazed at the hole up near the ceiling and said, "Guy was some piss-poor shot, or else he's got a vision problem, sees things upside down."

Hammersmith glared at him, his blue eyes flat and cold. He said, "Just see Ballistics gets the bullet."

The uniform nodded and hustled out of Nudger's office, carrying an opaque plastic bag containing the lump of lead that had been dug from the wall. Holding the bag with thumb and forefinger, well away from his body, as if it were something nasty. He looked like a dog walker reluctantly obeying a pooper-scooper law. Nudger wondered what the landlord would think of the hole in the wall. Considered hanging a picture over it, but knew it might look funny up there just a foot from the ceiling.

Hammersmith fired up one of his abominable cigars, fouled the office with putrid green smoke, and sat on the edge of Nudger's desk.

He said, "You draw a line between the bullet hole in the wall, the one in the window, and follow that angle, Nudge, and it leads to the window of a stairwell landing of the building across the street. On a level about fifteen feet below your window. Leads also to some conclusions."

Nudger glanced at the bullet hole in the window, then carefully moved out of line with it. This business of bullets zipping through the office scared him. He didn't like being at either end of a gun, but if he had his druthers he'd be the shooter rather than the shootee. "You're going to tell me whoever fired the shot wasn't really trying to hit me," he said.

"Well, it adds up that way. At the angle of fire, the only thing he could've hit would have been up near the ceiling. Probably couldn't even see you from where he was. You said you were in the other room washing your hands, didn't you?"

"Yeah. And now the law is washing its hands of this."

Hammersmith emitted a heavy fog of green smoke. Here was a man capable of closing airports. "Dammit, Nudge, you know better."

Nudger jammed his fists in his pants pockets and nodded. "Guess I do. Sorry."

"Also," Hammersmith went on, "that's an office building across the street. Guy couldn't have stood there waiting to get a clear shot at you, not with people maybe popping out of offices, coming and going. Too risky. He must have gone to the landing, made sure nobody was around, fired off a round through your window, then got the hell out of there. All within less than a minute."

"You find an ejected casing on the landing?"

"No. Nothing. And nobody in the building remembers seeing or hearing anything unusual around the time of the shot. Must have used a silencer. Those are bulky and a bitch to conceal, which adds to the impression the gunman didn't plan on waiting for a target, just wanted to send a high-velocity message into your office, get you to thinking. Worrying."

Nudger knew Hammersmith was probably right. He had in fact reasoned most of this out himself after calling the law. The Maplewood police had taken a look at the spent bullet and determined that the lump of lead would reveal nothing about the gun that had fired it. They had questioned Nudger, taken extensive notes, told him they'd assign extra patrols to the area, and then left to file their report. All very professional and ineffective, but there wasn't much else they could do. So somebody takes a shot at a window; these things happen, and there's seldom a reason or solution. Every once in a while somebody runs amok. How the world works. Change that, you'll have to call a psychiatrist, not a cop.

But Hammersmith had said he might as well run the bullet by Ballistics in the city, misuse the taxpayers' money, though he suspected all the lab could tell him was what the Maplewood police already knew: the bullet was larger than a .22 and was soft lead that had flattened slightly when it penetrated the window, then became even more misshapen when it entered the wall and, as luck would have it, became embedded in a hard wooden stud. He'd come across the city line between Saint Louis and Maplewood of his own accord, after Nudger had called him, and really shouldn't have had the uniform drive him. For a cop, Hammersmith could sometimes bend the law with an easy conscience. Nudger liked that about him.

"Question is, who'd be likely to shoot into your office?" Hammersmith asked. "That's a serious enough offense even if the bullet doesn't hit anyone. And there's always the chance of a ricochet. Or maybe a seven-foot basketball player being here to hire you and getting his skull creased."

"I've got enemies, Jack, but nobody I'd figure would do this."

"Owe anybody money you haven't paid?"

Silly question. "The electric company comes to mind."

"They got easier ways of turning out your lights."

Nudger took his hands out of his pockets. "I owe Eileen."

"Don't be an asshole, Nudge. Eileen wouldn't hire somebody to take a shot at you. Kill the goose that lays golden alimony eggs. Some motive. Besides, she's not that sort of person and you're damn well aware of it."

"Well, you know her better than I do; I was only married to her."

Hammersmith flicked ashes onto the floor and then sighted

carefully along his cigar at Nudger, as if taking aim with carcinogens. "You still on that Hiller thing?"

"Unless he's been found."

"Nope, he's still missing. Along with his secretary and all that money." Thoughtful blue gaze. Cloud of smoke. "Knowing as I do the average volume of business that parades through these plush offices, might I assume that's the only case you're working on right now?"

"Assume it," Nudger said. "So far, though, I haven't stirred up anybody who might . . ." Nudger glanced again at the bullet hole in the window. "You thinking Arnie Kyle?"

"Are you, Nudge?"

"I don't know. I'm not even sure how or even *if* he's mixed up in the Hiller disappearance."

"You asked about him when you were in my office down at the Third. Why?"

"He paid my client a visit. Asked for an envelope Hiller's secretary had left for safekeeping."

"Wait a minute—the missing secretary?"

"Uh-huh."

"Christ! You don't call that mixed up in it?"

"There's not necessarily a connection. I don't know what was in the envelope."

"Who does?"

"Whoever took it. It's missing."

"What about your client?"

"Never looked inside."

"You sure, Nudge?"

"Very. For what it's worth."

"Worth a lot to me," Hammersmith said. "But I'm afraid we're gonna have to talk to your client."

"I thought the police had it figured out that Hiller and his secretary ran off with city money and are living it up somewhere. Windsurfing and drinking piña coladas at taxpayer expense."

"Most likely it *is* that way. But now a shot's been fired at somebody looking into the matter, and you mentioned this envelope left by the secretary. You mentioned Arnie Kyle."

"Mentioned him yesterday."

"But not in the context of the envelope and the secretary."

Nudger knew the law, knew Hammersmith had no choice but to ask him about the case. Knew he'd have to give up his client's name. Adelaide hadn't instructed him not to; but if knowledge was power, why give it away?

Unless there was no alternative. He told Hammersmith who'd hired him. "We're talking about sisters here; that's why Kyle and the envelope might not be connected to the theft of the money and the disappearance of Hiller and Mary Lacy."

"So what do you think links Mary Lacy to Kyle?"

Nudger looked out the window, beyond the bullet hole, at the building across the street, where the gunman had set up and fired into the office. "Who knows? Maybe gambling. Or something political. Maybe something Mary Lacy didn't even know about."

Hammersmith said, "We talked with Adelaide Lacy."

"Right. You told her you had the case solved, her wallflower sister was away someplace tossing stolen money around and sleeping with her boss who she hated."

Hammersmith stood up, inhaled and exhaled heavily on the cigar. More green smoke. Getting to Nudger's stomach. The office would reek for days of a mixture of cooked nicotine and greasy doughnuts. Nudger would smell the same way. People would shy away from him. Stray dogs would sniff him, cough.

"Don't be cruel, Nudge," Hammersmith said. "You know how we have to approach these things."

"You still believe it?"

"Believe what?"

"About Hiller and his secretary."

"I'm not sure."

That was pretty much where Nudger stood.

About most things in life.

—— 59 ——

9

The county library was practically deserted this time of day. Too early for Baudelaire, not to mention Jackie Collins.

Nudger and Adelaide stepped into a room near the checkout desk. There were about a dozen microfilm viewers lining the walls, and there were file cabinets containing microfilmed copies of St. Louis newspapers dating back to the nineteenth century. The *Post-Dispatch*, the defunct *Globe-Democrat* and *St. Louis Star-Times*. Nobody was probing the printed past at the moment, so they could talk in private in the hushed little room that smelled of dust and history.

Adelaide had her blond hair pinned back and was wearing a skirt too short to belong on a librarian. But then her legs didn't belong on a librarian, either. Nudger cautioned himself about thinking in stereotypes. Shouldn't do that. It was a disservice to librarians, accountants, teachers, and the like. After all, his high school biology teacher had had legs like Adelaide's. Made it difficult to concentrate on dissecting frogs.

He said, "The police are going to talk to you. I had to tell them you hired me to look for Mary."

She seemed to make no big deal of that. "They've already talked to me, but they didn't say much that meant anything. I *want* them to talk to me again. If you've got them believing Mary might not have run away with Hiller, that's fine with me. That's part of the object of all this."

"I would say they're beginning to doubt," Nudger said. "Because of this morning." He told her about the unseen gunman in the building across Manchester, the bullet that had entered his office.

She seemed alarmed, yet strangely calm. "Are you sure it's connected with this case?" she asked.

He didn't want to tell her that at the moment this was his only case. "Yeah, I'm sure. None of my other cases involves Arnie Kyle."

She became thoughtful at the mention of Kyle's name. Nudger noticed that she had a short yellow pencil tucked behind one pale ear, almost lost in her swirl of yellow hair. "He'd really do something like that? Fire a shot at you?"

"No, but he has people on retainer who'd do things like that. And worse. Partly for money, partly because they enjoy that kind of action. Some of the folks working for Arnie Kyle cast real doubt on the theory of evolution."

She said, "You're afraid?"

"Ah, you picked that up."

"Seems odd to see a private detective afraid. You people are supposed to be hard-nosed and fearless. Like Mike Hammer." She lifted a hand in a vague gesture toward the mystery section out in the main library, where chaos became order and justice reigned.

"This is real life, Adelaide, and I'd like to make it last as long as possible."

"Want me to hire someone else?"

"I didn't say I was showing the white feather. I am saying this is a time for extra caution."

She nodded, considering, then said, "I agree. Did you go to Mary's apartment?"

"Yesterday. Mind if I keep your key to the place? Just in case?"

"Keep it. I don't have a use for it anymore. Find out anything there?"

"Nothing specific, but I came away with more of a sense of who your sister is." Nudger had almost said *was*. "It's the lair of an orderly—and if you don't mind my saying so—dull spinster."

"Well, I told you why Mary didn't have many male friends. I mean, after what was done to her. The rape was brutal, mentally debilitating, and it destroyed her respect for men, destroyed her self-respect. She felt dirty for a long time. Guilty, if you can imagine. As if *she'd* done something wrong. I know it shouldn't work that way, but it does. It's an emotional reaction. You'd have to be a woman to understand. For quite a while she was reclusive. I mean almost totally. Hardly ever raised her shades. She's lived by herself for the last ten years. Six years ago she got her job with the city, and three years ago she got the apartment in Richmond Heights. It's an improvement over the cheap rented room she lived in downtown. She's had to re-create herself, Nudger; do you understand that?"

"I think so."

"There's nothing in my sister that could possibly include her running away with Virgil Hiller."

"Doesn't sound like it," Nudger admitted. He became aware of something. Sniffed the air. "You smell terrific. What's that perfume you're wearing?"

"It's called Hot Shoulders. Why?"

Should be called Small World. "That's a Nora Dove perfume, isn't it?"

Her blue eyes flared in surprise. "I'll be damned. The detective knows his scents."

"Isn't that line of cosmetics only sold door to door? Something like Avon?"

"That's right. It's not carried in the stores."

"Who'd you buy it from?"

"No one. It was a gift from an admirer." She smiled a mysterious librarian's smile, as if only she had the key to the reference room of life. "I'm not nearly as shy as Mary."

A bespectacled man in a baggy brown sweater stuck his head into the room, then shuffled into the doorway. He was carrying a thick looseleaf notebook and a folded *Wall Street Journal.*

He smiled nervously and said, "I need the financial pages from October, nineteen twenty-nine."

Adelaide said, "This is the place."

He came all the way into the room and stood in front of the file cabinets, studying labels. The sweater had leather elbow patches. "Maybe if I read about the twenty-nine crash, I can figure out where the stock market's going next," he said. But he sounded doubtful, almost woeful.

The librarian in Adelaide sprang to life and she offered to be of service.

Nudger said good-bye and left the two of them bent over the file cabinet drawers, Adelaide helping the guy in the brown sweater try to do what Nudger was attempting: make sense of the present and divine the future by exploring the past. Somehow come out ahead when the smoke cleared. People had been working on that one since before Nostradamus and not doing well at all.

At least Nudger could exercise some control over *his* future; he was going to have lunch.

To add the spice of uncertainty to the afternoon, he decided to drive by Claudia's and see if she wanted to join him. The fall semester was just getting under way at Stowe High School, and she'd mentioned that this was the date for late registration and she had the day off. She was probably lounging around her apartment, maybe getting a few things done at home before settling down to the grind of a new school year. Domestic duties. Unsuspectingly sorting the wash or vacuuming. Soon-to-be-jealous Claudia.

Ah, she was home! Her tiny white Chevette sedan was parked in front of her apartment building on Wilmington. As Nudger got out of his car and crossed the street, a few of Claudia's neighbors stopped what they were doing to stare at him. What they were doing was raking nasty leaves off their manicured little lawns, or planting zoysia grass. Early fall was a good time to plant the sturdy grass; it was placed on lawns in plugs, rather like hair transplants, so that when spring came it could begin its insidious takeover of less hardy growth. Innocent Bermuda grass didn't stand a chance. Not even crabgrass. Nor was any other grass preferred in this part of town. People here were serious about their lawns. Even devout. In the pantheon of deities, zoysia was the god of South St. Louis.

Inside the building, away from prying eyes, Nudger climbed the steps to Claudia's second-floor apartment and knocked on the door.

She opened it almost immediately—a medium-height, slender woman with dark hair and whimsical brown eyes. A woman who grew more attractive with each minute spent with her, each angle she presented. Hers was a face that belonged in a Renaissance painting: oval, somber, with a too-long but otherwise perfect nose. There was a plainness yet at the same time an odd nobility about Claudia that carried with it a low-voltage but sizzling sex appeal.

She said, "It's you."

"You sound disappointed."

"Don't be contentious, Nudger. Come on in." She stepped back with a dancer's grace, her blue skirt swirling elegantly around slender ankles, her high heels leaving tiny indentations in the carpet. The outfit was a favorite of Nudger's and one she'd worn on dates with him. He realized she was dressed to go out. Oh-oh!

He went inside and she closed the door behind him lightly, as if she wanted to open it again soon to let him out and was making sure it wouldn't be stuck shut. The old Wilmington apartment was large and high-ceilinged, the sort of place common to the neighborhood. It had an old-fashioned crystal chandelier, fancy woodwork coated with layers of enamel, windows with wooden frames and venetian blinds, a brick fireplace that was no longer functional. Used and comfortable, a connection with the past. Nudger felt at home here.

Usually.

Claudia didn't try to brush him off with lies. Give her that much. She said, "I was expecting someone else."

"Biff Archway?"

"Well, yes."

"I was gonna ask you to lunch. Thought I'd splurge, take you downtown and buy you a steak."

She smiled. "Lying bastard."

"About the steak maybe."

He put his fists on his hips and walked over to the window overlooking the street, peering through the blind's wooden slats and half-expecting to see Biff Archway parking down there, getting out of his sports car, and jogging healthily toward the building. Cheeks rosy, teeth flashing white, barrel chest stuck out, powerful arms pumping like pistons. Nudger really disliked that guy.

"What are you looking for?" Claudia asked. He could tell by her voice that she knew what. She didn't like it when Nudger and Archway got together. The last time, it had resulted in Nudger being flipped about and flying through the air like a man gone berserk on a trampoline. Archway was an expert in martial arts, as he was in most things.

Nudger said, "Mostly I see zoysia grass."

"There's plenty of that around here. Too bad the stuff's not good to eat."

"Maybe it is. Tried it?"

"No."

"They say dandelions are delicious when they're cooked right."

"They say."

He decided to lay it on her. "I saw another woman last night."

"I'm not surprised; we make up more than half the population."

"I mean, I was out with another woman."

"Were you really?" She seemed only mildly interested. Hah! Wait till she heard.

"Name's Bonnie. A bright and beautiful young widow."

"That covers everything but rich. You didn't mention rich."

"Rich? I dunno. She's employed. A cosmetics executive."

"Where'd you and Bonnie go?"

Ah, her curiosity was up. "Dinner. Then her place."

"Which is where?"

Another question. Nudger liked the way this was going. He turned away from the window to look at Claudia, who had an eyebrow arched in what Nudger hoped was disapproval. Christ, he loved her! "She's got a house out in the county."

"Meet her through a case you're on?"

"Yeah. The Virgil Hiller disappearance."

"That the big-shot politician who stole from the city and ran away with his secretary?"

"I don't think that's exactly the way it happened," Nudger said. "Neither does Bonnie." Even as he spoke, he decided he'd better take it easy mentioning Bonnie over and over. He was messing with something potent here. A woman scorned could be a hellcat.

Claudia showed no reaction at the mention of Bonnie's name. She said, "Nudger, I'm glad you've found you can enjoy the company of other women. I feel good about you and this Bonnie person. Now maybe you can understand how I feel, realize this arrangement of ours doesn't mean I'm not still fond of you."

Huh? What kind of crap was this? He said, "You really think what you just told me makes sense?"

She glared a dark warning at him. "Nudger, don't start this conversation. Not now."

"When?"

"I don't know. We've had it before, though, and it leads nowhere except to an argument."

"What about tomorrow?" Very calmly: "Lunch tomorrow?"

"I have a doctor's appointment."

"You're sick?"

She seemed almost to smile at the concern in his voice. "It's a routine Pap smear; nothing to worry about."

"Dammit, Claudia—"

A car door slammed outside.

Nudger turned back to the window and saw Biff jogging across the street, away from his parked Mustang convertible, cheeks rosy, white teeth flashing, barrel chest stuck out, powerful arms pumping like pistons. A few of the leaf rakers halted work for a moment to wave at him. So much personal magnetism paper clips flew at him. Popular guy wherever he went. Especially with the women.

"That Biff?" Claudia asked.

"Sure. Don't you hear the trumpets?"

She shook her head at the hopelessness of trying to reason with him. "Help yourself to a beer, Nudger, then let yourself out."

She backed quickly to the door, and before he could say anything she was outside in the hall and the door was shut. He heard the clatter of her heels on the stairs. Heard the vestibule door open and close with a sound that reminded him of airlocks in science fiction movies.

He peered through the venetian blind slats again and saw Archway stop on the sidewalk and raise his arms as if to embrace her. She pecked him on the cheek, ducking in and out between his arms like a nifty bantamweight before he could touch her, and stalked toward his car. He shrugged and followed. Patient. Certain. Shoulders a little hunched, elbows slightly winged; a virile, confident walk.

As Claudia got into the car, she glanced almost angrily up at the window. Nudger thought of waving to her, but she'd lowered herself into the low-slung vehicle before he had a chance.

Archway wedged in behind the steering wheel. The red Mustang snarled what sounded to Nudger like a definite insult, then its tires dug in and it shot away from the curb and accelerated down the street. Changed tone and laid a few feet of rubber as Archway hit second gear in a speed shift. Probably he'd raced in a few Grand Prixs. An old guy washing his Pontiac tipped his baseball cap as the red bullet zipped past, doubtless wishing he were still young and hot-blooded. Then he bent again to the task of scrubbing his whitewalls until they looked virginal.

Nudger stood at the window for a long time, feeling the afternoon heat radiate from the glass, listening to the faint and desperate drone of a fly trapped behind the blinds.

Finally he trudged into the kitchen and got a can of Busch beer from the refrigerator. Put together a bologna sandwich. Got lucky and found some pickles.

Lunch, not as he'd planned it.

10

The hell with Biff Archway, and double-the-hell with Claudia. That was how Nudger felt at the moment, anyway.

He got a paper towel and wiped the crumbs off Claudia's kitchen table. Felt a few of them crunch underfoot as he walked over and threw away the wadded towel and his empty beer can. The can bounced with despondent, hollow thunks at the bottom of the empty wastebasket. Just the way Nudger's heart no doubt sounded. His hands smelled like bologna. He washed them, and they smelled like bologna and soap.

It gave him perverse pleasure to use Claudia's phone to call Bonnie Beal for another dinner date.

Bonnie's machine answered. He remembered she'd said she was doing temporary office work and wouldn't be home until five. And the kids were either at school or at a baby sitter. The oldest, Tad, would be only a high school junior or senior. At the machine's piercing tone, Nudger identified himself and left his office phone number. Then he hung up and called Hammersmith at the Third.

The desk sergeant, Ellis, asked who was calling, though

Nudger knew he recognized his voice. Procedure ran thick in cops' blood. Satisfied, Ellis then turned Nudger over to the crackling and clicking of the switchboard system. Lost among the microchips. Several minutes passed before Hammersmith came to the phone.

"Got the Hiller thing solved yet?" he asked.

"No, but I've got this feeling I'm further along than the police."

"Too many feelings, that's always been your problem, Nudge."

"Facts will follow."

"Maybe. I assume you didn't call to chat about the economy. So what can I do for you?"

"Anything on the bullet they dug out of my wall?"

"Yeah, it's what the Maplewood police thought. Lump of lead that tells us nothing. Maybe if it hadn't slammed into that hard wooden stud and flattened out it'd mean something. What we know for sure is that it's a bullet from a gun that was pointed toward your office window. That oughta be enough to inspire reason and caution in you, Nudge."

"Maybe you should question Arnie Kyle about it."

"There's an idea on par with arms for hostages. Kyle you don't question unless you got something stronger than suspicion. He's got layers of attorneys around him you have to peel back one by one. Incidentally, we talked to Adelaide Lacy a little while ago. Nice of you to warn her we were on our way."

"I didn't think you were gonna try to sneak up on her. Remember, she's the one the police wouldn't listen to in the beginning. You learn anything new from her?"

"For Chrissakes, Nudge, she's *your* client. You oughtta know everything *we* learned from her—which is basically nothing." He paused. Nudger heard the puffing and slurping of a cigar being lighted. Wheeze! Cough! "We share on this one," Hammersmith said, his words distorted by the cigar in his mouth. "What friendsh are for."

Nudger said, "That mean you'll call me right away if anything new turns up?"

"Coursh." Pause. "You gonna be home tonight, or at Claudia's?" He'd taken the cigar out of his mouth.

"Neither."

"Working late at your offish?" Back in.

"No."

"Shtake-out, like on telewishion?"

"No."

"Okay, be fuckin' myshterioush!" Hammersmith said, and hung up.

He had a fetish about hanging up first on phone conversations. Made him feel one up on the world. He knew Nudger would call later and leave him a number.

Bonnie had turned on the cute and invited Nudger for dinner with the family at her house. She must have figured why not? He knew the worst and would either stick or bolt. Maybe this way he'd find out she could cook, and that would count for something. If she could.

The subdivision ranch house on Pleasant Lane looked the same. Same tree growing through the white circle of stones in the center of the front yard, same grease-stained driveway, same air of . . . well, sameness.

Janet, the fifteen-year-old, answered Nudger's knock on the front door. She was wearing acid-washed jeans, scuffed brown sandals, and an untucked white T-shirt lettered MOUNTAINS OF LOVE across her undeveloped breasts. She looked him up and down.

"You got dressed up," she said.

Nudger was wearing wrinkled slacks and his threadbare brown corduroy sportcoat. "No tie," he pointed out.

She stared at him like a miniature hostile Bonnie, as if considering whether to admit him. Once inside, he might steal the silverware and rape the women.

"I'm only here for supper," he told her, "not to plunder." He flashed his winningest, most reassuring smile at her, pretending for an instant that he was Biff Archway. Just for an instant.

"I know," she said, warming up a few degrees to the Archway method. "Listen, Tad told me what he like said to you. He shouldn't have done that. Tad's a geek."

"He's worried about his mother," Nudger said. "I understand that."

Janet shook her head. "No, he's a geek."

"A geek's a guy who bites the heads off chickens in carnival freak shows."

"That ain't what a geek is at school."

"Maybe they behave at school," Nudger said.

"Did I hear the doorbell?" Bonnie appeared a few feet behind Janet. She was wearing a crisp pink dress and actually had a white apron tied around her waist. The word "frilly" leaped into Nudger's mind. On her left cheek was an unmistakable smudge of flour. The apron emphasized her tiny waist and generous breasts. Nudger felt as if he were making time with June Cleaver behind Ward's back. There was a kind of erotic domesticity about it all that he liked. He wondered if it was calculated.

"He didn't ring the doorbell," Janet said, "just knocked."

"Either way, invite him in. Where's your manners?"

"Manners are for phonies."

Nudger thought he could grow to like Janet. He wasn't so sure about Tad.

Janet solemnly stepped aside so Nudger could enter.

The living room had been picked up. Even the furniture was squarely aligned against the walls. Not a sign of dust, and there were vacuum sweeper tracks on the blue carpet, as if the floor had been colored in with pale chalk laid flat and moved in a series of wide arcs. From the kitchen wafted the scent, even the taste, of bread baking.

Bonnie wiped her hands nervously on the apron, smiled cute as you please, and said, "Hope you like spaghetti."

"One of my favorites," Nudger said.

As if in doubt, Janet said, "Really?" Candid and suspicious Janet.

He nodded. "Cut my heart out if I'm lying."

"Then you better lick your plate clean," said a Clint Eastwood voice that broke into a momentary yodel. Tad.

Bonnie's grin stretched wider, desperate. As if to make sure Nudger knew Tad had cracked a lame joke. He's only a boy, the grin said. You understand. *Don't you?*

Nudger thought, What the hell am I doing here?

Tad had on grimy Levi's, a thick black belt with an oversized silver buckle in the form a race car, and a black shirt with the arms cut off. A rose with a dagger through it was tattooed on his scrawny left bicep, above the scrawled blue-lettered words BORN TO BE BAD. The left side of his nose was smeared with grease.

Bonnie squinted at the grease and said, "Wash that face before dinner, Tad."

He glared at her. "I been workin' on the Plymouth."

"Now work on your face."

He shrugged and moved away angrily in a swagger that didn't belong with his skinny body. Made him look like a Slinky bounding down an incline.

"Told you," Janet said. "Geek."

"I made some martinis," Bonnie said. "I noticed you had one last night before dinner at the restaurant."

"Sounds great," said Nudger, who usually drank bourbon or beer and had forced down a martini last night only to impress her. Janet was staring dubiously at him. Little bitch had some kind of truth radar.

He crossed the living room and sat down on the plaid sofa. It was firm and uncomfortable and he'd bet it was the kind that unfolded to make a hard and torturous bed. He'd seen them at J. C. Penney's and just being near them had made his back ache.

Bonnie brought him his martini, complete with two olives impaled on a tiny red plastic sword.

It was a good martini if you had a taste for gin, which Nudger didn't. Bonnie excused herself and bustled back to the kitchen, while Janet continued to stare. Somewhere in the house an infant began to cry.

"That Belinda?" Nudger asked.

Janet shrugged. "Yeah. She's like always crying. That's babies for you."

"Guess so."

There was a loud grating noise and four-year-old James scooted into the room on a heavy-duty plastic truck with wide rubber wheels. It had some kind of ratchety mechanism to represent the roar of an engine. James had on jeans and a red shirt that was crookedly buttoned. He was barefoot. His straw-colored hair was unbelievably mussed. When he saw Nudger he grinned and said something like "Vroooooooroarr!" Short legs pumping crazily, he steered the plastic truck in ever-tightening circles until it toppled onto its side. James lay on his back as if horribly injured and began to kick the carpet, then roll, all the time grinning and keeping his eyes trained on Nudger. Wasn't often somebody new to show off to ventured into the house.

Tad slunk back from washing his face. The grease stain was a gray film now. Carlotta, the adopted Mexican ten-year-old, stood near him, gazing at Nudger with sad brown eyes, like the children he'd seen begging in south-of-the-border newsreels. The kind that inspired instant guilt. Belinda was still wailing. Even louder. Calling ships at sea.

Nudger took a long pull on the martini. It actually tasted pretty good.

Bonnie called from the kitchen, "Janet, help set the table. Tad, you get the chairs."

Tad said, "Shit!"

"I do nuffin'!" James yelled.

Janet moaned and trudged toward the dining room, kicking at James but missing as she passed. Tad groaned and followed her. Ask these kids to do something, they were in real pain.

Ten minutes later everyone was seated around an oval mahogany table in the dining room. A chandelier with a couple of hundred tiny bulbs glistened overhead. To Nudger's left, a bay window looked out on the yard next door, where a mangy golden retriever was shoving its plastic water dish across the cement. The sound the dish made was something like James's foot-propelled truck.

Janet dished up the salad. Gave Nudger three broken leaves of lettuce. Then she sat down, sighing as if she were celebrating her ninetieth birthday. Nudger glanced at Belinda, who was playing with the Rice Chex that had been placed on the tray of her highchair to placate her. James sat in a regular chair, but up on two phone books. Head thrown back, he was gripping his glass with both hands and draining it of the milk that wasn't dribbling down his chin. Janet was hungrily forking in the heap of salad she'd lavished on her bowl. Carlotta had disdained her salad and was gazing with Latin intensity at the platter of spaghetti in the center of the table. Tad was spearing a wedge of tomato over and over with his fork, as if tomatoes represented everything he hated. Bonnie smiled at Nudger. Happy family scene.

Still glaring at the tomato, Tad said, "Can't get the damned carburetor adjusted right."

"Must you always talk about cars?" Bonnie asked.

"Fuel mixture's too rich."

"*Must* you, Tad?"

"What else is there to talk about?"

Bonnie looked to Nudger for help. He took a generous bite of lettuce and finished most of his salad. He didn't have a tomato to abuse. Didn't have an answer. He couldn't imagine Tad chatting about the weather.

Janet said, "My civilization teacher's like out to get me. I mean, who *cares* where Tasmania is?"

"That would be geography, wouldn't it?" Nudger said.

"Sure, that's just what I mean. And who *cares?*"

"Tasmanians," Tad said. "They care."

Janet gave him a look that suggested he was other than human.

Tad said, "They got cars in Tasmania?"

"I dunno, geek."

Bonnie said, "Of course they have cars in Tasmania," and began dishing up the spaghetti, ladling rich red sauce over it. Nudger was glad. He'd worked up an appetite with that salad. The sauce had a pungent scent that almost brought tears to his eyes. Spicy. The way he liked it.

"Toyotas and Nissans, I bet," Tad said. "Them Japanese cars is everywhere, with their little four-banger engines."

The sauce was as advertised. Nudger thought the spaghetti was delicious. The accompanying bread was just as good. He helped himself to some Parmesan cheese. Bonnie could cook, all right.

"When *we* gonna get a new car, Mom?" Tad asked.

Carlotta spoke for the first time. "When Nora Dove says so."

Janet snickered.

Tad said, "Maybe the company'll give you a Corvette, hey? Goddamn, that'd be somethin'—Mom in a hot red Corvette."

Nudger could see it. Wondered why the picture was so incongruous to Tad. "Mom" was a pretty hot number herself.

James said, "Twuck."

"Cosmetics ladies don't drive trucks!" Janet sneered, a shred of lettuce stuck between her front teeth.

James said, "Twuck" again.

"He's asking for butter," Carlotta explained patiently. "He's talking with his mouth full—as usual."

Bonnie said, "Janet, you can reach; give your brother the butter."

"He can like reach it himself."

"Give it to him!"

Janet took a bite of spaghetti.

"Like to see Mom in one of them little four-wheel-drive pickup trucks," Tad said. "Deliver that Nora Dove shit any-where they ordered, she had one of those. Get one with a turbo-charged engine."

"Tad, shut up about cars!" Bonnie said. "Janet, butter!"

Janet reluctantly used her knife and plopped a wedge of

—— 76 ——

margarine on James's plate. He delicately picked it up with his thumb and forefinger and tried to throw it at her, but it slipped from his grasp and dropped to the floor. Bonnie didn't seem to have noticed. Janet was winding spaghetti around her fork and James was quiet.

The butter episode was finished.

Tad ate his spaghetti with noisy gusto, letting it trail from his mouth and sucking it in to swallow without chewing.

"Manners!" Bonnie cautioned.

Tad said, "You got a V-8 engine in that Granada of yours, Nudger?"

"Six cylinder."

"They ain't for shit," Tad said, and continued to slurp spaghetti.

Belinda had managed to reach Bonnie's salad fork and had accidentally stuck herself in the chin. She began to wail.

Janet said, "*Shut* up! Can't she just like *shut up?*"

Bonnie hugged Belinda and made soothing sounds. Woman didn't have things under control, but she had remarkable patience.

James began screaming and pleading for something, but no one could understand what he was saying.

So this was family life. Nudger's stomach was quivering and his head was starting to throb. He realized he'd left his antacid tablets at the office. Should have stopped and bought some on the way over here. Tylenol, too.

"I'm gonna get me a dual manifold and exhaust for the Plymouth," Tad proclaimed to no one in particular. "Eliminate some backup gas and add horsepower."

"You need to get like horse *sense*," Janet said.

"Up yours, slut!"

James was yelling louder. He threw a piece of hard-crusted bread at Janet. Belinda, who'd calmed down under Bonnie's attention, started screaming again, imitating James. Carlotta smiled wistfully.

Tad said, "You just ain't old enough to drive, so you're pissed."

Janet said, "Like screw *you!*"

Bonnie said, "Janet will clean up most of the mess, Nudger. The kids can have dessert here while we go out someplace quiet for coffee. That sound okay to you?"

Nudger said, "I guess so."

Over carrot cake and coffee at a Denny's franchise restaurant, Bonnie said, "Been kind of a whirlwind since Gary died."

Nudger studied her in the harsh fluorescent light. Not so cute at the moment. Like a well-worn Barbie Doll down from the attic. Fine lines swooping from the wings of her turned-up nose down to the corners of her strained red lips. Mascara smeared beneath the china blue eyes. Blond hair more lank than pert. There was a faint spattering of spaghetti sauce on the shoulder of her pink dress, like stains on her life.

"He had a minor heart attack," she said. "Survived that one, and we thought he was gonna be okay. Things had never seemed sweeter, since we'd almost lost them. Two weeks later another, massive attack took him." Her voice was weary and objective, as if she'd hashed all this out but still had a mechanical need to reiterate. "I was pregnant with Belinda when he died."

Nudger wasn't sure what to say. Hadn't dated many grieving widows. "Must have been rough," was all he could muster. It sounded feeble and insincere. He took a bite of carrot cake.

Chewed slowly. Somebody in a nearby booth must have ordered garlic bread; its sharp scent drifted to him.

"There are plenty of people have it rougher," Bonnie said. "We had mortgage insurance, so the house is paid for. Still, kids are more expensive as they get older." Nudger thought she might tell him the kids needed the firm hand of a father, but he supposed that went without saying. She grinned, for a moment young Doris Day without a care. Being cute was her armor, her defensive game plan for life, and there was nothing cute about maudlin. "Hey, we get by."

"That's what most people do," he said, "get by." He was seeing a new depth to Bonnie, a woman behind the facade.

She drew in a breath, took a long sip of coffee, knowing it was time to change the subject. "Making any progress on the Virgil Hiller disappearance?"

"I'm not sure. In my line of work, whether you're making progress is something you seem to find out all at once."

"You don't like being a detective."

"You can tell?"

"It's almost lettered on your forehead. Why don't you find another occupation?"

There was a question Nudger had often asked himself. "This one found me," he said. "Not liking it is the only way I'm not suited for it. Besides, it's more than an occupation. It's what I do. If you know what I mean."

"What you are," she said.

"That's right; seems to make little difference that I don't like it. Somehow it's become *me*. Or I've turned into *it*."

Bonnie finished her cake and rested her fork on the plate. "I'm going to deliver some Nora Dove to Gina Hiller tomorrow," she said. "Want me to ask her anything about her husband? Maybe she'd tell me something she wouldn't tell you. You know, woman to woman."

Off on a grand adventure—Nick and Nora Charles. "I don't want to use you that way, Bonnie."

"You wouldn't be; I volunteered."

True. And that did indeed put another light on it.

The waitress came and asked if everything was okay. Nudger knew that everything was never okay, but he smiled and said that it was. Let her have her illusions, not knowing they were as perishable as the lettuce.

Bonnie extended a hand to her plate and touched a cake crumb firmly, so that it stuck to the tip of her finger, then popped it into her mouth. She said, "I'm a born volunteer. Really."

"All right," Nudger said. "But don't ask Gina Hiller questions. See if you can move the conversation in the direction of the errant husband and then let her take the lead. Just listen."

Bonnie nodded. "And remember what she said, so I can tell you." She was already a pro at this game. She thought.

"Remember that deceiving people can be damned dangerous," Nudger told her, wondering if this was really a good idea.

But he could see that good idea or not, Bonnie was determined to play her role.

He asked if she wanted another cup of coffee, but she said no, she'd better get back home and make sure the kids hadn't leveled the house.

He thought she was probably serious.

After driving Bonnie home, Nudger aimed the Granada west on Manchester, then north on Lindbergh. Toward the address he'd looked up in the phone book—Paul Dobbs's apartment.

St. Louis's schizophrenic weather was at it again. Now that darkness had fallen, the evening had turned cold. Wind chill factor of thirty degrees, said the car radio, even though the temperature was in the low forties.

The Granada's windshield started to fog up, and Nudger switched on the defrosters. Helped some. He wished he'd brought a coat.

Dobbs lived in Chez Le Chic, an apartment project off North Lindbergh near the airport. It consisted of three L-shaped buildings, each built around a square swimming pool. The architecture was somebody's idea of French, with fancy shutters, hip roofs, and iron balconies. The rent was probably moderately high, mainly because of convenient location if you were some-body on the go. Nudger suspected the apartments were full of people other people called yuppies.

Dobbs's building was the Frenchest of all, constructed of white brick and trimmed in blue. Neatly pruned hedges lined the front wall on each side of the softly lighted entrance. The light was soft because it was coming from fixtures hidden in the shrubbery.

Nudger parked in a visitors' slot on the blacktop front lot, then went into the blue-and-white tiled foyer. Saw Dobbs's business card inserted in a plastic slot above the fancy brass mail slot for apartment 2B. Mail was jammed into the locked box. Some junk mail addressed to Dobbs was fastened together with a thick rubber band and lay on the tile floor beneath the stuffed mailbox. The top piece said Dobbs might have won a bamboo steamer; not as impressive as Mary Lacy's new Buick, but look what the guy was missing, not being home.

Just for the hell of it, Nudger pressed the button to buzz the apartment. Maybe Dobbs was back from Fiji, or wherever it was Hammersmith had suggested the photographer had dashed off to, and simply hadn't bothered or had time to collect his mail. Man on the run with camera and assignment. Like an old *Life* photojournalist in the forties. Hubba, hubba. Hammersmith was caught in a time warp.

Nudger leaned on the buzzer again. No surprise. The inter-com was silent.

He took the stairs to the second floor, then used his honed Visa card to slip the pathetic lock on 2B's door. Cheap apart-ment hardware. No problem. Sometimes Nudger *did* like being a detective.

He pushed the door open and stepped inside. Not so much fun now. Breaking and entering, this was called in courts of law. Carried a penalty of fine and imprisonment. Nudger's stomach was fluttering like hummingbird wings.

The apartment had about it the perfect stillness of places that had been sealed and unoccupied for a long time. In the sickly orange glow from the sodium streetlight, filtering in through the sheer drapes, he could see that it was furnished modern. Lots of low tables, a two-foot-high sofa that might be even more uncomfortable than Bonnie's. There were what looked like metal-framed modern prints or paintings on the walls, but when Nudger glanced at the one nearest him he saw that it was actually an enlarged photograph. Looked like a swirl of different colored liquids on a flat surface. There were dark spatters over the graceful swirls, like blood shed in violence, only they were different colors, too. He wondered if it was Dobbs's work.

The wall switch near the door turned on a squat yellow lamp by the sofa. There was a clear glass ashtray next to the lamp, ashes and two filtered cigarette butts in it. The butts were stale. The smell of them contaminated the air.

Swallowing the nervous lump in his throat, Nudger began nosing around the apartment.

Dobbs's closet and dresser contained plenty of clothes, which would indicate that if he'd gone somewhere on an assignment it wouldn't be for long. On the other hand, what did you need by way of clothes in Fiji?

After about five minutes, Nudger found what he'd really come here to see. The place where Dobbs kept his photographic equipment.

It took up most of the walk-in closet in the second bedroom. The inside of the closet was a mess; there was undeveloped film unraveled all over the place, and three expensive Canon thirty-five-millimeter cameras lay on the hardwood floor with their backs open.

The closet was set up to be a simple but functional darkroom. An enlarger lay on its side on a narrow counter. Bottles of developing chemicals and wash were knocked over on their shelves. Shallow metal trays were stacked crookedly in a corner. Half a dozen rubber-coated tongs lay in a clutter in the top tray. Developer had been spilled somewhere; its bleachlike scent permeated the closet.

A sudden noise from the living room made Nudger suck in his breath, fear clawing at his insides. The smell of the spilled developer suddenly made him feel sick.

Someone else was in the apartment, walking slowly toward the smaller bedroom that Dobbs used for sleeping.

Nudger heard the floor creak. Close to him. His heart scurried up into his throat and expanded there.

This bedroom would be next, he was sure. And he doubted if he was hearing Dobbs light-footing it around his own apartment.

Only one direction available. He eased his way out the sliding glass doors onto the rear balcony. Two stories below, the deserted swimming pool glimmered darkly in the moonlight, water black as licorice.

A deep, amused voice crooned from the room he'd just left, "Come out, come out, wherever you are." A parody of childhood. Taunting. Sadistic. Coaxing.

Nudger moved to the side of the balcony, almost bumping into a huge fern in a ceramic planter. Pressed himself against the cool hard bricks.

Beyond the opposite building he could see the streaming lights of traffic out on Lindbergh. The rushing sound of the cars was barely audible. A lonely whisper. There was no way off the small balcony other than through the bedroom, or by a Tarzan-caliber two-story dive into the pool, and it occurred to Nudger that he didn't know which end was the deep one. Fear jellied his knees and he tasted the metallic bitterness of bile at the base of his tongue.

"Getting a breath of night air, are you?" the voice said, playing this out, enjoying it. Nearer. Moving toward the open glass doors. "Well, you should enjoy breathing while you can. Something we all take for granted."

Nudger wasn't taking it for granted at the moment. He was paralyzed with the knowledge that breathing might be a bodily function soon denied him.

Then anger tipped the balance over fear and revived him from his transfixed state. *Nobody had the right to do what the* man in Dobbs's bedroom was threatening. *Nobody had the right to terrorize another human being this way. Especially if that human being was Nudger. That made it intimate and infuriating.*

Nudger was able to think.

To act.

He found sudden strength and lifted the ceramic planter to hurl at the man. The fern tickled his cheek, and small clods of dirt rained at his feet.

He waited, muscles strained; the rich loam in the planter brought the smell of the grave.

Then he had a better idea.

He yelled and tossed the heavy planter, fern and all, out over the pool. Then, simultaneous with the splash below, he drew back into the shadows at the very end of the balcony. Crushed himself against the bricks.

A large man wearing a black or dark blue suit ran to the balcony railing, skidded on his heels to a stop, and said, "Goddamn it!"

He gazed for a second down at the foam and ripples in the dark pool. Then he wheeled and ran back into Dobbs's apartment. Nudger saw the dull gleam of a gun in his hand. *Jesus! Meant business, all right!*

Nudger waited five seconds before he followed the man's path through the empty apartment. He could hear descending footfalls crashing on the back stairs.

He ran as silently as he could down the front stairs. His heart was banging an insane rhythm against his ribs, echoing in his ears. Urging him to hurry!

Then he was out the front entrance and racing across the parking lot to his car. Opening up his stride.

"Hey!" a voice yelled behind him.

Nudger didn't know whose voice. Didn't pause or look back. He had his key in his hand when he yanked open the car door. Had it in the ignition switch even before he was all the way in the seat. Twisting the key almost hard enough to break it.

The engine ground . . . ground.

Coughed.

Then roared to life.

Nudger jammed the shift lever into Drive and the Granada screeched from the parking lot like a wild thing set free, its right front fender ticking one of the brick pillars flanking the driveway. He yanked the steering wheel to the left, let it slide back through his fingers, then stomped the accelerator again. Luckily there was a break in the traffic on Lindbergh, or he might have caused a hundred-car pile up.

He got off Lindbergh as soon as he could. Took every side street too fast, skidding around corners, checking the rear-view mirror on the straightaways.

Ten minutes passed before he could assure himself he wasn't being followed. And it was a wonder he hadn't picked up a cop, speeding around like a teenage leadfoot. Like Tad. Even a few minutes ago he'd have given anything to see a police car in his rear-view mirror. Where were the traffic cops when you needed them? Out wasting their time chasing crooks? He'd talk to Hammersmith about this.

There was much he wanted to talk about with Hammersmith. He was sure now that Dobbs hadn't disappeared of his own volition, and that Mary Lacy hadn't simply fallen helplessly in love and run away with the irresistible Virgil Hiller and his stolen half million dollars.

Nudger had bought a fresh roll of antacid tablets while paying the cashier at Denny's restaurant. He popped three tablets into his mouth and chewed frantically but with a sense of relief. Some night this had been!

He drove toward home, wondering about tomorrow.

But the night hadn't finished with him. A few minutes before midnight he awoke sweating and clutching the thin sheet. His mind was free of his dream, but his body remained captive. His heart still pounded crazily, pumping fear along with blood. Not fear for himself, but for Claudia.

They'd been on a picnic, just Nudger and Claudia, in what he thought was Forest Park. Odd, because Claudia was big city and joked about not liking to step off concrete. Not the picnic type. But in the dream they were sitting on the grass, with sandwiches and paper cups and plastic forks spread before them on a white blanket. Everything on the blanket was white—except for a tiny black insect that scurried out from beneath a slice of bread.

Claudia had been laughing with her mouth open wide, but when she saw the insect she stopped laughing and said, "I hate them."

"Ants?"

"Not ants."

Nudger scooted sideways on the cool grass and leaned down to study the insect.

Claudia was right; it wasn't an ant. It was even smaller than an ant, with countless flailing legs and rapacious pincers. That was all the thing seemed to be, legs and scythelike pincers.

It stopped crawling, and that was when Nudger felt a cold fear that drilled deep, deep to the center of his brain.

He knew that the thing was aware of him. Staring back at him and emitting a malevolence that struck him like a fist, left him gasping.

Then another of the tiny creatures scurried out from beneath a sandwich.

Another.

Another appeared from between the white plastic tines of a fork.

Then they filled vision with motion. The white blanket was suddenly gray, covered with the infinitesimal creatures so that it seemed alive and undulating in pain.

Astounded, Nudger turned to draw Claudia's attention to the spectacle. Share it with her.

He couldn't see her.

He heard her scream.

Still hearing her scream, Nudger struggled out of bed and padded to the bathroom. He thought about running cold water on his wrists, but that might wake him so completely he'd never get back to sleep.

He relieved his bladder. Then he rinsed his hands and stood leaning over the washbasin, waiting for the ticking, soothing seconds to leave the nightmare far enough in the past so that it *was* nothing more than a bad dream.

Somehow the cold tile against his bare soles soothed him, rooted him in reality.

A long time passed before he lay down again.

A longer time before he returned to sleep.

12

Nudger caught up with Hammersmith the next morning at the Webster Grill and Cafe, where the lieutenant often had breakfast when he was working the early shift. Hammersmith was slouched in a booth near the front window, a piece of buttered toast halfway to his mouth. He put on an annoyed expression. Looked as if any second he might say, "Damn, can't I even eat in peace?"

"I wouldn't bother you at breakfast, only it's important," Nudger said, sliding into the booth to sit across from him. The booth benches at the Webster Grill were fashioned from old oak church pews that had been sawed in half and fitted against the walls. The ends of the benches had crosses engraved in them. High above the booths, ceiling fans rotated their wide blades slowly, as if to test the air rather than stir it.

On the other side of a low wooden partition, the cook worked in plain sight behind a serving counter. The tantalizing smell of frying bacon rode the air, thick enough to taste.

"How'd you find me?" Hammersmith asked.

"Called your house. Jed said you were probably here." Jed

was Hammersmith's teenage son, who was, so far as Nudger could tell, not at all like Tad. It was comforting to think Tad might be a mutant, but Nudger knew better.

"Gotta talk to that boy," Hammersmith said. He waved his fork. "Had breakfast, Nudge?"

"Yeah," Nudger lied.

"Sure. Why don't you order a wheat waffle? Those things are delicious." Hammersmith, however, was eating eggs, toast, and fried potatoes. Upping the old cholesterol count.

"I don't like health food."

"It's not sprouts or anything; it's a goddamn waffle. A zillion calories but worth it."

"Why the wheat then?"

"Forget the waffle, Nudge, and tell me why you're here."

The waitress, a pleasant woman with dark hair and eyes and a white bandage on her forefinger, came over and Nudger ordered coffee. He hadn't been by his office yet and gotten his usual cup of Danny's potent brew. Found that he actually missed the stuff. Could the body adapt to acid?

When the waitress returned he asked her how she'd hurt her finger. She told him a skiing accident. Nothing in the world seemed logical. He imagined a lodge full of skiers with bandaged fingers, sitting around a roaring fire and sipping Ovaltine.

After sampling his coffee—mere water compared to Danny's—Nudger said, "Suppose somebody let themselves into Paul Dobbs's apartment last night."

Hammersmith dabbed at his lips with a napkin, then wiped butter from a smooth-shaven jowl. Wobbled his head and straightened his tie like Rodney Dangerfield. "The suppose game, is it?"

"Attorneys play it all the time."

"Attorneys play all sorts of games."

"Let's play attorney."

"You mean broke in? Or with a key? As you know, Nudge, there's a difference."

"Is there really?"

"Uh-huh. 'Bout ten years." Hammersmith forked some egg

into his mouth, chewed, sipped coffee. He sure liked food; it was easy to understand how he'd put on so much weight over the years. "But let's keep on supposing. Let's suppose the person who got into Dobbs's apartment did so legally, and also happens to be a private investigator. Let's even suppose this person is you."

"For the sake of discussion," Nudger said.

"'Course." Another mouthful of egg, followed by coffee. Some fried potatoes. The breakfast was only half eaten, but going fast. "What did you find?"

Nudger told him about the disarray in Dobbs's closet-darkroom.

Hammersmith munched on a triangular piece of toast. "Interesting, Nudge. Happens I obtained a warrant and went through the Dobbs apartment myself, right after Adelaide Lacy came to us with her story."

"I didn't think the police took her story, or Dobbs's, seriously enough to look into."

"I'm going to level with you, Nudge. Confidence for confidence. It seems there are people who don't want the investigation of Hiller's disappearance to go in the direction of Paul Dobbs."

Nudger thought about that for a few seconds. "What sort of people? Higher-ups in the department?"

"Sure, but somebody's pressuring them. Politicos."

"How do politics enter into the disappearance of a man and his secretary? That's a police matter."

"For Chrissakes, Nudge, the guy was assistant comptroller. Politics. Something you never really understood. There's nothing sinister going on here; the fact is that Hiller probably *did* abscond with the money."

"So there might be political fallout. What about Mary Lacy? She deserves more than an investigation that pulls punches."

"I got a judge to issue a warrant so I could search Dobbs's apartment," Hammersmith reminded Nudger. "It's a matter of record, but on the other hand, I wouldn't want the information bandied about."

"So what did *you* find there?" Nudger asked.

"The same nothing you did. Only when I was there, Dobbs's darkroom was neatly organized."

That was news, Nudger thought.

"Also, I talked to some of his neighbors. They said his job often took him out of town on short notice."

"This time he didn't bother to stop his mail," Nudger said. "His box was jammed full and there was even a stack of junk mail beneath it on the floor."

Hammersmith toyed with his coffee cup. "There were only a few pieces in the box when I was there. I got the key from the manager and checked. Nothing but ads."

"Something else happened when I was at Dobbs's," Nudger said. He described his run-in with the big man carrying the gun.

"Guy must not know much about you," Hammersmith said, "or he'd have figured you wouldn't have dived off a second-story balcony into a dark swimming pool. Nevertheless, clever, that deal with the potted plant. So give me a description—of the big guy, not the plant."

"Well over six feet, with a lot of weight but not much fat. He moved smoothly, like an athlete. Maybe dark hair, but I'm not sure. He was wearing a blue or black suit. It might have been an automatic in his hand, a big one, large caliber."

"Big, athletic, blue or black suit. He doesn't change that suit, we got him."

"It was dark," Nudger pointed out. "He didn't stop and pose so I could identify him later." He was getting irritated with Hammersmith's wisecracking. "The thing is, this means somebody else is interested in Dobbs's disappearance. That somebody is probably Arnie Kyle, and he was looking for something in Dobbs's darkroom, or else making sure all of the film there was exposed and couldn't be developed. That must be why he opened the cameras and tossed them on the floor."

"I don't think Kyle owns a dark suit," Hammersmith said. "Not as far as we're concerned, with the evidence you've given me." He was finished with breakfast. Reached into his shirt pocket and withdrew a cigar, though he didn't remove the wrapper. A threat. A way to let Nudger know the conversation was about over.

"So what are you going to do now?" Nudger asked.

"Same thing I've been doing—sit with my hands tied. I told you, Nudge, politics."

"Politics stink."

"You bet. But I accept them as a fact of life, and you don't."

"Don't have to. I'm not a civil servant."

Hammersmith smiled. "And your hands aren't tied. Make sure your tongue isn't, either, when it comes to what you find out." He scooted his bulk out of the booth, then reached in his pocket for his silver lighter with a flame like a blowtorch. He fired up the cigar. A woman in a nearby booth looked ill and waved her hand in exaggerated fashion in front of her face. That kind of thing didn't faze Hammersmith. The whole world should smoke. "Gotta get down to the Third, Nudge, before crime takes over the city. Things in your life seem to be gaining momentum; you be careful you don't get run over by them."

"I'm always careful."

"Almost always." Hammersmith rested a hand on Nudger's shoulder for a moment, then glided over to the cash register. Despite his obesity, he still moved as he did twenty years ago. A younger man inside his bulk, the past inside the present.

Nudger saw him inform the cashier that he, Nudger, was paying for breakfast. Her gaze followed Hammersmith's pudgy, pointing finger.

Then, with a puff of green smoke, Hammersmith disappeared out the door. Might have been smiling.

The waitress ambled over. She was definitely smiling.

Nudger thought what the hell and ordered the wheat waffle.

13

As he parked the Granada at the broken meter across the street from his office, Nudger decided he could use another cup of coffee. Even a cup of Danny's.

There was actually a customer in Danny's, an old man wearing a heavy brown wool sweater despite the morning warmth. Mingled with the sweet aroma of fresh doughnuts was the acrid scent of mothballs. Sunlight that had streamed through the window lay in a golden trapezoid on the floor. A fly spiraled upward through the broad, dust-swirling beam and then flitted wildly against the window, as if mad for more warmth and light.

Nudger stood at the opposite end of the counter, away from the old guy who was death to moths. Danny drew a large cup of coffee from the steel urn and, since Nudger was standing, stuck a plastic lid on it. Carried it over to place it on the counter in front of Nudger and said, "Your lady's upstairs waiting for you."

Oh-oh! "Eileen?"

"That's not the lady," Danny said, "that was your wife."

Nudger stared at him. Danny wiped his hands on his gray towel, apparently not realizing he'd cracked a joke. Incredible.

"Didn't mean to scare you, Nudge. It's Claudia up in your office. Hey, you want a doughnut to go with your coffee?"

"No thanks," Nudger said. "Already had breakfast."

Carrying his warm foam cup, he moved toward the door.

Behind him the old guy in the sweater said, "This here's s'pose to be a jelly doughnut, but there ain't no jelly in it."

"Sometimes the pockets get off-center," Danny told him confidently. "Take another bite and jelly'll squirt all over you."

Nudger pushed through the door and got out of there before that happened.

He trudged up the creaking stairs and opened the door to his office.

Claudia was half leaning, half sitting on the edge of his desk. She was wearing a high-necked white blouse and a muted green plaid skirt, high heels, a gold pin on the blouse. Said, "Danny let me in."

"He told me."

Nudger placed the foam cup on his desk, walked around, and sat in his squealing swivel chair. Claudia stood up straight and turned to face him.

He said, "How come you're not out at the school?"

"I phoned and told them I'd be late this morning. I wanted to talk to you."

"Will you *look* at that," Nudger said, nodding toward the window. "Damned pigeons come right up to the glass and stare in."

Claudia smiled. "You're being evasive."

Nudger knew she was right. He was afraid of what she'd come here to tell him. Did she want to stop seeing him altogether? Was she going to hike across the country with hardy Biff Archway? Was she going to invite Nudger to her and Archway's wedding? Was that it? There was a dreadful cold weight in his chest. Come close to losing something, see how much it means to you.

Claudia said, "I left you abruptly yesterday. That was wrong of me. I want to apologize."

Nudger's spirits lifted. The pigeon fluttered against the glass and flapped away. Not only was she not going to tell Nudger something he didn't want to hear, she was here to ask his forgiveness. Maybe she'd thought about him going out with Bonnie Beal. Maybe gotten at least a tiny bit jealous. Delayed reaction. Possible.

He waved a hand in casual dismissal. "No problem. I understand." Magnanimous Nudger.

"Do you really?"

No. "Yes."

She managed to put together another smile. The cruel morning light tried hard but couldn't do a thing to her; she was beautiful. "How was your . . ."

"My date?" How had she guessed? Or had she been about to say something else?

"Yeah."

"Fine. How about yours, with Archway?"

She shifted her weight to her other leg, touched a lean finger to her blouse collar, as if to make sure it was buttoned all the way up. "The usual."

Nudger didn't want to know what that was. Said nothing. The silence grew huge and threatened to turn on them.

Claudia cleared her throat and said, "How you doing on the Hiller thing?"

"All right. It's his secretary I'm looking for, actually."

"I know. Hammersmith told me."

"You saw Hammersmith?"

"Ran into him downtown. We talked a while."

"About me, apparently."

"Sure. Hammersmith worries about you."

"He shouldn't."

"He does. He's your friend. So am I. He asked me to keep an eye on you, not let you do anything dumb. I told him that was a tall order."

Nudger picked up a pencil, stared at it, and dropped it on

—— 96 ——

the desk hard. It bounced and rolled under the phone, leaving its lead point behind. He didn't like Claudia and Hammersmith conferring about him. Friends trying to help could cause more harm than enemies trying to hurt.

Claudia said, "You're being an ass, Nudger."

He looked at her, knew she was right. This *friend*. He realized that was what really irritated him, that she should refer to him as a friend. After what they'd been to each other, done to each other.

Claudia laced her fingers in front of her and stood in an oddly prim, little-girl posture. "I guess what I came here for was to make sure things are the same between us."

"You mean on hold? In limbo?"

"No," she said, showing just a hint that he'd miffed her, "I wouldn't describe it that way. Not at all. We see each other."

He sighed. See each other in dreams, he thought. "You afraid of ants?"

"No. Why?"

"Just wondered." He pried the lid off his cup, managing to tear the plastic and prick his finger, and stared at the rising steam. He wasn't going to drink the coffee; his stomach was bucking. "I suppose we do see each other," he said. Trouble was, Archway seemed to be seeing more of Claudia than he was. And putting in quality time.

She walked around the desk and bent down gracefully. Kissed him on top of the head where he was just beginning to go bald. He grabbed her wrist but she grinned and pulled away. Had on a jangly gold bracelet that tinkled like gypsy finger cymbals. Gorgeous queen of the gypsies.

He said, "Dance for me."

"*What?*"

"Never mind."

"Don't be impetuous, Nudger. I've got to get to the school if I want to keep my job. No time for nonsense."

"Time should be made."

"I'll be home this evening. Time can be made then. Why don't you drop by?"

"You'll dance?"

"Something better."

"Better?"

She sort of pirouetted out the door. Nudger thought he heard the tinkle of finger cymbals, but it must have been the bracelet.

He listened to the fading tap of her high heels as she took the stairs fast, in a hurry to get to her work. Amazing how women could run down stairs in shoes like that. So much about women amazed him.

He stood up, walked to the window, and looked down.

She was crossing the street. Paused to let a westbound semi rumble past, held down her skirt so the breeze wouldn't give passengers a leg show. It reminded Nudger of when Adelaide Lacy had crossed the street toward the doughnut shop the day she'd hired him. Images orbiting forever, like radio signals in the ether. More *déjà vu* every year. On the opposite sidewalk, two executive types in dark business suits momentarily broke stride to glance at Claudia in surprised and brief admiration. The way men look at women.

Her white Chevette was parked half a block up, where Nudger hadn't noticed it. She climbed in behind the steering wheel. He saw the little car shudder as its engine started. It trembled eagerly. Then it bolted away from the curb and disappeared in dappled sunlight, picking up speed.

Nudger turned away from the window and sat down again behind his desk. Stared at the backs of his eyelids. Thought about the coming evening.

Something better.

14

Nudger sat in his desk chair, swiveling back and forth, staring out the window at the sky trying to make up its mind about what kind of weather to send at the city. The way he couldn't make up his mind about Mary Lacy. About what kind of woman she was. It was something he couldn't quite get a handle on, and it might have a lot to do with what had actually happened to her and Virgil Hiller.

Hiller had been a politico firmly plugged into the old boy network. A man of compromise, with others and doubtless with himself. No major surprise that he'd succumb to the temptations of an extramarital affair and half a million dollars. But Mary Lacy—if she was as her own sister described her—was another matter. It was difficult for Nudger to imagine her playing the other woman for a guy like Hiller. And if Hiller was dead, as Dobbs's photograph strongly suggested, then where was Mary Lacy?

Nudger decided it might be a good idea to get some insight into Mary not provided by sister Adelaide, or by merely snooping around Mary's apartment.

He locked up the office and drove back to the flat on Hoover, in search of a nosy neighbor.

He only had to knock on two doors before he came up with Mrs. McCloy, the elderly widow who lived in the unit directly above Mary's. As soon as Nudger had given her his vague cover story about being an insurance investigator determining the status of Mary Lacy's policy, Mrs. McCloy showed an uncommon willingness to gossip. Nudger's attentive ear was just what she'd been waiting for all these empty days.

She was a tiny, withered woman with wispy gray hair and watery blue eyes. There was a shrewd angularity to her thin lips, as if they were constantly pursed as she calculated, but it was probably due to badly fitted dentures rather than mental adroitness. She was wearing an embroidered pink something that might pass for either a robe or a dress. Nudger decided it was a robe. There was about her the scent of the old—a faint mingling of stale perspiration and spilled medicine, of musty final chapters.

"I just put on water for tea," she said hopefully. "'Less you'd prefer coffee."

And Nudger had been worried about lack of cooperation. He told her tea sounded great and followed her short, stooped frame into her living room. No wonder the elderly were the favorite targets of con men.

The living room probably looked the way it had twenty years ago. A threadbare sofa with curved mahogany arms, a matching wing chair, a worn oriental rug, an arrangement of black-and-white portraits in oval Bakelite frames, a painted brick fireplace with a studied arrangement of artificial flowers in front of its opening. Nudger didn't remember a fireplace in Mary Lacy's apartment; he wondered if there was one and it had been walled up.

The weather had decided to be cool, at least for the moment, and Mrs. McCloy had the thermostat set on high. It had to be eighty degrees in the cluttered apartment. Nudger immediately regretted his acceptance of the tea offer. Hot caffeine drinks when he was already overheated made his heart race. Someday the old pump might shake itself to pieces.

Mrs. McCloy gave a sly, crooked smile and limped into the kitchen. Just you wait, the smile said. I'm not a gossip, but we'll settle in all cozy with our cups of hot tea and I'll have something very important to tell you. Since you asked.

Above the mantel was a large crucifix, and on the opposite wall hung a poster-size print of Moses watching the recently parted Red Sea close on the hapless pursuing Egyptian army. It might not have been historically accurate, but it sure was graphic. Moses seemed unmoved by all the suffering. Wore a kind of smug, serves-you-right expression. On the mantel was an oval-framed black-and-white photograph of a hatchet-faced man in a World War Two army garrison cap. The late Mr. McCloy, no doubt. He was staring three-quarter-face into the camera, wearing the same expression as Moses. Except for something in the eyes. Mr. McCloy had the most avaricious eyes Nudger had ever seen; pure greed huddled in them and peered out like reclusive sea creatures.

Mrs. McCloy limped back into the living room with a round wicker tray containing a china teapot and two matching cracked cups with a rose pattern on them. Nudger told her no thanks on the cream or sugar, and with an unsteady hand she poured him a cup of tea and gave it to him. The delicate cup rattled like a glass engine on its saucer until he took possession.

Nudger carried his tea to the old sofa and sat down, careful not to splosh any of the hot stuff onto his hand as he sank into the cushion. Mrs. McCloy settled down opposite him in the wing chair, looking lost in its enfolding vastness. She balanced her saucer firmly on one knee, took a sip of tea, and said, "Now we can talk." As if tea were a necessary lubricant for the larynx.

Nudger said, "I was wondering how well you knew Mary Lacy."

"Weller than she thought," the old woman said, the tilted set of her lips almost arcing into a smile. "These old buildings, sound carries through the vents something awful. Gotta watch what you say, you don't want it to become common knowledge."

Ah! This interested Nudger. "Really? You could hear through the vents what went on in Miss Lacy's apartment?"

"You betcha."

Nudger sipped his own tea. Bitter, with tiny leaves bobbing in it like flotsam from a cup-scale sunken ship. "I guess," he said carefully, "over time, through the ductwork, you formed some kind of opinion of Miss Lacy."

"Uh-hm. Wasn't what she seemed, that one. Oh, nice enough, but not what she seemed." She sniffled. "Nope, not at all."

"In what way?"

"I mean, she *seemed* respectable. All stiff-backed and proper. But at least once a week a man with a beard'd come to her place late, stay about ten minutes, then leave."

Ten minutes. Nudger tried to imagine what might have gone on in ten-minute increments. Thought about Claudia. Hmm. Quite a lot, maybe.

Mrs. McCloy leaned forward. This was it; she was about to cough up the pearl. "Like Mr. McCloy often cautioned me, I'm far too apt to see the good in folks. But it came to me eventually, Mr. Nudger, that Miss Lacy wasn't the upright Christian everybody thought." She tilted her head and waited for his reaction. Watched him the way a bird watches a worm.

Nudger said, "Between you and me, I'm not surprised. Some people will take advantage."

"It was drugs she was buying from that man."

Huh? "You're sure about that?"

She nodded almost fiercely. "Real sure. Don't you think I'd verify something like that before I'd pass it on? Some kinds of pills she said she needed to make her sleep, then some kinds to help her come all the way awake in the morning. So she could put on her makeup and face the world, I heard her say one time. She couldn't just say no—not that one. Downers, uppers, reds, yellows, that's some of the kinds I heard them talking about. I watch TV, know what that sorta talk means." Now she did smile. Nudger was beginning to dislike this sweet old soul. "I know something else, too."

He pretended more awe than he felt. "Something *else?*"

"Was a woman come to visit her now and again."

Nudger didn't understand at first. "A friend?"

"More'n a friend, I can tell you. Lots more."

Oh-ho. "What about men friends? She have any of those?"

"Not a one. Every now and again, though, this woman'd turn up, stay the whole night. I'd see her leave about seven in the morning. Half hour later, Mary Lacy'd go prancing out to her car, all dressed neat as a Sunday school teacher, on her way to that city government job of hers." Another prim sip of tea. Very proper. But an amber drop clung for a moment to her withered lower lip and then plummetted to leave a tiny, spreading dark stain on her robe. Like acid, Nudger thought. "No gentleman callers, Mr. Nudger. She weren't no bisexual, I can say for sure."

"You mentioned a bearded man."

"Oh, him. I guess you could say he was a caller. But I told you, he was all business, him and his pills, and stayed only about ten minutes."

"You tell the police any of this, Mrs. McCloy?"

"Nope. Police never asked. Talked to me for only a few minutes, they did. Just wanted to know what kinda hours she kept, and if she'd been acting strange lately. Well, she kept regular hours, all right. It's what she did with 'em that'd surprise some folks."

"Considering the police think she ran away with her male boss," Nudger said, "don't you think this is important information?"

"Maybe. I'm telling *you*, ain't I? Thing is, Mr. Nudger, I don't have any love for the police. Nor did Mr. McCloy. I called 'em ten times last month to get that Mr. Adler down on the first floor to park his pickup truck somewheres other than directly below my window. At first they was polite, then they got downright rude to me. Like I ain't paid taxes all my life. Go look out the window, Mr. Nudger. Just you go and look."

Nudger leveled his teacup, stood up, and walked to the window to look outside.

There was a rusty black Ford pickup truck parked at the curb. Several greasy car engine components were scattered over its bed, along with pieces of scrap lumber and some empty beer cans.

He didn't know exactly what was expected of him. "It's out there," he said, and returned to the sofa.

"You betcha it is. And after all my phone calls and complaints. Think I'd tell anything interesting to the police? Do you?"

"Guess not," Nudger said.

"Don't that provide one heck of a view? A work vehicle parked there most all the time. Makes the neighborhood look like a junkyard. Mr. McCloy'd raise holy b'Jesus if he was alive today." Some small part of Mr. McCloy would remain alive as long as she lived.

"Er, when this woman stayed the night . . . how do you know what she and Miss Lacy did?"

Mrs. McCloy chuckled deep in her throat. A phlegmy, ugly sound. "Bedroom ductwork's right alongside the bed, Mr. Nudger. I might as well been in the same room with 'em. Not that they know'd nor cared, the way they acted. Lord be merciful! Such sounds you never heard."

"Know what the woman looks like?"

"Some. I seen her from the back a few times when she left. Big woman, tall and broad, with thick brown hair combed straight back like my aunt Sarah used to wear hers."

"How'd she dress?"

"Sarah?"

"Mary Lacy's friend."

"Always the same—tight blue jeans and a sweatshirt or T-shirt. The jeans had little silver things going down the seams, so they glittered when she walked. She thought that was attractive, I s'pose."

"Studs?"

"Beg pardon."

"Silver studs? On the jeans?"

"I'd call 'em that, surely. Though I was never much of a hand with needle and thread. Mr. McCloy bought all our clothes. Had a fine job with the railroad. But that went by the by when the unions got gutless."

"Did you ever hear Miss Lacy call the woman by name?"

"Never. Called her lotsa things, but not her name. They had like pet names for each other, and they changed all the time."

"What about the man with the beard?"

"He was never in the bedroom."

"I mean, did you hear his name?"

"Skip, I think she called him. Never a last name. Just Skip. They was only seller and buyer, them two. Here's your little pills, here's your money, and have a nice day."

"Did you get a good look at the bearded man?"

"Nope. Same as the woman. Seen him from the back, is all. Wiry little fella with lotsa black hair and that bushy beard. Beard was kinda reddish, maybe. Never seen how him nor the woman got here, either. Took the bus and got off at the corner, for all I know."

Nudger was almost afraid to ask. "What about other visitors?"

"None to speak of, other than a sister came to see her about once a week. Pretty blond thing."

Adelaide.

Nudger suddenly felt confined in the overfurnished, claustrophobic apartment with the old lady who smelled of dust and medicine. He wanted out. Had to get out.

He pretended to finish his tea, then placed the half-full cup and its saucer on a doily on a nearby table. There were lace doilies all over the place, on tables, draped over chair arms and backs, like ornate, sepulchral leaves that had floated down and stuck there. He stood up. Made himself smile. The smile part wasn't easy.

"Thanks for your help, Mrs. McCloy."

"You gotta go?" She sounded distraught.

"Afraid I do."

"Well, glad we had the chance to talk, Mr. Nudger."

That was for sure.

She put down her tea, straightened up out of the grasp of the wing chair, and wobbled with him to the door.

"It ain't like I'm a common and nosy old woman, eavesdropping on the neighbors. It's just that, nighttime especially, sounds drift right up through the ductwork."

"One other thing," Nudger said. "If Miss Lacy had a, er, girlfriend, why do you suppose she ran away with her male boss?"

Mrs. McCloy seemed surprised that he'd ask. "Why, the money, Mr. Nudger. Like Mr. McCloy always said before he died and left me a poor widow, everybody does everything for the money."

When she smiled at him this time there was no mistaking the calculating cast to her parchment features. Eyes like the ones in the oval frame on the mantel.

He gave her ten dollars, peeling it off slowly in ones so it seemed like a lot. Money, money.

She grinned wickedly, Mr. McCloy's widow, and stuffed the bills into the pocket of her robe.

5

Nudger was sure he knew Skip. Small-time, grubby, and groovy Skip Monohan, who lived in a run-down apartment over on Waldemar and did nickel-and-dime deals in stolen merchandise and minor drug deliveries. Skip did a lot of business in Maplewood, where Nudger's office was located, and adjoining Richmond Heights, where Mary Lacy lived. She was on Skip's route, so to speak.

As Nudger drove down Manchester toward Waldemar, he thought over what Mrs. McCloy had told him about Mary Lacy. He wasn't sure how much of it he believed. This was, after all, gossip from the mind and mouth of a snooping old woman. Possibly nothing more. Maybe Skip could corroborate the drug part. Or cast more suspicion on it.

But suppose everything Mrs. McCloy had said turned out to be true. So Mary Lacy liked women, and that made it all the more unlikely she'd run away with Hiller. Unlikely, but not impossible.

Nudger supposed it made sense that Mary had found love in the arms of one of her own sex, considering how his had treated her. Or was that sound reasoning? Nudger's own heart had been kicked around like a rock on the way to school, and still he returned to women, with longing and hope in soul and groin. On the other hand, he'd never been violently raped by a member of the opposite sex, as had Mary Lacy. Hmm. He was getting confused. Better stay with facts instead of speculation.

Skip's apartment was near the corner, with a view of the gray and depressing closed Scullin Steel mill across Manchester. The mill wasn't going to reopen; there were occasional rumors of a shopping mall to be built on the site. The city needed another one of those, all right. Despite big talk and big plans the past several years, the partially razed steel mill remained like a sprawling, miserable monument to outmoded industry. Long gray buildings with high opaque windows; rusting cranes and winches; a few empty and deteriorating rail cars still languishing on the siding. A line of scraggly pine trees, planted along Manchester by the city to disguise the ruin, only added to the depressing view. Even a guy like Skip Monohan didn't deserve to look at this every morning.

As he parked by the mill, Nudger gave it a shuddering glance. Then he locked the Granada and crossed the street.

It was a six-family building, with a sharply peaked roof, tar paper siding designed to look like bricks, and windowpanes that were either cracked or replaced with water-stained cardboard. The entrance was flanked by small, recently planted evergreens; maybe the building's owner had stolen some of the city trees across Manchester. The tree on the left was brown and dead. Its green partner was polelike and pathetic, and would be lucky to make it through the merciless St. Louis winter that was haunting September like a specter.

Nudger pushed into the tiny, tiled vestibule. Smelled stale vomit and urine. Saw nothing original about the graffiti. Who scrawled this stuff? Had anyone actually seen a human hand at work on it? What kind of person spelled "women" *w-i-m-i-n!* He noticed there were no names in the slots above any of the mailboxes, and the lock on every box had been punched out. He trudged up the wooden steps and began knocking on doors.

No one answered his knocks.

The third door he rapped on swung open, and he saw that the apartment was littered and hadn't been occupied for quite a while. He tried the other two doors. They, too, were unlocked and squeaked open to reveal vacant units.

Afraid Skip Monohan had changed addresses, as folks of his ilk did often, Nudger made his way to the second floor. A mouse scurried around a crumpled paper bag on the landing and disappeared into the shadows of the baseboard. Nudger probed the bag tentatively with his foot. Empty. The higher he climbed, · the more the building smelled like a public toilet.

Two of the second-floor doors were unlocked and led to empty and abused apartments. One had the blackened remains of a small campfire in the center of the ruined hardwood floor. Probably not built by Boy Scouts.

Ah. The door to the third unit was locked.

Nudger knocked.

Got no answer. Skip knew who he was. Skip knew everyone. Knew about them, too.

Nudger shouted, "Skip, Nudger here. I leave without you talking to me, there's a uniform in your near future."

Silence. Long minutes.

"Next stop's police headquarters, Skip. The chief's waiting to hear from me."

Nothing but echoes through the empty building. Bouncing off all that enameled wood and cracked plaster. Mimicking the mean and desperate lives that had been played out there.

Nudger gave up and was turning to walk away when the door opened.

"I knew who it was," Skip said. "Seen you drive up. Heard you kicking around downstairs." He tried out his broken-toothed smile, young guy on the way to early death. There was an amiable Irish face beneath the decay. Clean him up, trim his hair and beard, take a few hard years off him, and he'd be the nice-looking type you'd like to see date your daughter—if only his eyes didn't now and then look like Charles Manson's. "Been in the B and L lately?"

"Lunch last week," Nudger said. The B and L was a small and inexpensive diner at Manchester and Sutton, near Nudger's office, where he'd seen Skip a few times hunched over a bowl of chili.

Skip looked as if he could use a meal now. He was thinner than Nudger had ever seen him, wearing paint-smeared pleated pants he'd probably filched from a dumpster. No shoes, and nothing to keep him warm up top except for tattoos. They were the crude, one-tone blue tattoos of the sort done by inmates in the state penitentiary: snakes, daggers, bound buxom women. Tattoos paid for with cigarettes, the currency of the incarcerated. The word TRIUMPH was tattooed on Skip's wasted right forearm. That was a laugh.

Skip said, "So whatcha want, Nudger?"

"Maybe you could invite me in." Nudger pointed to the paint-spotted pants. "Unless you're busy sprucing up the place."

Skip grinned again. "I have decorators come in and do that kinda thing." He stepped back to let Nudger edge past him.

Nudger caught a whiff of Skip's foul breath, then found himself standing in the middle of an amazingly littered room. There were empty beer cans, wine bottles, crumpled fast-food bags from White Castle, a faded pink bra (Nudger wondered where *that* had come from; what kind of wimin would spend time here?), stacks of yellowed newspapers, piles of wallpaper that had peeled off the stained plaster walls. One corner had been cleared to allow room for a battered kerosene heater and a rumpled mound of blankets. Taken by surprise by a pang of pity, Nudger said, "Times rough, Skip?"

"You fuckin' know it, man!"

Skip shut the door and walked over to stand near the heater, which wasn't burning. He moved with a slow limp, as if his knees ached and would feel that way for the rest of his life.

"All I want's some information," Nudger said.

Skip snorted. "Good! 'Cause that's about all I got to give."

Nudger kicked aside a huge dead cockroach and walked farther into the apartment. The bare floor and walls amplified the sounds of his steps. "Ever make any deliveries to a woman over on Hoover? Mary Lacy?"

Skip wiped the back of his thumb across his runny nose, then wiped the thumb over his chest, as if he were wearing a shirt. "Tell you straight out, I could use some bread, Nudger."

Nudger knew he didn't mean enriched white. He reached for his wallet again, for what made the wheels of the world go round. He said, "Ten do it?"

"C'mon, Nudger. This is a normal business expense for you, ain't it?"

Thinking he'd have a difficult time asking Adelaide Lacy to cover bribes, Nudger said, "This is more personal. Ten'll have to do."

"Won't, though."

The wallet slid smoothly back into Nudger's hip pocket. "Your choice."

Before Nudger could so much as move, big bluffer Skip said, "Ten'll buy a couple of what I need at that."

Nudger handed him the ten-dollar bill. "The money's not counterfeit, so it oughta buy straight information."

"Nothing there not to be straight," Skip said, tucking the wadded bill into the pocket of his pleated paint pants. "I was told the lady's name and address so I could make a regular drop to her."

"Who told you?"

"Don't ask me that, Nudger." It was a plea. Skip didn't want to be put in a vise, where he'd spent so much of his life. Naming the people he worked for could be fatal, and in ways not pleasant.

"All right, but do you know how they got her name? I mean, how'd somebody like that make the contact?"

"Whaddya mean, 'somebody like that'? You'd be surprised by some of my regular customers."

"Guess so," Nudger said. "Dumb question, but it stands."

"Well, I never talked to her much."

"But you talked to her some. Must have listened some."

Skip shuffled his bare feet on the wood floor. Nudged the dead kerosene heater with an unwashed big toe. "All I can tell you is she met somebody at a drugs and alcohol rehab center. Looked him up later and said she was accepting his offer to supply what she wanted, when she wanted it. The arrangement was made. Nothing really unusual, you know? I took her the goods. Simple as that."

"You having anything to do with Arnie Kyle these days?"

"Damn! That ain't a fair question, Nudger." Real fear here. But then anyone like Skip might show alarm at the mention of Kyle's name.

"Guess it isn't. I didn't ask it. What rehabilitation center was Mary Lacy in?"

"That I don't know."

Nudger said, "What sort of stuff you take her?"

"Minor league shit. Something to put her down, something to get her up. Mini-whites to keep her going. A little Mexican brown now and then, but other'n that it was all pills. No hard stuff, no needle goods. This was just a lady needed a little help getting through her days and nights."

"How often did you deliver?"

"Enough to keep her in the pills. Like I said, that must have been her main thing, just the pills. Probably 'cause she went off the booze at the rehab center. That happens, you know?"

"I've heard."

"That's all I know about her. I mean, she was just a customer. I ain't had a call to deliver to her for over two weeks."

"You don't know she's disappeared?"

Skip's eyes widened, then flared up with that Charles Manson look, a combination of self-pity and rage. Frustrated by a world that gave no quarter and played tricks. He backed a step toward the window, as if he'd like to whirl and soar through it and escape everything bedeviling him. Maybe someday he'd do exactly that. "Christ, no! How could I know that? Hey, you ain't dragging me into a police case, are you, Nudger?"

"Not likely."

Skip shuddered, then wrapped his arms around himself as if a cold wind had roared through the apartment. He needed the ten dollars all right; Nudger was what junkie luck had provided.

"Tell you this," Skip said, "she was a nice lady. Real shy and polite."

"You talk about her like she's dead."

"Whoa! Hey! No way, Nudger! I don't know nothing about her other than she was a nice sorta person. Had some job or other with the city, didn't she?"

Skip was an expert at playing ignorant. Or maybe he really was ignorant about the disappearance of Mary Lacy and Hiller. This wasn't the kind of guy who kept on top of the news. Still, Nudger didn't want to appear naïve. Seem to believe everything a pin cushion doper told him.

"She was the mayor," he said. He headed for the door.

"For all I know, Nudger, that's the fuckin' truth. I mean it, man."

"Use the ten to buy kerosene for that heater; it might get cold tonight."

"Sure. What'd you think I wanted it for?"

Some put-on, Skip.

Nudger's footsteps echoed through the lonely building as he went downstairs.

A large man wearing a well-cut black suit was standing behind the Granada with a foot propped on the rear bumper, like a cop about to write a parking ticket.

Only this was no cop. When he saw Nudger approach, he straightened up and grinned. Broad shoulders, waist about the size of a fashion model's. Despite his muscular bulk, a curiously sunken chest. He had a pale complexion, wavy black hair, eyebrows so black they seemed painted on, eyes even blacker than the brows. Button eyes. Shark's eyes. Eyes beyond cruel and into cold detachment. He looked like an embalmed weight lifter in a tailored suit.

"You're Nudger," he said. Not a question. "The three of us

should take a walk." He motioned with his long head toward the gray, deserted mill. "Maybe you'll learn some things about the steel industry."

Nudger had stopped about ten feet from the car. "Three of us?"

"You, me, and Mr. Browning." The expensive suitcoat was held aside briefly to reveal the checkered grip of a large-caliber automatic in a black holster.

Who was this guy? Probably not one of Tad's friends, here to warn Nudger not to feel up Bonnie in the back of the car.

With feline grace, the big man moved around to walk directly alongside Nudger. Though they were side by side, he somehow managed to lead the way toward an opening in a chain-link fence. Then beyond some rusting railroad tracks and across a debris-littered field, toward a grimy gray building the size of an airplane hangar. A gloomy scene, not at all the stuff of Currier and Ives prints.

The man with the gun said, "You had me thinking you were a hell of a high-diver." His voice was vibrant yet controlled. A deep voice, but with an underlying shrill rasp that cut into the consciousness. Like the singing of a saw as it whines through hard wood. And it carried the same taunting, sadistic quality Nudger had heard while cowering on the dark balcony of Paul Dobbs's apartment. "Two-story swan dive. Figured maybe I was dealing with somebody oughta be training for the Olympics. Maybe you should check on that, see if they have a plant-throwing event."

Nudger wished he were training for the Olympics now. Anywhere but here.

Beyond the deserted steel mill, traffic on Interstate 44 swished past, rolling to and from downtown, too far away to help. Part of another world. A safe world.

The gray building loomed before them. It seemed to absorb the sunlight and transform it into something ominous.

The big man said, "This is where they used to melt down the scrap metal." He smiled like a pleased cadaver. "Turn up the heat to about a zillion degrees, sizzle hard steel down to nothing. Everything in this world's got its melting point. Interesting, huh?"

Nudger agreed it was interesting.

Tried not to think about it.

Kept walking.

16

In the cool shadow of the gray building, the big man gripped Nudger's elbow in a painful signal to stop. He moved around so he stood facing Nudger, then put on his icy cadaver grin. Said, "What were you doing at Dobbs's place last night? I mean, besides magic tricks on the balcony."

Nudger's nervous stomach crawled up into his throat, grew fuzz, and made it difficult to answer. "Looking around."

"That's what you're doing right now. What you're usually doing when you're not sleeping. I'm looking for a more specific answer." The automatic slid out of its black holster. Alligator. The holster was alligator skin. The barrel swung around to point at Nudger. The big man held the gun casually and with a frightening familiarity, as if he shot people every other day and thought about as much of it as putting out the trash.

Nudger decided sure, he could be more specific. "I was trying to find something that might give me an idea about why Dobbs disappeared and where he went."

"Disappeared? Dobbs is a free-lance photographer. You know how it is with those guys, live out of a suitcase. Maybe he upped and flew off to some exotic country to take snapshots for *Time* or *Life*."

"I've heard that theory. And it could be the truth."

The man in the neat black suit stepped nearer, his finger curled around the gun's blue steel trigger. "I think you should subscribe to that theory. Regard it as gospel truth."

Nudger's heart slammed against his ribs almost hard enough to break them. "I suppose I could do that."

"Sure you could, because it makes sense. Don't you think?"

"Perfect sense."

An airliner rumbled high overhead; Nudger wished he were on it, even now, after deregulation.

"You're a private cop," the man said, "working for that Adelaide Lacy cunt."

Nudger didn't know what he was supposed to say to that. He nodded acknowledgment.

"She's the best-looking of the two sisters, that's for sure. Got that something about her says she'd give you a high old time in the sack. Wouldn't you say that Virgil Hiller guy ran away with the wrong sister?"

"I'd say so," Nudger agreed. The man with the gun *did* have a point.

The gruesome grin. The gun barrel dug into Nudger's stomach. "Then say it."

"Wrong sister."

The gun barrel gouged deeper, causing Nudger's breath to leave him in a whoosh. "Say Virgil Hiller ran away with his secretary."

"That's it, all right." Nudger gasped. "Ran away with his secretary."

"And the money. Christ, let's not forget the money!"

"The money," Nudger repeated dutifully.

The barrel of the gun came away, up, up, pressed painfully into the bridge of Nudger's nose, directly between his eyes. His knees were suddenly nonexistent, and his legs began to quiver. He was sure he was going to melt faster than the scrap metal that had been processed here. Fall to the ground and dissolve all in one squiggly motion.

"Don't forget any of what you said," the big man told him. "Hiller and his secretary ran away with the money and are probably fucking their brains out under the palm trees somewhere. A really simple matter, stop to think about it. Kinda thing happens all the time, only it doesn't make the news. You think?"

"I guess so," Nudger said. "Yeah, I think so, in fact."

"Then you can find better ways to spend your time, wouldn't you say?"

Nudger started to nod, then realized he might jiggle the gun and set it off. "Better ways," he agreed.

Holding the gun steady, the big man reached down with his free hand, gripped Nudger's testicles with a chilling kind of skill, and squeezed.

Agony drilled through the marrow of every bone in Nudger's body. He heard his shrill gasp and sank to the ground, curled tightly in the fetal position. Nausea and pain paralyzed him. He wished only that he could lose consciousness and escape what was happening. What he'd become. And he was terrified of what might happen next.

The man with the gun leaned down, smiled at him, and pressed the barrel to Nudger's temple. Nudger began to shake. He watched in horrible fascination as the manicured finger tightened on the trigger. The nail was so neat, probably painted with clear lacquer.

The trigger moved.

The gun clicked on an empty firing chamber.

As Nudger dropped into cold blackness, he heard the man's soft but high-pitched sadistic giggle, and he plunged all the way through time to when he was twelve years old and heard that same laugh from a school yard buddy who was one-by-one snapping the legs of a newborn puppy.

Even before he remembered what had happened, Nudger realized he'd vomited. He could smell it, and his cheek was resting in the mess. He was reminded of the stench in Skip Monohan's apartment building. *God, this was horrible! Sickening! What it must be like for down-and-out alkies almost every day.* Nudger decided that next time a wino approached him on the street for a handout, he'd give generously.

When he tried to move, the pain in his groin jolted through him like high voltage, and he knew where he was and how he'd gotten there.

Using his arms, his body still curled tightly against the pain, he pushed himself away from the vomit. The effort exhausted him and he passed out again, but he didn't think it was for long.

Without budging, he looked around as far as his field of vision would permit. Dark bare earth. In the distance, a chain-link fence, a line of pine trees. Movement—a car shadowing past beyond the trees. The sky had darkened and he estimated it was late afternoon. He'd been lying here unconscious for hours. He moved slightly so the arm of his sportcoat crawled up his wrist. His watch read 3:05.

When he glanced at it again it was 4:15, though he didn't remember time passing. Maybe the sun had done a sudden sprint across the heavens.

Some of the pain had left him. Gingerly, he made himself sit up, leaning his back against the wall of the gray building. Looked out on a gray world. Beyond a corroded piece of industrial equipment, and the rusting railroad tracks, he could see the drab brick buildings on the north side of Manchester.

Using the wall for support, he managed to struggle to his feet. He brushed dirt from his clothes. Took a cautious step away from the wall. Teetered, but stood up all by himself. Baby's first step. Quite a feat.

He thought about the vomit and wiped his sleeve over his face. That made him feel amazingly better, cleaner. He chanced taking another step or two and found the process less painful than he'd imagined.

A shard of dread pierced his mind. He spat most of a bitter taste from his mouth, then took lurching strides toward the street.

After a zigzag course across the field, he stumbled across the railroad tracks, kicking rocks and almost tripping over the ties. Then out beyond the line of sickly pines.

Traffic was heavier than he'd anticipated. Early rush hour, people heading west from their jobs downtown. Home to drink and dinner. Kids and mortgages. The straight life.

Ignoring the glances of passing drivers, he crossed the street and made his way into Skip Monohan's apartment building.

The man with the gun hadn't asked him why he'd seen Skip, though he must have known that was where Nudger had just come from.

Trusting the old wooden handrail to support his weight, Nudger fought his way up the stairs to the second floor and limped down the littered hall to Skip's apartment. Saw the door standing open.

The trash-strewn apartment looked the same except for the cold kerosene heater lying on its side. A puddle of fuel was soaking into the bare floor, stinking up the place. At the edge of the puddle lay a ten-dollar bill, half of it discolored and plastered to the floor with kerosene.

Skip was gone.

When he'd finished with Nudger, the man in the black suit must have crossed the street.

17

Hammersmith said, "You oughta quit being stubborn, Nudge. Go see a doctor."

Nudger squirmed painfully in the hard wooden chair before Hammersmith's desk at the Third District station. It was too warm in the office, not making things easier. He could feel a sticky coating of perspiration inside his clothes. "I'd know if I was hurt bad enough to need a doctor."

"Sure, you know all about the human anatomy. Whether anything's broken, or you're bleeding inside. Whether you'll be able to have kids even though your balls have been wrung out like a dishrag."

Nudger said, "I feel better."

"From what you described, you'd have to with every passing second. Somebody does that to you, there's no place to go but up when it comes to feeling better." In something like disgust he dropped another cloth-bound mug book into Nudger's lap. Dropped it harder than was necessary. Vicious way to make a point.

Making an effort not to show pain, Nudger placed the book

on top of the one he'd been leafing through and opened it. Some of the holes around the metal ring binders were torn, causing a few of the pages to stick out at odd angles. Had to turn the pages carefully.

There, on the third page, was the man in the black suit, staring straight into the camera as if amused by it. Confidence and cruelty glittered in the dark eyes. The profile shot showed a handsome tilt of nose and strong chin. What made the face brutal came from inside.

Hammersmith noticed Nudger's reaction and glided his bulk around to loom behind the chair. Nudger could hear him breathing like an asthmatic.

"Him," Nudger said, pointing to the dark features set in the pale complexion. Eerie. There was something about the man's mere photograph that inspired fear.

The photos were numbered and the identities of the subjects were listed on a separate sheet of paper in the back of the book. But Hammersmith didn't have to consult the directory. He said, "Uh-hm. That's Jack Palp. Works for Arnie Kyle."

Nudger wasn't surprised by the Kyle connection. "What do you know about Palp besides his employer?"

"Sure you wanna hear?"

"I asked."

"Guy's a bad, bad boy, Nudge. Got into trouble in the early seventies and had his choice of going to prison or into the army and Vietnam. Chose Vietnam and won a lotta medals for upping the body count. Came back and got involved with the sorta people who appreciated his unique talents. Palp's barely missed homicide indictments twice that I know of in the last five years. Who knows how many other jobs he's pulled we never linked with him. He's a neat, clean worker." There was a touch of admiration in Hammersmith's tone; pro acknowledging pro, however grudgingly. "A craftsman."

Nudger felt a chill. "What are you saying, that this guy's a hit man?"

"He was," Hammersmith said. "Kind that liked his work.

—— 122 ——

Kind that was born to it. Then a couple of years ago he went to work for Kyle."

"Doing what?"

"Sorta thing was done to you."

Nudger took a last look at the amused, confident face staring up at him from the photograph. Handsome guy who reminded him of death. Who'd made death his trade. The heavy cover of the book fell closed with a flat, slapping sound. The End. "What about Skip Monohan?"

Hammersmith took the mug books from Nudger and dropped them on his desk, moved back around the desk, and sat down. Laced his pudgy pink fingers. "Monohan's gone, that's all. You're the one thinks there's some connection between that and what happened to you."

"What do you think?"

"Unofficially, same as you. But maybe I'm not as firm on it. People like Monohan move around like they sit down someplace it burns their ass. Odds are always good you wouldn't find him where you saw him last. Especially after the kind of conversation you had with him. Bound to make him itchy."

"If you assign a detail to search Scullin Steel," Nudger said, "you might find Monohan."

Hammersmith smiled with maddening tolerance. "One of your hunches?"

"Guess you could call it that."

"Monohan might be off on a high somewhere, or busy doing whatever it is creeps like him do when they're not tripping or stealing money for drugs."

"Maybe in Fiji helping Paul Dobbs snap photographs."

Hammersmith arched a white eyebrow. "Smart mouth'll get you nowhere, Nudge."

Hadn't so far, Nudger conceded.

His stomach was twitching and he felt as if a mule had kicked him in the genitals. He didn't feel like arguing with Hammersmith; he felt like driving home and soaking in a hot bath. Maybe after that going over to Claudia's for some sympathetic sex of whatever sort he could manage with his damaged equipment. He hadn't forgotten the "Something better" she'd mentioned this morning. It had stuck on the fringes of his mind like a catchy melody. He wouldn't be able to perform but she could soothe him, hold him, make it all well. Almost well, anyway. Certainly better.

"I guess you want me to put out a pickup order on Palp," Hammersmith said.

"It's a thought."

"A thought's all it is, Nudge. No witnesses. And he'll be able to account for his time, probably working for a charitable cause. Your word against his any of this even happened."

"That oughta count for something—my word against his."

"Counts only with me, Nudge. You know that."

Nudger knew. It would be futile trying to tie Palp in with Nudger's aching core. Or with the disappearance of Skip Monohan, who wasn't called Skip for nothing. Unless Skip's body was found and it offered some kind of lead. If he was actually Palp's latest victim.

"I'll see to it somebody takes a thorough look around the grounds at Scullin Steel," Hammersmith said. "Another waste of time, but a favor for you."

"I guess you'll apologize if they find Monohan's corpse."

"In that eventuality it's Palp should apologize. For being so uncharacteristically stupid. He's not like most goons, Nudge; guy's got a brain. Went two years with top grades down at the University of Missouri in Columbia before he maimed an instructor after an argument over a coed. Professor of history. Palp spent a few hours with the poor guy, and now the professor's history himself; went off to teach in Guatemala or some such place. Too scared even to press charges against Palp, though Palp didn't know that at the time and agreed to the army deal."

"How'd Palp get hooked up with Arnie Kyle?"

Hammersmith laughed. "How would he *not?* They complement each other. Kyle's full of meanness, but he's no physical tough guy. Comes to maybe having to spit blood, Kyle'll bluff and then back away. There's no bluff in Palp. He was a dog, he'd bite without a warning growl."

"He warned me today."

"That was Arnie Kyle warning you."

"Which means there's more to the Virgil Hiller disappearance than a political hack absconding with the funds and his secretary."

"Not necessarily. It looks like Mary Lacy and her envelope and Kyle are mixed up together, but it probably has to do with drugs and not Virgil Hiller's disappearance. Or maybe Kyle was supplying her with a lesbian prostitute and blackmailing her. Be just like him. Lots of possibilities with these kinda folks."

Nudger had thought of that, but hoped Hammersmith wouldn't. Should have known better. Time to get him back on track. "That photo of Dobbs's shows Hiller dead, and you know it."

"To know is not to prove, Nudge."

"Especially when the powers that be don't want something proved." Nudger knew Hammersmith would take only so much of this. He was himself a masterful politician in a limited arena, which was what had enabled him to rise in rank. But he was also an honest cop.

The conflict in Hammersmith must have made him feel ornery. He pulled a cigar from his pocket and unwrapped it. Fired it up and puffed mushroom clouds like a series of atomic detonations.

Nudger decided not to fight the inevitable nausea. He braced himself for the pain in his groin, stood up, and moved toward the door. Walking was a chore.

Hammersmith said, "I heard someplace acupuncture's the best thing for what's bothering you, Nudge."

Nudger winced. "Let me know what you find at Scullin, all right?"

"Or *don't* find."

Hammersmith was determined to be difficult. Nudger knew

he didn't like it that his superiors had put him in a position where he had to act against his cop's instincts. Didn't like being squeezed in a vise.

Wishing he hadn't thought of that vise analogy, Nudger waved good-bye and left Hammersmith squatting like a corrupt Buddah in his desk chair, obscured by foul green incense of his own making.

Nudger had slipped a Fathead Newman jazz tape in his Sony portable, then slowly and painfully lowered himself into a bathtub full of hot water, when the phone in the other room rang.

He said, "Damn!" and gripped the smooth rim of the tub to lever himself to his feet. Slipped and almost fell, splashing water out of the tub to spread over the tile floor. Hit your head, good way to drown. He straightened up gradually and high-stepped carefully out of the tub. Wrapped a towel around himself. A clumsy kind of dance. Newman played accompaniment.

Five rings already. Whoever was calling might hang up.

Dripping water and leaving damp footprints on the carpet, he hurried toward the jangling phone. After the hot, humid bathroom, he felt chilled. That made his testicles feel as if they were being twisted like taffy again and caused him to walk hunched over, shivering. God, this was fun!

He snatched up the receiver on the seventh ring, gazing at his glistening hand and wondering if phones ever electrocuted the wet and the hasty. Pressed the plastic to his ear anyway. Might as well get it in the brain direct. Zap! End it quickly; lots of pain but brief. Over.

Bonnie's voice said, "Thought you might not be home."

Bonnie, Bonnie. Nudger liked and admired this woman, but he was increasingly sure they were hopelessly incompatible. Bonnie and her brood of unruly kids, her noisy suburban lifestyle. Her hostile son. But Nudger always had trouble summoning up the courage to break off relationships clean. And he had to admit he was flattered by the healthily attractive Bonnie's persistent adulation.

"Home," he said cheerily.

"Catch you at a bad time?"

"Naw."

"I delivered some Nora Dove to Gina Hiller today and we had quite a conversation."

Nudger got a better grip on his damp towel, which threatened to fall. "Oh, about what?"

"I think it'd be better if I told you in person." Very coy. Cute, even on the phone. "Want to meet at Denny's restaurant tonight for coffee?"

Nudger hesitated.

"Nudger?"

"Okay, I'll be there. About seven?"

"We better make it eight, if that's all right with you."

"Sure. See you then."

He hung up. So much for Claudia. So much for "Something better."

He backtracked along his damp footprints and again lowered himself painfully into the bathtub.

Soaked.

Probably the wrong end.

18

Nudger sat alone sipping coffee at Denny's until 8:20, when a waitress veered over to his booth and asked his name, then told him he had a phone call.

Bonnie.

She apologized for standing him up, explained that she had car trouble, and asked if he'd drive over to her house and pick her up. Nudger thought it was almost as if she were planning on using enough time to prevent him from possibly dropping by Claudia's apartment later tonight. Did women have this subtle telepathic thing going? Like dolphins?

Twenty minutes later, still tasting the bitterness of four cups of coffee, he pulled into Bonnie's grease-stained driveway on Pleasant Lane and saw her Nora Dove station wagon, its hood raised, parked at an angle near the garage. Tad's long, jaybird legs, clad in faded jeans, were all that was visible of him as he lay over a front fender to worm as far as possible into the unfortunate car's engine compartment. He was wearing beat-up, club-toed brown boots that made his feet look like Frankenstein's monster's.

Nudger got out of the Granada, hop-stepped over a grease stain, and walked toward the front porch. Tad must have heard him drive up, heard the car door slam, but remained draped over the Chevy like a slain deer.

Ten-year-old Carlotta answered Nudger's ring and stood smiling wistfully up at him without speaking, somber brown eyes like deep-glazed saucers, holding onto the knob of the open door with one tense hand for security. Did this one always look like a poster girl for waifs?

Nudger smiled back. "Your mother home?"

Carlotta nodded, her smile fixed, her dark eyes unblinking. She was so small and vulnerable. How could she not have been adopted? Nudger was ready to adopt her now. She released the knob and stepped back, jamming her tiny fists into the pockets of her flowered skirt.

Nudger stepped inside. Called, "Bonnie?"

It was Janet who wandered in from the kitchen, sipping from a two-liter bottle of sugar-free Pepsi. Dabs of flesh-colored makeup were visible on her forehead. Much changed from one generation of teens to another, but the war against zits was constant. "Mom's putting on different clothes. Belinda like spit up on her."

Nudger said, "Oh."

Janet was wearing a white blouse and amazingly tight Levi's that inhibited her walk and probably hurt. She set the Pepsi bottle on a table where it would leave a ring and said, "I'm goin' someplace. Gotta look tough. You think I should wear my blouse like this?" She tucked it in tightly. "Or like this?" She plucked at the material with her thumb and forefinger so it wasn't quite as taut. Nudger saw no significant difference.

He said, "First way. Definitely." He was wising up.

She crammed the material back into her Levi's around her seventeen-inch waist. Sort of wobbled about in the painted-on pants and raised and lowered her arms tentatively, as if testing. Yep, she could still move, though some compressed internal organs might have ceased functioning.

She ducked her head, looked at Nudger with a hopeful grin, and said, "Got any loose weed?"

"Nope. Don't smoke the stuff."

"You one of those *Reefer Madness* geeks?"

"One of those who don't do dope," he told her. He sounded, even to himself, like a moralist on a soapbox.

"Why don't you?"

"I know people who do and wish they didn't. A few who don't and wish they never had."

Janet said, "I'm not sure if that makes sense."

James ran into the room, carrying a plastic automatic weapon that looked so real it gave Nudger the creeps. A replica of an Israeli Uzi, the terrorists' favorite. Leveling the gun expertly, he took a shot at Nudger, then at Janet, each time making a repetitive chucking sound and spraying saliva. His eyes were fierce. He was dressed in tiny camouflage pants and shirt, wore a red bandanna around his blond head. Said, "Both you's dead!"

Janet said, "Fuckin' geek!" and was immediately blasted again. James curled his upper lip at her, as if annoyed she'd survived the first hail of bullets.

Nudger wondered why Carlotta had been spared. Turned to ask her and found she'd faded from the room. Maybe she waged silent guerrilla warfare against James.

"Wanna stick wif a knife on it," James said. "For my birf-day."

Nudger said, "What?"

"Stick wif a knife!"

What was wif—with this kid? "You mean a bayonet?"

Nudger had struck on the right interpretation. James grinned maniacally and charged Nudger, jabbing at his stomach with the barrel of the plastic gun. Sore and not moving well, Nudger barely hobbled out of the way. Almost. Caught a glancing blow on the hipbone. James spun on his heel and took a run at Janet. She sneered and shoved him against the wall and he fell. Began to cry.

Bonnie's voice said, "Don't pick on your brother!"

Janet let her lower jaw drop, made an "Uh!" sound through her nose, then rolled her eyes straight up out of sight into her skull. She tucked her blouse in tighter and minced from the room in a huff. James wiped a camouflaged sleeve across his nose and mounted an attack against an imaginary enemy in the kitchen. Nudger could hear his heels clattering on the tile floor as the foe was met. Something metal dropped with a loud clang. Maybe a tank had been destroyed.

Bonnie looked cuter than ever. She had on a denim skirt, plaid short-sleeved blouse with a western cut and pearl buttons, and blue Nikes with those socks with fuzzy balls on the heels. Her hair was mussed just so, her face was scrubbed and radiant, and her wide blue eyes shone. She looked ready to square dance all night.

She sashayed over to Nudger in the Nikes, pecked him on the cheek, and sort of dosey-doed around him to the door. "Sorry about the inconvenience," she said. "Tad tried to adjust something on the Chevy and can't get it back together. You ready to go?"

"Er, who's gonna watch the young ones?"

"Janet."

"She said she was going out."

Bonnie looked surprised. "She told you that?"

"Thought she did. And she was taking a fling at fashion."

Bonnie set her jaw and squeezed a " 'Scuse me" through clenched teeth.

She strode toward the back of the house with purpose, hips switching, skirt swaying, little fuzzy balls jiggling on her heels.

A door slammed. Then something else slammed—maybe a foot on the floor. The vibration carried through the house. Nudger heard loud female voices from another room as Bonnie and Janet went at it like a couple of pit bulls. Some of what they were saying drifted in: ". . . Always hated you! . . . Don't *care* if you die! . . . *Your* responsibility! Like, *God*, I can't *stand* it here!" Carlotta had reappeared in ghostly fashion and was smiling knowingly at Nudger, ageless and wise.

Five minutes later, Bonnie glided deliberately back into the living room wearing a strained smile. "Janet's decided to stay home after all," she said. She drew a deep breath that made her ample breasts test the buttons on the plaid blouse. They held, but thread was stretched. "Shall we go?"

"Sure." Nudger moved to the door and opened it for her.

Bonnie bent low and kissed Carlotta on the forehead, then with her usual pertness bounced out onto the porch.

She was seated in the Granada by the time Nudger opened the driver-side door and scooted in behind the steering wheel.

As he backed from the driveway, he saw Tad raise his head from beneath the hood of the Chevy and glare at him with raw hostility.

Back at Denny's, Nudger switched to tea.

Bonnie had apparently worked up an appetite arguing with Janet and asked for a large order of French toast.

When the waitress, a pimply, enthusiastic teenager who'd introduced herself as Stephanie, was gone, Bonnie grimaced and said, "Kids are a trial."

"Looks that way."

"Ever thought about being a parent?"

"Not for long." But he had, with Claudia.

"It's hard to see from the outside, but believe me, it has its rewards."

Nudger wondered.

Still bubbling over the fact that they'd entered her life as customers, Stephanie returned with the food, placed it on the table, and assured them that if they needed anything else— anything at all—they should call for her. Her skinny body almost vibrated with her eagerness to please. Then she wedged the curved edge of the empty tray into her waist, spun lithely on her sandaled heel, and left them. Everybody should like their work so well.

As she was pouring a quart of blueberry syrup over her plate, Bonnie said, "I delivered Gina Hiller's Nora Dove order today and got her talking about her husband, just like we planned. Wasn't hard to do at all. The poor woman needs somebody to talk to. I can tell you this, she really doesn't think her hubby ran away with his secretary."

"She have a theory?"

"Uh-uh. She's totally confused about why he should leave her. And he lived like a king around the house. She said he mistreated her, but he had for years."

Nudger dropped his soggy teabag onto his saucer. Watched it form a brown puddle that would cause the bottom of his cup to drip when he lifted it. "Oh? Mistreated her how?"

"Well, that's what I asked. She was vague, but I got the idea Virgil was really more of a pitiless dictator than a king at home, even with his kids. One of those total control types, if you know what I mean. Like Ralph Kramden. But Gina says he loved all of them, and it looks to me like she loved Virgil back. You know how some women are."

Nudger did. Some women.

Bonnie used her knife and fork daintily to saw off a generous piece of syrup-logged French toast, stuffed it into her mouth, and chewed. "Something else," she said, almost choking as she swallowed. "Gina told me she got a phone call last night from Virgil."

Nudger's turn to choke. He gagged and coughed. Kept his lips pressed together but came very close to letting his last sip of tea escape and dribble down his chin. It took him a few seconds to recover.

Bonnie grinned. Her teeth were stained blue from the syrup, but somehow it didn't look bad. "Not really Virgil, silly. At least Gina doesn't think so." She dabbed at her mouth with her napkin, then poured even more syrup on her French toast. Didn't like the idea of it soaking in and disappearing.

Nudger needed to get this straight. He interrupted her as she was about to raise another bite on her fork. "Hold on. You saying somebody called Gina Hiller and identified himself as her husband?"

"That's it. Didn't fool *her*, though."

"What did this person say?"

"That he was someplace where he was happy and not to

———— 133 ————

expect him back home. And he apologized for any pain he'd caused the family, but he said some things just had to be because of fate."

"He mention Mary Lacy?"

"Nope."

"How'd Mrs. Hiller reply?"

"She didn't say anything, she told me. She was so surprised she just listened. Then, when she realized it wasn't her husband talking, only somebody claiming to be, she slammed down the receiver. The conversation lasted about half a minute, the way I get it."

Nudger took a sip of tea and felt a few drops spatter into his lap. Not hot. Tea from the saucer. "Some crackpot playing a practical joke," he speculated out loud.

"Maybe. He did call her Boobsers, she said."

"Boobsers?"

"His nickname for her." Bonnie smiled, looking a lot like a blond Linda Ronstadt in heat. "You know—pillow talk."

"So that narrows it down to a crackpot who knew Hiller or his wife. Knew them intimately enough to have received that kind of personal information, maybe over lunch or a few drinks too many."

"It could actually have been Virgil Hiller," Bonnie said. "Maybe Gina just didn't *want* it to be him. Didn't want to hear what he was saying. Freud had a name for that kinda behavior. I read it in a magazine or someplace, but I can't remember it. Maybe later I'll go through the alphabet, and I'll probably think what it is."

Nudger said, "Hmm."

Bonnie finished off her French toast, licked syrup from her lips. "You're awful quiet tonight."

"Not feeling my best." Nudger told her about his visit with Skip Monohan, and his subsequent run-in with Jack Palp. Unloading the burden of his day. Pretending she was Claudia. It worked, up to a point.

"Poor man," she said, glancing down in the direction of his injured genitals as if the table were transparent. Claudia had never called him "poor man." At times like these she leaned more toward mock sarcasm, and then gentleness. Bonnie said, quite seriously, "I'd like to kiss it and help make it all well."

Nudger couldn't avoid staring at the cleavage visible above the top button of her blouse. He felt an overpowering urge to rest his head on the soft swell of breast. She'd stroke his hair. She's smell like Nora Dove. Maybe Hot Shoulders. Probably got the stuff wholesale. The entire line. Every part of her probably smelled terrific.

Kiss it and help make it all well . . .

Suddenly Stephanie was standing over their table, hands on her narrow hips, smiling down benignly. "Everything all right?"

Nudger said, "It will be."

19

They drove to the Coral Court Motel on Watson Road, an art deco creation infamous as the scene of countless romantic trysts. The cabins were constructed of glossy tile and had rounded corners and reminded Nudger of public restrooms yanked inside out. The feature that had gained Coral Court its reputation was that each cabin had a garage with an overhead door, so no suspicious spouse or hired private detective could see a familiar vehicle parked out front. Complete privacy was assured. Once inside the motel, lovers were lost to the outside world. Lovers have always liked it that way, so the motel had thrived.

Nudger checked in and paid in advance. Thought of signing the name "Smith." He'd never registered at a motel as "Smith" or "Jones" and thought it might be a hoot. Signed in as Mr. and Mrs. Nudger. Then he parked the Granada in the cabin's garage while Bonnie stood waiting, her shoulders hunched, her arms tightly folded, making herself smaller in an effort to achieve invisibility as she glanced uneasily at passing traffic on Watson Road.

After lowering the squealing overhead garage door, he unlocked the door to the cabin. He had this vague idea that she expected him to hoist her high and carry her over the threshhold, as if his back wouldn't crack out of joint. But she simply smiled up at him nervously and stepped inside.

He switched on the light to reveal red shag carpet and the usual motel furniture: double bed, mass-produced dresser, vinyl chairs, matched reading lamps. In a corner squatted an old Philco console color TV.

Bonnie said, "I haven't done this since . . ."

"I know," Nudger said gently.

He asked if she wanted him to go out for some ice and something to drink. She said no.

"What then?" he asked, and she snaked an arm around his neck and kissed him on the mouth. Kissed him again, using her tongue. Getting over her shyness. The years "since" were falling away.

Nudger undressed in a hurry, but Bonnie had already scooted into bed beneath the covers by the time he peeled off his socks. He switched off the lamp and turned on the TV without volume for a night light. An Australian football match. Even the players didn't seem to understand the rules.

She probably actually hadn't since. Once ignited, her fire was volcanic. She was all warmth and softness and desperate motion. On top. On the bottom. Nudger listened to the headboard banging into a groove in the wall and that was the only sound in the world and Bonnie's hot breath was the only air. He was surprised by how much he wanted her. The sharp and spiraling ecstasy that took him over. He heard her breath catching rhythmically in her throat—or was the sound coming from him? Didn't matter.

Over too soon.

Nudger said, "Jesus!" and lay on his back trying to take in oxygen. A little scared by the burning in his lungs.

Bonnie said, "You love me?" Then, when she saw him hesitate, she grinned and said, "Don't answer that."

Good thing. He could only have croaked an answer she wouldn't have understood.

The next time was less frantic. Love was at least equal if not better the second time around, even at Coral Court. As he climaxed, Bonnie did, or pretended beautifully.

A kind of peace settled over the quiet motel room that held the musky scent of their lovemaking. There was a lot to be said for dropping out of the world, even for one night.

Lying on his back, Nudger ignored the rivulet of perspiration zigzagging over his bare ribs like an exploring beetle. He laced his hands behind his head and listened to the traffic hum by on old Route 66, which had become Watson Road after the legendary highway was rerouted. Time did that to things, even the seemingly unchangeable, altered their direction almost before anyone realized it while the world spun on.

Beside him Bonnie lay silently staring at the ceiling and smoking a cigarette. He'd never seen her smoke before, but she'd had half a crumpled pack of Salems in her purse. He felt the warm pressure of her thigh against his, the slight brush of her upper arm whenever she raised the cigarette to her lips. She'd indeed kissed him where he hurt and made it better. He felt so much better he was totally relaxed, drowsy, his discomfort and confusion momentarily forgotten in the afterglow of passion. Bonnie was nothing if not therapeutic. Made him content, hidden away here, car inside the garage. His eyelids weighed ten pounds each and were impossible to keep open. Why keep them open? he asked himself. Couldn't come up with an answer.

Welcomed total darkness . . . the oblivion of sleep.

"I've been thinking," Bonnie said, and exhaled smoke in a drawn-out hiss. "You suppose Virgil Hiller really *did* phone his wife?"

"Could be," Nudger answered drowsily. A draft played over his stomach and chest. The room was warm and all he wanted to do was sleep. He was no twenty-five-year-old kid anymore. Didn't want to be. Usually.

Bonnie sucked noisily on her cigarette. Reminded Nudger

of Hammersmith and his cigar. Theorizing the way Hammersmith did, too. Got Nudger's sleepy, sated mind turning lazily. Maybe the man on the phone had actually been Virgil Hiller, and Gina didn't want to admit it even to herself. Possible. Maybe Freud was right, even after all these years and in *Psychology Today*, or *People*, or wherever Bonnie had acquired her drugstore psychiatry. Didn't have to be Vienna. He pictured Bonnie in Vienna, with a goatee and monocle. Crazy. Lounging in one of those gondolas—no, that was Venice. If she couldn't cure her patients she could sell them cosmetics, send them away perfumed and happy. Happy for sure. He felt himself dropping into deep sleep. Fine. Where he wanted to go. The warm breeze again, the scent of sex. He was drifting on a canal in Venice-Vienna, drifting . . .

Bonnie said, "Ohmygosh, we better get outta here!"

The gondola capsized. Nudger's eyes flew open. "Huh?"

She switched on the lamp and all of a sudden he felt as if he were in center field at Busch stadium in a night game.

Her voice was frantic. "It's almost midnight!"

He sat up. "Yeah?" What was the deal here?

"Janet's watching the young ones. Nudger, I can't stay out all night. God, Coral Court! This is bad enough!"

Bad enough? He didn't think so. Not bad at all. But Bonnie had a point about Janet. Set an example for the girl, get home at a reasonable hour. Made sense. Damned if it didn't.

" 'Kay," he said sleepily, "see what you mean." He sat up on the edge of the mattress and searched the floor for his socks. Found one. Pulled on it so it wasn't wadded. A start.

Bonnie was out of bed and striding toward the bathroom. For a moment he couldn't look away from her compact, perfect body. All firm curves and softness. Large breasts jiggling slightly as she picked up her pace. In the bright light he noticed red marks on her buttocks where he'd gripped her. Except for that, the woman actually looked like a *Playboy* centerfold. Gravity-defying mammary development and a smooth, tucked-in tummy. Amazing! He'd have to check and see if she had a staple for a belly button.

He heard the hiss and roar of the shower and decided to wait until he got home to wash away the evening. More important to get Bonnie back in her house on Pleasant Lane and setting a sterling example for the kids. Janet couldn't bitch next time she was told to make curfew.

Nudger wrestled into his pants. He decided Janet would probably bitch anyway. And come home whatever time she chose. He was learning about kids. It wasn't like on "Brady Bunch" reruns.

Where was that other sock?

At ten minutes to one he steered the Granada into the grease-and-shadow-stained driveway on Pleasant Lane. The Nora Dove station wagon was parked straight in front of the garage now; maybe Tad had put right whatever it was he'd messed up under the hood.

There was only a dim light glowing behind the drapes of the living room window. All the little Beals in bed?

Nudger said, "Want me to come in?"

Bonnie shook her head. Smiled. Doris Day by moonlight. "Better if you didn't."

She was right, Nudger figured. The evening had run its course.

"It looks like they might all be asleep in there," he said.

"Only if they exhausted themselves earlier."

Nudger didn't ask her what she meant by that.

She said, "I enjoyed tonight."

Well, sure. "So'd I."

She kissed him quickly on the cheek, got out of the car, and flounced up onto the porch. She still looked pert, even though her hair was less strategically mussed and her skirt and blouse were wrinkled. Coral Court would do that to you. Had been doing it to people for generations.

He waited until Bonnie was inside, then backed the car out of the driveway and accelerated down Pleasant Lane.

He wasn't tired. Being awakened immediately after falling asleep always left him this way. Hyper. Restless. The way Mary

Lacy must have felt the nights she popped pills delivered by Skip Monohan. The missing Skip Monohan.

Nudger took Manchester Road east, but he didn't turn onto Sutton, where his apartment and a warm bed waited. Instead he continued east until Manchester became Chouteau, then made a right turn on Grand.

He drove to Oleatha Avenue and went by Adelaide Lacy's apartment. The tidy brick building was illuminated by dusk-to-dawn outside lights and by a nearby streetlamp, but her windows were dark. Behind those windows Paul Dobbs had paid two visits, one to show Adelaide the photograph of Virgil Hiller, the other to warn her not to cross Arnie Kyle. And Arnie Kyle and his enforcer, Jack Palp, had dropped in to raise some hackles and blood pressure, and demand an envelope that was no longer where Adelaide had placed it. An envelope given to her by Mary for safekeeping. An envelope that might concern the disappearance of Hiller and Mary, but, considering Kyle's business, possibly had to do with Mary's penchant for illicit drugs and sex and her vulnerability to blackmail.

To add to Nudger's bewilderment, Hiller had been seen by the city comptroller and the mayor the day *after* Dobbs had taken his photo, so presumably *before* he'd disappeared along with Mary. Four people disappearing, if you counted Dobbs and Monohan—and Nudger did. What it all meant was beyond Nudger, but it seemed that contact with the Lacy sisters was bringing real disruption in people's lives. That was something to think about, all right.

The car Nudger had watched Adelaide get into after she'd left his office, a tan Dodge sedan, was parked at the curb a few buildings down. As a helpless concession to crime, a yellow sign dangling in a back window said, THIS CAR DOESN'T HAVE A RADIO. The rear bumper wore a sticker that said, STAY HOME, READ A BOOK. Good advice, Nudger thought. Kept folks out of trouble.

He tapped the Granada's accelerator and drove back to Grand Avenue. Cranked down the window so he could breathe fresh night air as he cruised past the small shops lining both sides of the street. The shops were closed now, their windows dark and giving back the lighted reflection of his passing car, his own form sometimes visible behind the steering wheel, obscure and anonymous. He knew where he was going, where he'd been going from the time he'd driven away from Bonnie's house.

Claudia's windows were dark, too. But at the end of the line of cars parked at the curb on Wilmington was Biff Archway's red sports car.

Looked like Archway's car, anyway. Red Mustang with a black convertible top. Nudger studied the license plate but couldn't remember the number on Archway's car.

Nudger told himself to ease up. Unreasonable jealousy had gotten him into trouble before, made him play the fool. How many red Mustang convertibles did Ford Motor make in a year? Couple of hundred thousand?

How many were sold in the St. Louis area?

Out of those, how many might find their way to Wilmington Avenue?

To Claudia's block?

Other than Archway's?

He decided he didn't like the odds.

More awake than ever, Nudger headed for home.

The car that followed him had its right headlight aimed way too low. Gave it the look of a half-closed yellow eye.

Nudger thought immediately of Jack Palp. Then he told himself he had the jitters. Manchester was a major east-west thoroughfare; the car simply happened to be going his direction. The driver probably lived out in Chesterfield and was sneaking home from the girlfriend's. Or boyfriend's. Nudger had done plenty of divorce work in west county. It was prime area for real estate and adultery.

But when he turned off Manchester and drove down Sutton, the droopy-eyed car stayed behind him.

He parked in front of his building and the headlights stopped half a block behind. Gazed at him like the mismatched glowing eyes of a crouching cat.

Staring into his rear-view mirror, Nudger was considering staying in his car and driving to police headquarters, when suddenly the headlights rose slightly as the car behind him accelerated and came straight at him. Rubber on pavement screeched like something enraged and tortured.

His heart jump-started into a frantic beat. Automatically he reached forward and twisted the ignition key to turn over the Granada's engine and get out of there. Realized too late he hadn't turned *off* the engine. The starter engaged and howled noisily and his response was to twist the key too far in the opposite direction and kill the motor.

His sweat-slick fingers slipped off the key as he tried again to start the car. He kept fumbling, not making any progress.

The oncoming headlights illuminated the inside of the Granada, then swerved.

A shout. A shriek.

Tad's old gray Plymouth shot past, then did a nosedive and skidded to a stop. Left a twin trail of rubber; tires might last a week that way. Looked as if a dozen teenage boys were crammed inside the Plymouth.

Tad! Not Palp! Whew!

Still shaking, Nudger climbed out of the Granada and stood in the street. Faced the Plymouth with his hands at his sides.

High Noon in the dark.

The Plymouth didn't move. He could hear its old engine idling roughly, see clouds of oil fumes belching from beneath its rear bumper. A skinny male arm was draped out of one rear window, pressed against metal to swell the bicep.

After a few minutes an empty beer can flew from the Plymouth and bounced clanking across the pavement to stop, spinning, near Nudger's feet. It was a paper-thin aluminum Coors can and hadn't made much noise. Maybe not enough to wake the neighbors and further sully Nudger's reputation. He didn't need neighbor problems.

A light winked on in a window across the street. An angry male voice yelled, "People tryin' to sleep here, asshole!"

The rear end of the Plymouth dipped so the bumper almost scraped, and it screeched down the street and turned the corner. Oil-laden exhaust fumes settled like soiled fog beneath the streetlight.

"Keeps up, I'm gonna call the cops!" the nonsleeper shouted.

"No need!" Nudger told him, probably not loud enough for the man to hear.

Nudger thought the Plymouth might go around the block and reappear at the opposite corner, but he heard the growl of its motor fade.

A sudden night breeze sent the beer can rolling, humming shrilly on concrete until it wedged with a faint *clink!* against the curb.

The street remained dark. Quiet. The time for teenage menace was over.

Nudger let himself relax. He wiped his hands on his pants legs and plodded upstairs to his apartment.

Tad would never know how glad Nudger was to see him.

20

The next morning Nudger caught Hammersmith in the Third District station house parking lot. The lieutenant had just climbed out of his unmarked blue Pontiac when he saw Nudger approach. He stood next to his private parking space and waited, nodding to fellow officers on the way to or from their cars. Flashing the old Barney Miller smile.

Today's schizo weather was starting off warm, and the lieutenant had his dark blue uniform jacket neatly folded and draped over a huge arm. His powder blue shirt was flawlessly ironed, his smooth-shaven jowls spilling over the collar. Flat blue eyes took a trip over Nudger with the slightest spark of curiosity.

Nudger said, "I was on my way in to see you."

"Pleasant morning, Nudge, we can talk out here."

It *was* a pleasant morning, except for the yeasty smell from the nearby Anheuser-Busch Brewery.

Irritated, Nudger said, "Afraid to talk about Virgil Hiller inside? Think your office might be bugged?"

"Maybe."

Nudger was startled. Hammersmith seemed serious.

"I told you, Nudge, there's pressure from above not to push a nose or anything else too far into the Hiller disappearance. Pressure from immediately above in the department, and then from above that."

"All that pressure from above and above. Sounds like you're at the bottom of the sea."

"I'd agree with you, only it's still possible to sink."

"I know. Politics. But hasn't it occurred to anyone that Hiller's supposed to have run away with half a million dollars of taxpayer money? I mean, even if you see it the official way—that he bolted with his secretary and the money—isn't there some political gain to be made by at least getting back the loot?"

Hammersmith stared down at the blacktop and frowned. A small moth flitted sluggishly around his head and then circled away into the slanted morning sunlight. September already. The moth didn't have much longer; the temperature might plunge below freezing any hour. "It's more complicated than that, Nudge."

"In what way?"

"In a way I'm not sure of myself. But I can sense the complication."

"Haven't you always told me I could afford hunches and you couldn't?"

"Sure. Because you're a private cop and I'm not."

"Then how come you're paying attention to what you sense this time? Why not just act on the facts?"

"Let's be fair, Nudge. I've also said you don't have a gnat's navel idea of what politics is about, and that's why you never would have risen much beyond patrolman. Even if you'd stayed in the department, with your stomach wound tight as the inside of a golf ball."

"Being a good cop goes beyond politics."

"Only if you wanna be a good cop who spends all his time walking a beat or giving out parking tickets." Hammersmith put on a mildly pained expression. "Christ, haven't you at least learned that much after all these years? By politics, Nudge, I'm not talking about kissing ass—though that's part of it sometimes. I mean knowing what matters and what doesn't. Adapting to the lay of the land. Knowing how and when to compromise."

"And this Hiller thing is one you compromise on? Tune out the facts and look the other way?"

"More or less."

" 'Scuse me if I don't buy it."

Hammersmith appeared about ready to spit on the ground. A blue vein pulsated in his temple so fast it seemed to writhe. "Facts, huh? There's a word you toss around kinda carelessly, Nudge. Guy disappears with his secretary and a bundle of money. *That's* fact. Just what have you shown me beyond that?"

"The photograph Dobbs took."

"Photograph, huh? Don't photographs prove a lot? I've seen photos of flying saucers, Nudge. Look so real you'd think you could board them and fly to willy-nilly land just like that. I could even scare you up some folks'd claim they made the trip."

"What about Arnie Kyle's involvement? And Palp working me over."

"Kyle's involvement's with the secretary's sister and some envelope nobody's seen. That's if you take the sister's word that any of it ever happened. As for Palp playing rough with you, where are your witnesses?"

"Think I'm lying?"

Hammersmith shook his head and let out a long breath. "No, Nudge. I'm just saying that if you wanna break through and make Hiller's disappearance other than what it appears, you need something more. Gimme half a break, hey? I mean, you're talking to the only guy on the department hasn't slammed the door on all doubt. I told you, I think you might be onto something—emphasize *might*—but officially I have to see it differently."

Nudger knew Hammersmith was right. In the context of

his position, anyway. He had little choice other than to tell Nudger what he was saying—that you bucked the higher-ups when you had the ammunition, but not before. A basic rule of survival in any bureaucratic jungle.

Hammersmith said, "Notice I'm the only cop talking to you at all about this? Officially or un?"

"I've noticed," Nudger said.

"Which brings me to the thanks I deserve for sticking my professional neck out and ordering a search of the Scullin Steel site."

"You've got my thanks," Nudger told him. "You know that."

"Guess I do."

"So what did you find at Scullin?"

"What anybody'd expect. A field littered with the debris of a closed and partly razed foundry. Mostly chunks of building material and industrial crap. Stuff I couldn't even tell you what it was. Pieces of this and that, but no pieces of Skip Monohan."

"Then Palp must have taken him somewhere else. I'm sure Monohan knew something and had to be shut up."

Hammersmith said, "Monohan's probably sleeping in a flea-bag hotel where you don't sign the register. It might have been you talking to him that made him go to ground."

"Might have. But Palp had to see me leave after I talked to Monohan; I can't imagine him *not* crossing the street and finding out about the conversation."

"Could be that's what he did. But that doesn't mean murder, Nudge."

"You'd think it might, if you'd chatted heart to heart with Palp the way I did."

Hammersmith paced a few steps, dragged a fingertip over his unmarked Pontiac, then faced Nudger with a no-nonsense expression. There was a long clean streak in the dust on the car's fender. "Here's what we got: Jack Palp, an Arnie Kyle henchman who doesn't mind killing."

"Likes it," Nudger said, remembering Palp's eyes.

"Okay, likes it. Scary guy. Then we got Skip Monohan, a

small-time drug mule with no mailing address since the state penitentiary, and whose business is to be invisible. You say Palp scared you, and you can't find Monohan. So what would you have me do now, Nudge? What?"

Nudger watched half a dozen uniforms take the steps and disappear inside the station house. Several of the night shift officers were maneuvering their cars out of the lot, on the way home to breakfast. Thinking things other than cop thoughts.

"I dunno," Nudger said. "I really figured you might find Monohan at Scullin."

"We tried."

"I know you did, Jack. Thanks."

"You already thanked me; don't get sickening. Listen, Nudge, I better get inside. Some things to go over at muster. Hiller's not the only crime needs attention."

True for Hammersmith, but not for Nudger.

He said good-bye to Hammersmith and watched the obese lieutenant glide with his peculiar fat man's grace into the shade of the low brick building. In through the glass double doors. Wavering and fading out of sight beyond them. Like strolling into another dimension.

Something brushed Nudger's arm and arced away to light for a moment on Hammersmith's car. The September moth again, flitting around doomed and not knowing it. Reminded Nudger of someone.

He shivered in the bright sunlight and then walked toward his car parked in the captain's reserved slot.

What was it Palp had said? Hiller and his secretary ran away with the money and were someplace fucking their brains out under a palm tree. Maybe Palp believed that and maybe not.

So many people were trying so hard to believe it that Nudger found believing impossible.

2

Hammersmith was only part of the reason why Nudger had struggled out of bed so early. Braved the perils of morning traffic while the sun, hovering low over the Mississippi, blasted through the windshield and made his eyes ache.

After leaving the Third District station, he drove to Claudia's apartment, parking half in shade, half in sunlight in front of the old U-shaped, brick building just past seven-thirty.

As he got out of the Granada, he glanced up the street. The red Mustang convertible was gone from where it had been parked last night. A white work van was there now.

Nudger sidestepped a rusty tricycle with a shiny new bell attached to its handlebars, pushed open the door to the vestibule, and began climbing the steps to the second floor. An old gray-haired guy he'd seen in the building before edged past him on the landing, smiling and nodding a good morning. Alert for his age. Neighbor of Claudia's. One who could probably tell him a few things about Claudia and Biff Archway, Nudger thought. Maybe someday he'd ask. The detective in him.

He knocked on her door, waited a while. Then he heard a

faint sound and thought he felt the subtle vibration of her approaching footsteps.

She was nyloned-barefoot when she opened the door, wearing a plain green dress with a white collar. Her uncombed hair was a dark, wild bramble, as if she'd spent the night tossing her head from side to side. Nudger thought about the red convertible again. Biff Archway. Oh, the bastard!

Claudia smiled at him and contorted her arms to reach behind her and button the back of the dress. The effort made her small pointed breasts jut beneath the green material. She said, "C'mon in, Nudger."

He did, and she finished with the dress and raked her fingers through her tangle of hair. Mussed it more. Made it look better, though. He didn't say anything while he tried not to let his gaze roam around in an attempt to find some sign, some residue of the contemptible Archway's presence.

"You're an early bird today," Claudia said.

"Thought I might catch you before you left for work."

"You regard me as a worm?"

"Huh?"

"That's what the early bird catches: the early worm."

"I don't see you as a worm," Nudger said. He did glance around. "You alone?"

She frowned, then she padded over to where her black high-heeled shoes were lying near the sofa, pointed in opposite directions. Sat down and slipped the shoes on, bending forward gracefully. "What kind of question is that?"

"I dunno. How about that worm question? Don't be touchy."

She stood up, much taller now. Goddamn queenly. "Why are you here, Nudger?"

"To see you, is all."

"This is the first time you've been in the neighborhood and casually dropped by at seven-thirty in the morning."

"Is it?"

She said, "Let's go into the bedroom." Said it brusquely so he'd know what she meant. Not what he wanted.

He followed her, watching the sway of her lean hips wearing

out the green dress from the inside. She had on just the right amount of rose-scented perfume or cologne. He remembered that scent in bed. Other memories kicked in.

Bed. The first thing he looked at when he stepped into the room. Far as he could tell, only one person had slept in the double bed. One pillow wrinkled and fluffed up, the other smooth. Blankets turned back only at one corner.

Claudia said, "I need to get ready for work and get out of here. I harp enough at my students for being tardy. Don't want to give them any openings." She sat on the stool at her vanity, in front of the oval mirror, and began brushing the tangles from her dark hair. Watching her mesmerized Nudger and gave him an oddly restful feeling. The hairbrush made a sound like water rushing as she pulled it through with each stroke. The strokes got longer as the tangles were worked out.

Nudger shook off his hypnosis, crossed the room, and sat down on the long radiator, which was warm and dug into his buttocks. He wouldn't sit there very long.

Claudia stared into the mirror as she diligently worked the hairbrush. "I thought you were coming by here last night. Waited quite a while for you."

"I tried to make it, but something got in the way."

Her dark eyes found his in the mirror. "Well, we didn't exactly have a firm date." *Shhhwiish!* went the brush.

"I did drive past here last night," he said, "but it was too late to come in."

No change of expression on her lean features. "You have a key," she reminded him.

Nudger couldn't decide if she was putting on an act. He imagined the scene if he'd let himself into the apartment and tiptoed into the dark bedroom, blundered into the bed before realizing he was the three that made a crowd rather than company. Just the thought made him almost uncomfortable enough to cringe.

He said, "Archway have a key?"

She glared at him from the mirror, out of that flat world on the other side of the glass, not breaking rhythm with the brush.

Shhhwiish! "No, only you." A flicker of something in her eyes, around her lips. "And me, of course."

"Good. Apartment keys shouldn't be given out like pecks on the cheek."

"That's something I knew."

Okay. Nudger was feeling better. The red Mustang convertible must not have been Archway's. A neighbor's. Somebody who'd already left for work. Archway and Claudia were due out at Stowe High School at the same time weekday mornings; it figured that if he'd slept with Claudia he'd still be here. Nudger shrugged off his contentious mood. Acting the jealous idiot again. No reason to be angry with life and with Claudia. Not over last night, anyway.

"Last night," Claudia said, putting down the brush, "where'd you go instead of coming here?" She turned her head slowly and carefully from side to side, as if balancing something on it, to check in the mirror how her hair looked.

"Work," he said. "That disappearance thing, Virgil Hiller and his secretary."

She said, "Hm," and adroitly wound her hair in a bun in back, pinned it neatly so that only one errant wisp escaped. He decided not to tell her about the stray wisp. Nobody loved perfection. Not really. "Look okay?" she asked.

"Great."

"Stakeout or something?"

"Huh?"

"Last night."

"Er, yeah. Something like that."

"Still seeing that Bonnie?"

"Off and on."

"Kind of a vague term."

"I guess it is. Or maybe it's just the English teacher in you that thinks so." What was happening here? He hadn't come to Claudia's to be interrogated. Hadn't she heard of the traditional double standard?

She stood up and turned to face him, a light of concern in her dark eyes. "Nudger, you getting along okay?"

—— 153 ——

"Sure."

"I mean, with this Bonnie woman?"

An image of Coral Court jumped into his mind. Glazed tile. Rounded corners. Curves. Flesh. Art deco love nest. "Uh, yeah. Well as might be expected."

Claudia grinned, walked over, and kissed him on top of the head. The radiator suddenly got hotter.

She said, "I don't suppose I can stop loving you, Nudger. You're in my blood like tiny white corpuscles."

She walked from the bedroom into the kitchen. He followed, weighted down with guilt. He shouldn't have come here. Bad, jealousy-inspired idea.

"How'd it go at the doctor's?" he asked. "The Pap smear?"

"I don't know yet. They'll call."

"That the usual thing?"

"All routine. Hang around after I leave," she invited. "Make yourself some breakfast. Eggs and plenty of orange juice in the refrigerator."

"Thanks, but I'll grab something to eat at Danny's."

"*Is* there something to eat at Danny's?"

He contemplated a Dunker Delite. "Maybe I'll have an egg here, some toast."

Claudia moved to the table and picked up a clear glass mug half full of mud-colored coffee. Took a sip, made a face, and then carried the cup, along with an egg-smeared plate and knife and fork, over to the sink. She dumped the rest of the coffee down the drain, then ran some water over the dishes and flatware and left them in the sink to be dealt with when she got home. A neat housekeeper, but in streaks.

"Gotta run or I'll be late," she said.

She tried to get away with only pecking Nudger's cheek, but he grabbed her upper arms and kissed her full on the mouth. Gave her a good one. She returned the kiss, but only perfunctorily, her lips pressed tightly together. No way to kiss back or lick a stamp. Obviously a woman in a hurry.

"Dammit! No time for this, Nudger."

"You taste like toothpaste."

"Complaining?"

"No."

She clacked over the floor in her high heels, into the dining room. Nudger drifted along behind her. "Where'd I put that briefcase?" she mumbled to herself.

"There," he said, pointing to her vinyl attaché case propped on a chair in the living room.

"Ah, thanks." She strode over and scooped up the case. "Tenth grade English exams," she said, as if explaining the importance of the contents. Her tone of voice suggested the case actually contained something other than school papers. Perhaps nuclear war plans. Maybe pornographic photographs. Or was Nudger searching for secretiveness in her? Getting paranoid about her and Archway.

He said, "I'll walk you to your car."

"Okay. But no time for a long conversation."

"Agreed. Even though I'm lonely."

She hesitated at the door. Speared him with those dark eyes. "*Are* you lonely?"

"For you."

"I'm usually here. You know that."

Maybe with Biff Archway. "Yeah, I know." At least he was sure that she'd spent last night alone.

She led the way downstairs and outside. Hadn't locked her apartment door. Nudger would be back up there in a minute, scrounging around for breakfast. He'd surprise her, he decided, and wash the dishes. Assuage some of his guilt about last night.

Claudia reminded him to lock up when he left the apartment, then lowered herself behind the steering wheel of her tin-can-sized white Chevette and shut the door.

Nudger said, "I love you. Love me?" She couldn't hear him but she read his lips through the windshield and smiled and shook her head hopelessly.

He turned and walked back toward the apartment, listening to the Chevette's starter grind.

The little car's engine was stubborn about turning over. The battery faded fast and the grinding sound turned into a low grating noise, then a woeful mechanical moan.

Nudger stopped walking. Claudia was out of the car, standing with her arms crossed, her feet planted as wide as her skirt would permit. She was staring at the car with an angry, puzzled expression, in the way she might stare at a loyal dog who had inexplicably snapped at her.

When he'd made his way back to her she said, "I guess I'm not destined to get to work on time this morning."

"Why buck destiny? You could come back upstairs, spend the morning with me."

"No, Nudger. But you can help me get my car started."

"Will there be a reward?"

"In heaven."

"That's right up there," he said, pointing to her bedroom window.

"Sometimes," she told him, "you disarm with charm. But not this morning." She moved into the street and raised the Chevette's hood. "It's done this before. It'll start, only I ran the battery too low."

"I've got jumper cables in the trunk of my car," Nudger said. "Nobody's parked in front of you; I'll drive around and we'll get it started."

He jogged across the street and climbed into the Granada.

Wilmington was too narrow for him to make a U-turn, so he drove to the corner, turned around, and pulled to the wrong side of the street. He parked almost nose to nose with the Chevette, leaving just enough room between the two cars for him to stand and hook up the jumper cables.

He got out of the car and walked around to open the trunk. Saw that several of the neighbors were watching from their stoops and windows.

Claudia stood alongside her car, waiting. Looking worried about a classroom full of teenage girls with no teacher. How would the school know they were unattended? When one of them broke down and notified the office? When the decible level soared high enough to alert the rest of the school?

It occurred to Nudger that the trunk key was on the ring with his ignition key, which was still in the switch on the steering column. He retrieved the keys, then returned to the trunk and worked the lock. Lifted the lid.

This was odd.

There was a rolled-up rug in the trunk. Looked like a cheap imitation oriental. A big one. One he'd never seen before.

He found a corner of the coarse material and tugged it loose from where it was pinned against the rubber trunk mat, yanked up on it.

Something white and angular became visible. He wasn't quite sure what it was, so he braced his knees against the bumper and leaned forward for a closer look.

Said, "Ah, Christ!" and jumped back in horror as he realized he was staring at an elbow.

22

Hammersmith said, "A dead body in your car, Nudge. That's not a moving violation but it's serious."

They were standing on the edge of a lawn across the street from where Skip Monohan's corpse was being removed from the Granada's trunk. Rigor mortis had made it difficult to unroll Monohan from the oriental rug. Now the attendants were working his arms back and forth, loosening them just enough so they could get them down and zip the rubberized body bag around him and transport him to the morgue. They were having a tough time. Monohan was defying authority even in death.

There were half a dozen police cars angled into the curb, and the street was blocked off at the corner. Claudia hadn't made it to work on time. She was up in her apartment, probably still being questioned. Most of her neighbors were out on the sidewalk, staring silently at the police working the scene. This was the sort of spectacle they'd longed to witness, but now, seeing it, they were sobered.

Finally Monohan was snugly zipped into the bag, strapped

to a gurney, and wheeled into the back of an ambulance. An attendant slammed the double doors and jogged forward to the vehicle's passenger side and climbed in.

The ambulance drove away slowly, no siren or lights, while every eye followed it avidly until it turned the corner. Death on a quiet street.

Now that the body was removed, the crowd's interest seemed to have waned. But only a little. They were nothing if not nosy, Claudia's South St. Louis neighbors. The way it was in this part of town. Very traditional and judgmental. The kind of area where you could organize a quiet lynch mob.

"Now are you planning on picking up Palp?" Nudger asked.

Hammersmith hitched a thumb in his belt, near his holstered Police Special, and nodded. "Yeah, we'll talk to him. Talk to you, too. Case it's escaped your thoughts, it was your car Monohan was found in."

Nudger was getting tired of trying to jar the law out of delusion when it came to anything even indirectly connected with Virgil Hiller. Hammersmith should know better than this. "And it was me who told you Monohan might have been killed," Nudger reminded him. "Me who eventually found the body, phoned the law, cooperated fully."

"Sorry, Nudge, but—"

"Don't tell me it's just routine."

"But it is. And you know it."

Nudger tried to convince himself Hammersmith was right, but he was still rattled from opening his trunk and finding Skip Monohan instead of jumper cables. All morning he'd been driving around with company and not known it. His stomach was twitching and he felt nauseated. He broke into a new roll of antacid tablets. Chewed and swallowed two of them and hoped they'd help. He didn't have the nervous system for getting involved in murder. He should be selling software or appliances, where nothing got slashed but the prices.

He remembered then: no blood in the trunk. "How'd Monohan go?" he asked.

"Strangulation. Thin wire around his neck. Yanked so tight it's almost completely embedded in his flesh. Very little bleeding, though. The rug soaked up most of it."

Nudger thought, You don't bleed much once your heart stops pumping. He touched his stomach with his fingertips and chomped another antacid tablet.

"Why are they staring at me?" Hammersmith asked, looking at the knot of neighbors across the street.

"You're standing on the zoysia."

"Oh." Hammersmith moved a few steps onto the sidewalk, and the crowd visibly relaxed. He lived out in Webster Groves, a near suburb that was a sort of unruly forest with streets and houses. He was partial to crabgrass and wildflowers and didn't fully understand why South St. Louisans had this compulsion to constrict and discipline nature.

Glancing up at Claudia's apartment, Nudger thought he caught a glimpse of her at a window. Or maybe he'd mistaken a blue uniform for a green dress. The curtain settled back into place; illusion behind glass. Whoever was at the window had turned away and disappeared.

Hammersmith methodically fired up a cigar, his smooth, fleshy cheeks puffing in and out as he made bellowslike noises and got the ember glowing bright red. "The way I read it," he said, "Palp saw you leave Monohan's place, then intercepted you and had his little chat with you at Scullin Steel. Left you there unconscious, went back and killed Monohan, and then loaded the rolled-up rug—with Monohan inside—into the trunk of your car."

"Sounds likely," Nudger said.

Hammersmith emitted a greenish thundercloud, then removed the cigar from his mouth and gazed at it as if he were talking to it instead of Nudger. "'Cept for a few things. Such as, how'd he get your car keys?"

Nudger had thought about that while waiting for the law to arrive. "Took them outta my pocket when I was unconscious at Scullin, then put them back after he'd killed Monohan and loaded him into my car's trunk."

"Why would he do that?"

"He wanted me to be surprised when I found the body. The idea was to scare me. Underscore the warning he gave me at Scullin."

"Could be. Or his idea of a joke, maybe. There's no accounting for some people's sense of humor. 'Specially hit men, though they're usually slapstick fans. Go for Gallagher, the Three Stooges, acts like that." He deftly peeled a flake of tobacco from his lower lip, rolled it to nothing between thumb and forefinger. "And the rug?"

Nudger shrugged, trying to imagine Jack Palp hawing over the Three Stooges. It was conceivable. "He probably had the rug in the trunk of his car. Maybe a guy like that carries an oriental rug just for the purpose of transporting murder victims."

"Oh, it all falls into place," Hammersmith said, "if you're telling the truth."

"You know I am."

"Sure I do. But what about Captain Springer?"

Leo Springer was a cop who went by the book, as long as he could revise it to his advantage. He and Nudger got along something like the Roadrunner and coyotes. "Think the little weasel-faced bastard'll see me as a suspect?"

"Yes and no," Hammersmith said. "Mostly no. But he might try to change that. You're not one of Springer's all-time favorites on the planet."

"Any of Monohan's neighbors see Palp coming or going with the rolled-up rug?" Nudger asked.

"There aren't many neighbors, but they were questioned at the time of the Scullin search. They saw nothing, which isn't surprising. The neighborly thing to do on Monohan's street is to keep your head down and your mouth shut."

"Even if your neighbor's been murdered?"

"Especially then. We do our best with what we got, Nudge, but right now witness protection in this city isn't for shit, and potential witnesses know it."

Hammersmith had that right. It seemed that every week

the *Post-Dispatch* ran a story about an indicted criminal going free because a witness had died or disappeared. Even if the accused were indicted, he often had friends in whose interest it was to create examples and teach object lessons to other, potential witnesses. The violent message had been driven home: if you couldn't be blind and deaf, be mute. Possibly Monohan's neighbors had chosen the wisest course.

Yellow lights flashed as a tow truck rounded the corner. A uniform moved a red and white police barricade so the truck could roar through a tight maneuver and then back up the street, chain and hooks clanking against its stubby iron boom.

Nudger said, "Oh, no!"

"'Fraid so," Hammersmith said. "We're gonna have to impound your car, Nudge. Shouldn't be for long. I'll try to put a rush on things and get it back to you by tomorrow morning, maybe even tonight."

Nudger watched the dusty white truck edge to the front of the Granada. The driver, a wiry little guy in greasy brown coveralls, jumped down from the cab and worked the winch. When he was satisfied he'd played out enough slack, he got down on his hands and knees to hook the tow chain to the car's undercarriage.

"How am I supposed to get around?" Nudger asked.

"Maybe Claudia will lend you her car."

"Maybe the department could give me a loaner to drive."

"We're not an insurance company, Nudge."

Nudger watched as the whining electric winch raised the front of the Granada. A couple of clumps of dirt fell from under the fenders.

The driver climbed back into the truck, got the yellow roof-bar lights flashing, and pulled away from the curb. The barriers at the end of the block were dragged to the side again, and the low rear end of the Granada disappeared around the corner.

"Talk with Claudia," Hammersmith advised. He shoved his cigar deep in his mouth and glanced at his watch. "Better do it now, sho we can get down to headquartersh, get your official shtatement." He blew green smoke, then removed the cigar and looked at it with a nicotine fiend's tender satisfaction. "You know how it is, somebody gets murdered, red tape, forms to fill out. Inconvenience all around, 'specially for the victim."

"Maybe now the department bureaucrats will look on the Virgil Hiller disappearance in another light."

"I doubt it, Nudge. Politics."

"There's a word I don't like."

"Like it or not, politics are the stuff of life."

It was just like Hammersmith to say something like that. And at a time like this. Made Nudger mad. "We both know politics are bullshit."

"Well, bullshit's the stuff of life. You and I been in our jobs long enough to realize that, hey?"

Nudger had no answer. He started across the street toward Claudia's apartment. Behind him Hammersmith said, "I'll wait for you here, Nudge. Give you a lift downtown."

Nudger hadn't planned on riding the bus.

When Claudia let him into the apartment, he couldn't tell if she was angry or scared. Maybe she couldn't make up her mind. He decided not to ask about borrowing her car, which still hadn't been started.

He said, "I'm sorry about all this."

"Guess you are."

"Better call the service station about your car," he said. "You better get out to the school."

She paced to the window, looked outside at the neighbors still milling about, some of them no doubt staring back at her. "A corpse in your car, Nudger. God . . ."

"Nature of the business," he said. "You know that."

She turned to face him, the light at her back streaming golden through her dark hair. He could barely make out her features. This body in the trunk had struck her as serious. She said, "I'm afraid for you."

"So am I."

"This about the Virgil Hiller case?"

He said it was. Brought her up to date and told her about Skip Monohan. He wondered if he was doing it so she'd be even more afraid for him. She wasn't afraid for Biff Archway, whose job cast no danger and who could probably take on the Mafia singlehanded anyway.

Claudia shook her head slowly from side to side and then crossed her arms. He wasn't sure what that reaction meant. "What happens now?" she asked.

"I drive downtown with Hammersmith, go through the routine."

She considered that for a moment, standing motionless in the golden sunlight. Dust swirled in the brilliant, slanted beams; Skip Monohan would soon be dust. "Good God," she said, "you're not—"

"A suspect? No, not really. They want to make sure I waltz through all the steps, is all. Kinda thing they do as part of the job."

"Is this the 'just routine' we read about in novels and see on TV shows?"

"Depends on the book or the show, I suppose. But there's no reason for worry. Everybody downtown wants to cover his or her ass. That's what this seems to be all about."

"But Monohan's body was in the trunk of *your* car."

"Don't be an alarmist," he said, trying not to be alarmed. "It's only politics." He remembered what Hammersmith had told him. "You know how it is; politics are the stuff of life."

"Of death, too."

Why hadn't he pointed that out to Hammersmith? She wasn't cheering him up. "Hammersmith's waiting outside. I better get going."

Claudia walked over and placed her palms on his cheeks, scrunching up the flesh around his eyes and staring hard at him with her sexy stern-teacher look. "You be careful for both of us, understand?" She fit her lips against his, let the kiss linger. Warm. Nice.

"I try never to be brave," he told her, when she stepped away.

"But you have lapses."

He assured her he'd be careful enough for two, then tromped downstairs to ride to headquarters with Hammersmith.

Chewed a couple of antacid tablets on the way.

23

It was past noon when the machinery of the law finally spat out Nudger. His interrogation had been uncommonly thorough, and most of it had been conducted by Leo Springer. Springer had been his usual nasty self, but at the same time there'd been an odd sort of decorum to his questioning. His insults had been carefully phrased so their impact was more in their tone and timing than in the actual wording. As if he suspected that someone somewhere would be reviewing his actions. Scrutinizing them.

Another odd thing: when the law was done talking with Nudger, he was told they were finished with his car and it would be parked in the City Hall lot across the street. Here was efficiency without precedent. And, so far, without explanation.

A small-time drug dealer had been killed and then dumped in Nudger's car trunk, and everyone was tiptoeing. Moving carefully along dotted lines.

Except for Nudger, who seemed to blunder into one dilemma after another.

He staggered out of police headquarters into a day that had turned cool. A steady drizzle was drifting down from an iron gray sky that seemed to hover ten feet above the tops of buildings.

Exhausted, he assured himself he wouldn't melt in the rain and didn't bother running to his car. The drizzle felt like cold pinpricks on his face and the back of his neck. The nasty wet stuff might soon turn into snow. Nudger could remember St. Louis September snowfalls that had brought the city to a white and silent halt. On the other hand, it might be ninety degrees by tomorrow morning. If you don't like the weather, give it a minute or two and it might change.

Tucked beneath one of the Granada's windshield wipers was a soggy slip of white paper. As was often the case, the left hand of the law hadn't known what the right hand was doing. The right hand had written a citation because the left hand had steered the Granada to an unauthorized parking space.

Nudger thought briefly about going back inside and having the ticket taken care of, then figured the hell with it and stuck it beneath a wiper of the car next to his. Big new Cadillac, not quite a block long. Maybe the mayor's car.

Nudger drove north to Market Street, then headed west. Before leaving the police station, he'd phoned the county library and was told this was Adelaide Lacy's day off. Another phone call revealed that she'd followed the advice of her car's bumper sticker and was home reading a book. Said she was, anyway. She was waiting for Nudger now, at her apartment.

She could wait a while longer; she'd told him she liked to curl up at home on rainy days and had no plans. Librarian talk.

Nudger found a parking spot on Market across from Union Station and fed all his loose change to the meter. He went inside and had a Super Slinger for lunch at Hodge's Chili Parlor, a spicy concoction of tortilla, eggs, and hot chili, topped with a tamale. He loved the things, and since his stomach was already twisted and bleeding, he figured the taste would be worth the pain.

That was because the taste came first.

He'd finished his roll of antacid tablets by the time he knocked on Adelaide's door. Even chomped and swallowed a linty stray tablet he'd found hidden in the depths of his sport coat pocket. His stomach seemed to have converted it all to acid.

When she opened the door, Adelaide said, "You look shorter."

Nudger realized he was slightly bent over from abdominal pain. His stomach and his still-aching groin were working in concert to make him suffer. Doing a bang-up job.

He caught the title of the book she was holding with one finger inserted between the pages to keep her place: *The Single Woman's Manual of Personal Growth.* He said, "Maybe you're taller than last time we met."

She lowered her blue eyes to glance at the book, got his meaning, and smiled. Invited him in with a sideways tilt of her head. She'd applied the slightest tint of violet eye shadow to her eyelids. For him? Or maybe it was makeup left over from yesterday, when she'd spruced up for Voltaire, Hemingway, and *The Reader's Guide to Periodical Literature.*

She shuffled to the side to make room for him to pass; he brushed her shoulder as he entered. She smelled faintly perfumed and soapy, as if she'd just showered and washed her hair.

The apartment was clean and neatly furnished. It even smelled clean, like its occupant, as if there might be an air purifier toiling away somewhere out of sight. There were brass-framed museum prints of no particular style or period on the walls; here a Picasso, there a Manet. A small oak bookcase with glass doors squatted over by the window, crammed with paperbacks. Not a big place, but comfortable.

Looks deceived. Nudger lowered himself into the chair and found it unyielding. No way to settle into it. His stomach didn't approve of him sitting down.

"I was about to get myself a cup of tea," Adelaide said. "Want one?"

"Glass of milk, if it's not too much trouble." There was conflicting medical opinion about the effects of milk on a nervous stomach. The white stuff seemed to help Nudger, especially when it was warmed, so he drank plenty of it. He couldn't remember seeing a nervous cow, and they had *two* stomachs.

Adelaide looked surprised, but she said milk was less trouble than tea and then turned and walked through the adjacent dining room into what Nudger assumed was the kitchen.

A microwave oven emitted a series of high-pitched beeps in the kitchen. Sounded like a kid learning to play some of the electronic crap that passed these days for musical instruments. Nudger had possessed an extensive collection of old jazz recordings before he'd sold most of it a few years ago to pay his rent and his back alimony to Eileen. Music by musicians, not technicians.

Adelaide soon returned carrying a white cup and a short, wide glass of milk. She had a smooth, sensual walk and the milk didn't slosh in the glass. She was wearing brown slacks, tighter than they should have been at the crotch, and a light beige sweater. Her blond hair was pinned back, but not as severely as she wore it in the library. Nudger remembered what Jack Palp had said about Hiller running away with the wrong sister.

When she handed him the glass he was surprised to find that it was warm.

"I remembered your stomach problems," she said. "I can get you cold milk if you'd prefer."

"Nope," he told her, "this is great. Exactly what I need." He sipped the milk and his stomach immediately calmed, as if signaling him that this was what it had been waiting for, only he'd been so dumb as to send down a Super Slinger instead.

Adelaide switched on a floor lamp to shoo away any outside gloom that might have crept in. Then she sat down in a corner of the sofa, curling her legs beneath her. She was wearing brown sandals without socks, had nice ankles. She placed her steaming cup on the broad sofa arm and waited.

Nudger said, "Your sister ever mention a guy name of Skip Monohan?"

"I don't think so. Why?"

He told her why.

For a minute or so afterward, Adelaide swirled her tea around in her cup, staring into the miniature whirlpool. "I guess I shouldn't be surprised Mary was—is—on drugs. She's been under stress for years. The kind of deep down, repressed stress that isn't visible to other people but that tears away at your insides."

"The rape?"

"What it did to her. She couldn't trust people after that. And she was too sensitive to what they thought about her. She imagined things."

"What kinds of things?"

"Oh, sometimes that people were staring at her. Looking down their noses. What happened left her permanently soiled—in her mind, anyway. And suspicious." Adelaide unconsciously floated a hand up to the side of her head and mussed her hair over one ear. She was wearing earrings, Nudger noticed. Dangling trinkets that looked like tiny silver seashells. She shook her head and the shells swung on their delicate silver chains and sent patterns of reflected lamplight dancing over her shoulders. "For God's sake! The idea of Mary becoming romantically involved and running away with Virgil Hiller is so ludicrous."

"The police don't think so. Not officially, anyway." Nudger tilted back his head and drained his glass of milk. Wiped away a white mustache. Reminded him of when he was a twelve-year-old kid. Where were the Oreo cookies? "This where Arnie Kyle sat when he came to visit you?"

"No. As I recall, Paul Dobbs sat there. Mr. Kyle sat on the sofa, where I'm sitting. Is it important?"

"I expect not. I'm just curious."

"Dobbs sat on the sofa on his first visit, when he showed me the photograph. I remember because he spilled some of his tea on the cushion." Apparently tea was her standard fare for visitors. Kind of genteel. "Next visit—when Mr. Kyle was here—he sat in that chair. He and Mr. Kyle both had tea, but Mr. Kyle didn't touch his."

"I wish you wouldn't call him 'mister.' He doesn't deserve your respect. He probably has something to do with your sister's disappearance."

"Do you think so? He seemed concerned about her when he was here. Strange to say that, I know, but that's the impression he gave."

"He's an expert at giving whatever impression the occasion calls for. Was Jack Palp with him?"

"The man you think killed Skip Monohan?"

"Uh-huh."

"No. Not here in my apartment. But Mr.—I mean Kyle said there was someone waiting for him outside."

Nudger rotated his empty glass slowly between his palms. "Adelaide, you think Mary might have had any other secrets?"

"Such as?" She sounded remotely offended.

"A neighbor said there was a butchy-looking woman who visited her frequently."

"Butchy?" Her face reddened. "Oh." She shifted position on the sofa so that one of her legs came out from under her. Barely touched a toe on the rug. "I'm sure Mary isn't—that way. But I couldn't blame her, after what happened. I mean, it left her with this deep distrust, this fear and dislike of men. But honestly, I can't imagine her with another woman. That's so bizarre. On the other hand, I can't imagine her with a man. I guess what I'm saying is that I don't want to believe it. After all, she's my sister. But anything's possible."

Nudger had known that. Every day seemed to offer proof. The world was like a kaleidoscope given a fresh shake each morning.

"That would make it highly unlikely she'd be with Virgil Hiller," Adelaide observed.

"Make it less likely. But the idea isn't to prove she's not with Hiller. We want to find her."

"You will, Nudger. Don't be discouraged." Here she was bucking him up. Not what he'd anticipated. He sure could inspire a client to have confidence in him. How difficult was it, he wondered, to break into sales or management at one of the big corporations in town?

He said, "It only seems to be getting more complicated."

"Something will happen soon."

It already had, Nudger reflected. To Skip Monohan.

He thanked Adelaide for the milk and stood up.

She stood also, balancing her cup again on the sofa arm, and moved to show him out. He'd been worried about upsetting her, but she sent him on his way with a beautiful reassuring smile.

It was tough to read either of the Lacy sisters.

The rain had stopped when Nudger parked across the street from his office. He saw half a dozen bicycles leaning on their kickstands outside the doughnut shop. Through the steamy window he could see Danny busy behind the counter, waiting on the bikes' prepubescent riders. Introducing them to Dunker Delites. Kids might bend a few spokes when they rode away.

Without interrupting Danny, Nudger opened the street door to the office and climbed the creaking wooden stairs. Unlocked the office door and pushed it open. Stepped inside and was hit immediately with the sensation that he wasn't alone.

A voice said, "Who did your office? Salvation Army?"

The man who'd spoken was leaning casually with one hand on Nudger's desk, the other in the pocket of his expensive gray suitcoat. He was about fifty, average size, had neat, straight salt-and-pepper hair combed straight back, and oversized glasses with droopy silver frames that lent him a sad yet alert expression. His mouth was the kind that was always turned down at the corners, above a jutting chin so deeply dimpled you could lose a fingertip in it.

Nudger recognized him from newspaper photos and occasional local TV coverage.

Arnie Kyle.

24

Nudger involuntarily glanced around the gloomy office.

Not moving, Kyle read his mind and smiled. "He's outside waiting in the car, Nudger. Jack makes a strong impression, doesn't he?"

Nudger said, "Kind of guy people remember, all right." He walked over to the window and looked down. Snow hadn't fallen. In fact, the rain had stopped. A big black Lincoln was parked on the other side of Manchester. They'd figured Nudger would check the street; the driver-side tinted window was rolled down so he could clearly see Palp sitting in the car, drumming his fingers on top of the steering wheel and staring straight ahead. He was wearing a dark tie with his black undertaker's suit. Maybe he'd read somewhere the ominous look was in.

Then Nudger saw something else that disturbed him. Half a block up the street another car was parked. Another driver sat, staring toward the office. Tad Beal in his ancient gray Plymouth.

Damn! The last thing Nudger wanted was for Tad to barge into the office and try to get adult and tough with Kyle and

Palp around. Teen World would be over and he'd grow up in a hurry, stay alive if he was lucky.

"Jack's a patient guy," Kyle said behind Nudger. "He'd wait out there all day, just like a well-trained Doberman. But if I was to press the button on the little sender I got in my pocket, the beeper on Jack's belt'd go off and he'd be up here on the run and primed for action. Something for you to remember."

Nudger turned around. Kyle's right hand was still casually inserted in his suit coat pocket, finger on the Destroy Nudger button.

Nudger said, "Why didn't you bring him up here on a thick leash?"

"'Cause we're gonna have a little talk it'd be better Jack didn't hear. That way, if the law questions him, he can honestly say he knows nothing about our conversation."

"Preserving his deniability but keeping him in the game."

"Exactly. Just like they do in Washington."

"The American way, I suppose."

"Nothing for you to be scared about, though," Kyle said, "long as I got your full cooperation."

Nudger sat down behind his desk. The swivel chair squealed and Kyle looked nervous. Nudger hoped his finger didn't twitch on the button. Once set in motion, a joyful killer like Palp might be hard to stop. Might object to suffering a kind of coitus interruptus. "What sort of cooperation?" Nudger asked. But he could guess.

"Listen," Kyle said, "it's a shame about old Skip Monohan, don't you think?" Kyle wasn't ready to get to the point. Wanted to lay some groundwork.

"He wasn't so old," Nudger said. "Never had much chance to make senior citizen."

"Sure he had a chance," Kyle said, moving closer. "Same chance you got. It's a great country—everybody's got a chance. He could have kept his lips together, minded his own business."

"I'm minding *my* business," Nudger told him. "Says what it is on the door. Investigator. I investigate. I got a client. Besides, how do you know Monohan told me anything?"

"How do I know he *didn't!*"

There was the problem. Nudger's as well as Kyle's. Made Nudger's stomach bounce around.

"Better if you stop your investigating," Kyle said. "It'd be inconvenient for you, anyways, from Hawaii."

Nudger said, "This is Missouri. No ocean. No islands. Corn and soybeans. Been years since I saw a palm tree."

Kyle used his free hand to draw a thick yellow envelope from an inside pocket. He held it up so Nudger could get a good look at it. "Plane ticket for tomorrow afternoon, Nudger. To San Francisco and then Honolulu. It's great in the islands this time of year. Oh, and there's also fifty thousand in small bills for you to have yourself a good time with something left over. Lay around, sip pineapple drinks, ball a hula dancer. That's what I mean by cooperating with me. Not so tough, eh?"

Nudger looked away from the envelope with effort. Fifty thousand. *Gulp!* He said, "How come you want me to stop searching for Mary Lacy?"

"Easy. 'Cause she's with Virgil Hiller."

"And you don't want him found."

"Ah, but I do. Only I want *my* people to find him."

Nudger didn't ask why; the question filled the room.

Kyle said, "It wasn't only city money Hiller ran away with."

"And when you do find him?"

"If you cooperate, you got my promise: The Lacy cunt'll be set loose from whatever happens. This isn't about her; she's just a bit of excess trim that doesn't interest me in the slightest."

Nudger sat wondering what were the odds. Of Kyle telling the truth. Of his promise being good. Of Nudger's stomach surviving the guilt if he accepted Kyle's offer. Of the rest of him surviving if he refused it.

"Don't decide now," Kyle said, slipping the envelope back into his pocket, patting the pocket. "Give yourself a while to think things through."

"What if I tell you it'll be business as usual?"

Kyle shrugged inside the elegant suit. "Guess you and Jack'll have another conversation. He feels as strongly about this as I do. As strongly about everything. Jack and I are of the same mind. It's his job."

"How's Hiller owe you money?" Nudger asked.

"Gambling debts."

Logical.

Kyle said, "He fancies himself a high roller, but the only way he ever rolled was downhill and over the edge. He was in the hole plenty. What he usually did was dip into city funds to set his tab right. This time instead of dipping and paying, he dipped and ran."

"Any idea why?"

Kyle shook his head. "Love, maybe. Fucks up people's thinking sometimes."

"What I hear about Mary Lacy," Nudger said, "Hiller would have had to kidnap her."

"You mean about her being a lizzy? Don't believe everything you hear, Nudger. 'Less it's from me. Mary Lacy went both ways."

"Way I understand it, she didn't even go *one* way."

"We don't know everything about her private life. All that intimate stuff. Looks like Hiller did, though. Knew enough, anyway. Pretty simple. Maybe he got her pregnant and she's got some inhibition about abortion. Had no choice but to run with him if she wanted to stay an honest woman. Maybe they're even married by now. All kinds of possibilities, Nudger. But best for you if you don't explore any of them."

Absconding with your boss and stolen money didn't sound to Nudger like staying an honest woman, but this was no time to argue fine points.

Kyle wrinkled his nose. "What the hell's that smell?"

"Doughnuts. From downstairs."

"Shit! How do you stand it?"

"You get used to some smells, don't even know they're around. Even though other people still know." He gave Kyle a tight grin; what the hell, Palp was down in the car. "Some days this office stinks worse than from doughnuts."

"You being a wise-ass, Nudger?"

"Not my nature."

"I wonder."

Still with his hand in his pocket, Kyle backed smoothly to the door. He moved backward with great confidence, as if he had rear vision.

"I suppose Palp has an alibi for when Monohan was killed," Nudger said.

"Ask the law; they already had him downtown and worked on him, checked out his story. It didn't take long. Jack's attorney saw he was treated right and the matter handled quick as possible. Everything goes smooth when there's cooperation on both sides. That's what I'm trying to get across to you."

Nudger said, "Was Monohan murdered so you could scare me into backing off the Hiller case?"

"Hey, how should I know?"

"You know."

"I know you're in a game that's too big and fast for a guy like you. Mile over your head." He glanced around the shabby office. "Loser, that's you. Two-digit IQ and bank balance to match."

"It isn't that. I don't feel compelled to put up a front."

"Or to pay for one. Listen, there should be a sign on the wall behind your desk, Nudger. Know what it oughtta say?"

"OUT TO LUNCH?"

"Uh-uh. DEEP WATER."

Kyle sort of slid out the door. Removed the hand from his pocket, then took the steps fast. Nudger heard the street door open and close.

He strode to the window and watched Kyle cross the street. Dapper guy with a jaunty walk. World by the short hairs, but right now a little worried. Possibly plenty worried. He glanced up at the office window as he got into the long black Lincoln with Palp. As the car eased away from the curb, it revealed a sweeping dark reflection of the street.

—— 177 ——

The Lincoln oozed down the block and slowed as it passed Tad sitting in his junk Plymouth, then picked up speed and merged with traffic pulling out of the K-mart parking garage.

Nudger went downstairs and walked along Manchester toward the Plymouth. There were puddles on the sidewalk. He sloshed through one and got his left sock wet. Great!

Tad was alone in the car. He leaned forward to reach the ignition, and the engine turned over and rumbled, but he didn't drive away.

Nudger walked up to the Plymouth's passenger side. The window was cranked open. He leaned down, hands on knees, and peered in at Tad, who was coiled awkwardly behind the steering wheel in the manner of scrawny teenage boys. He was wearing dirty Levi's and a green insulated vest over a white T-shirt. Nudger wasn't surprised to see a large grease smudge on his neck. He said, "Tad, I want you to stop following me."

Tad stared straight ahead and spoke in a tough-guy monotone. "This is a free country and a public street, ain't it?" Bogart lived. And he was civic minded, just like Arnie Kyle.

"You're likely to get hurt."

Now Tad glared at Nudger. Young Basil Rathbone again. "By you?"

"No. By somebody it'd be better you never met. It has to do with my work."

"Yeah, big-shit private detective. Like on TV. You think I'm scared? Well, here's a flash—I ain't."

"You don't have to be scared to get hurt. I want you to stop tailing me."

"Sure. And I want you to stop fuckin' my mom."

Nudger stared at him. Tad was barely constraining himself; the muscles in his pimpled, grease-marked face were jumping.

"Gonna tell me you ain't fuckin' her?" he challenged.

Nudger didn't know how to deal with the question. With teenagers. This one in particular. He slapped the top of the car in frustration.

"You dent that and you're dead!" Tad screamed.

"Christ! Take it easy. No harm done." Nudger forced himself to be rational. "Listen, I'm not going to hurt your mother. She wouldn't be with me if she didn't want it that way. You don't mind if she has a life, do you?"

"I do if you're in it."

"She should drive around and sell cosmetics, do temporary office work, and be mom, is that it?"

"Fuck you, Nudger!"

Here was a lad beyond reason. Maybe he'd settle down, make sense when he hit thirty. If he made it that long. Didn't wind up like Skip Monohan.

"You're two-timing her anyway," Tad said.

"You really are sticking to me, you persistent little punk. Listen, I see people on business. Some of them are female."

"I ain't dumb, Nudger."

"Oh, aren't you? That was a dumb stunt last night, you and your friends raising hell outside my apartment."

"Never know when I'm gonna turn up," Tad said. "Gonna follow you whenever I want. Be on you like flies on shit."

"You're in over your head," Nudger said, and abruptly realized he sounded like Arnie Kyle. "Messing with something dangerous. You don't understand what I'm trying to tell you."

Tad wasn't listening. His long, skinny arm snaked to the dashboard and he punched a button that turned on the radio. Heavy metal rock music blasted through the car. Not good rock. The electronic din Nudger hated. The lead singer screamed, "Do it! Do it! Do it!" and drums and a synthesizer took over. Enough to cause an earache.

"Jesus, Tad, you're so big on mother figures, why don't you ease up and listen to Madonna?"

Tad didn't hear him.

Nudger gave up. Walked back to the office. The music drifted after him and he found himself moving to the beat.

Didn't like that.

When he went back upstairs and looked out the window, the Plymouth was gone.

25

Nudger tried to get in touch with Hammersmith by phone at the Third District and was told the lieutenant had gone out to lunch. Desk Sergeant Ellis either didn't know or wouldn't say where, but Nudger had a pretty good idea.

Half an hour later he was pushing open the heavy wood door of Ricardo's restaurant on Locust Street. It was where Hammersmith usually ate lunch—the restaurant mainly responsible for changing the lean and handsome patrol-car officer of yesteryear into today's corpulent, desk-driving bureaucrat. The menu was Italian, the food was good, and the way the place was sectioned off by thick oak partitions provided privacy for confidential conversation. Plenty of deals between cops and informants, and attorneys and clients, had been cut at Ricardo's.

Nudger's appetite kicked in as he sniffed the pungent, garlicky scent that hung heavy in the air. He spotted the familiar gray top of Hammersmith's head above one of the oak partitions and began working his way there through the maze of round tables and angled, polished wood. Bumped his head on one of those damned hanging potted ferns. The thick carpet and drapes absorbed sound. Not only was the talk of diners muted, but even the clink of silverware and dishes was barely discernible.

It was almost two o'clock and most of the lunch crowd at Ricardo's had left. About a third of the red-clothed tables still had diners seated around them. Nudger exchanged glances with a cop he knew—a sergeant on the vice squad—who was talking with a bearded guy in a wooly gray sweater. The cop quickly looked away from Nudger and gave no sign of recognition. Nudger responded in kind. Or rather, didn't respond. Police protocol at Ricardo's.

Hammersmith was alone at his table, finishing off a large plate of spaghetti and meatballs. There were crumbs from garlic toast all over the tablecloth. His red napkin was tucked in his collar and covered the front of his shirt to act as a bib. There was a dusting of crumbs clinging to the napkin. Some dark spots of spaghetti sauce. Nudger had seen enough of spaghetti for a while.

Hammersmith looked up as Nudger approached. He slowly lowered his fork, and took a sip of red wine. Smacked his lips in appreciation even though it was probably cheap house wine. What did he know? He was more Cookie Monster than gourmet.

Nudger sat down.

Hammersmith lifted the lower half of the tucked-in napkin and dabbed at his lips. "Fun morning, wouldn't you say, Nudge?"

"Disney World."

A heavyset waitress with hair darker than Claudia's angled over and smiled at Nudger. Said, "Sir?" as if he'd summoned her.

He asked for a glass of milk. She stuck the tip of her tongue out of the corner of her mouth and wrote that down carefully on her order pad, as if it contained twelve syllables, then smoothly avoided a cluster of departing customers and headed for the kitchen.

"Oughta try the spaghetti," Hammersmith advised. "The special today."

Look what it's done for you, Nudger thought, recalling the

dashing Hammersmith of a decade ago. He said, "My stomach'd tie it in knots instead of digesting it."

"Still riled up about this morning, eh? Listen, Nudge, you know that was just Springer getting his jollies. Little jackoff's got some Hitler in his blood."

"Springer I can endure now and then."

"What, then?"

"It's not every day I find a dead pusher in my car," Nudger said.

"But it is every day somebody finds a dead pusher somewhere."

"The job's making you callous."

"You'd be better off if it had made you that way."

"The problem's not only this morning," Nudger said. He held his silence while the raven-haired waitress returned with a single glass of milk resting in the middle of a round tray. Placed the glass on a napkin in front of Nudger and then departed gracefully with the empty tray held level in exactly the same manner, as if she were still balancing something on it. We're all slaves to habit, Nudger mused.

He leaned forward in his chair and told Hammersmith about his confrontation with Arnie Kyle.

When Nudger was finished talking and settled back, Hammersmith took another sip of wine and sat silently. His pale blue eyes seemed to be focused on his empty plate.

After a while he said, "Tried to scare the bejesus outta you by making a gift of Monohan's remains, then offered to buy you off the case. The old one-two sales pitch, eh? Works with vacuum cleaners and aluminum siding."

"*Did* scare the bejesus outta me," Nudger corrected.

"Hm. So how 'bout it? You thinking over Kyle's offer? You going to Hawaii? Spend your money on suntan lotion and grass-skirted beauties?"

"It's not my money, it's Kyle's. I haven't got it yet and I don't want it."

"You know the alternative to tropical paradise."

"Yeah. Jack Palp."

"Bad-ass Jack."

"Not exactly a Boy Scout," Nudger agreed.

"Matter of fact, Nudge, he *was* a Boy Scout. One of those advanced, explorer scouts. Probably even helped old ladies do this or that. Palp's not your usual hard-core juvenile delinquent who graduated to big-time crime. He had an exemplary upper-middle-class boyhood and adolescence until he went from super scout to Special Forces and traveled to Vietnam. They say that's where he learned to enjoy killing while he was winning all his medals. What a difference time and place make, eh? Weren't for Nam, Palp mighta been a zillionaire high-powered executive or a killer lawyer."

"Eileen's lawyer."

"Maybe at that."

"Palp's why I wanted to talk with you," Nudger said. "Kyle said you brought him in for questioning on the Monohan killing."

"Sure did. He was cooperative, him and his attorney. And why not? Palp was on the other side of the state in Kansas City until late this morning. Got the airline tickets to confirm it. Got people in K.C. to substantiate his presence there. You shoulda seen his performance; it was stellar. He played the harried but understanding citizen, eager to help the law if only he hadn't been born innocent of a virgin the hour before."

"Where he *really* was yesterday was in St. Louis, laying a scare on me and then murdering Monohan."

"Yeah, but you know how it is. A pro like Palp doesn't make that kinda move without setting it up. Somebody else probably flew to Kansas City under his name. He had the alibi worked out with his buddies."

"All solid citizens themselves, I'll bet."

"Solid and scared."

"So Palp walked?"

"Yep. Told you ahead of time that'd happen. But it was interesting to hear his story. Inventive yet simple, and impossible to disprove."

"What now?" Nudger asked.

Hammersmith surprised him. "This now, Nudge. I'm gonna

stick my neck out a little farther, do some serious police work. But that's not for anyone but you and I to know."

Nudger grinned. "Then you admit this mess runs deep?"

"I think of it more in terms of running high. Which is why I had to ignore it, and why I can't any longer. I'm gonna have to buck the pressure from above." He ran a finger along the rim of his water goblet, made the glass sing. "Here's how it is: We got a political hack in the city runs off with taxpayer money and his secretary. No big deal. Then we got all this restriction from on high. Still no big deal—city politics. Also we got a prime bad man like Kyle somehow involved, even if indirectly. Not too surprising there, either, seeing as certain political types and guys like Kyle run as a pack. But you lump it all together and it starts to smell very much out of the ordinary."

"You knew all that almost from the beginning," Nudger said. "What changed your mind about spending time and effort on this?"

"Now we got murder. That makes it serious."

"It was serious before. It was murder before. Something else changed your outlook." Curious Nudger. Persistent. Way to get into trouble.

Hammersmith's thin pink lips arced down in a sour expression. "We bring in a guy like Palp, Nudge, and the pressure from up top doesn't let up. Just the opposite. We gotta see every one of his rights are protected and every box is checked. Gotta give Palp more legal advice than his lawyer's giving him. Treat the bastard like he's August A. Busch instead of some Murders-R-Us menace. Didn't set right with me."

"Guess not."

"Leads me to believe Kyle's telling it straight when he warns you about being out of your depth. Something big's happened. Maybe still *is* happening."

Nudger's stomach suddenly felt queasy. He downed half his milk. Hammersmith's instincts were usually on target. Nudger had been carrying a similar opinion almost since the time he'd seen Dobbs's photograph of Virgil Hiller motionless at his desk in the Arcade Building. But to hear Hammersmith say it brought home the potential danger even more than had Kyle's visit to the office.

Hammersmith unwrapped one of his cigars and dipped an end deftly into what was left of his wine to improve the tobacco's taste. Placed the soggy part of the cigar in his mouth and set the dry end ablaze with his silver lighter's blowtorch flame. But if the tobacco tasted better, it smelled the same. Horrible. Stomach-assaulting.

Nudger placed a couple of dollar bills on the table and pushed back his chair and stood up, as Hammersmith had probably planned.

"Leaving without finishing your milk, Nudge?"

"Yeah. Looks like it's turning green."

Hammersmith smiled. Inhaled. Exhaled. Diners in the no-smoking section glared. There was no protection from nuclear drift.

"Keep in close touch," Hammersmith said, "and I'll stay in touch with you. You and me against the world, Sancho. No windmill too big."

"Windmills don't strangle people with thin wire," Nudger said, thinking he'd been compared with Don Quixote too many times for comfort.

"Never been to Holland; wouldn't know."

"Jack Palp's no windmill," Nudger said, aggravated with Hammersmith for cracking jokes. Hell with him, if he felt that way.

As he was leaving he heard Hammersmith say, "Aloha, Nudge."

Holland. Hawaii. In an Italian restaurant.

Hopping all over the world.

Maybe that was why Nudger felt as if he had jet lag.

As Nudger drove west on Chouteau, he thought about what he'd told Tad about not wanting to harm Bonnie. True, maybe, but was he nonetheless being unfair to her and to himself? Nudger knew, really, that her attraction to him was based more on their mutual hard circumstances than on love. Not that there wasn't something *like* love between them. If Bonnie had at first seen Nudger as a potential meal ticket, she knew now that his ticket was punched.

Nudger switched on the wipers to clear the windshield of the sudden and gentle September rain. To the west, over St. Charles, the sky was a slanted bar of blue beyond low gray clouds. The shower wouldn't last long. Staring mesmerized beyond the metronome strokes of the wiper blades, he admitted that the Nudger-Bonnie affair was limping along on a cross-current of sympathy and little else. Well, good sex, too. That counted for something. A lot, actually.

And of course there'd been his desire to make Claudia jealous. That hadn't worked at all; she was still seeing Biff Archway more often than she saw Nudger, he was sure. He was also sure that the honorable thing to do was to break off his affair with Bonnie. To be fair to her and to himself. And to her wild brood.

It was, he decided, his manly duty.

He stopped by his office and checked with Danny to see if anything was going on. Danny said nope, there sure wasn't, except for an old gray Plymouth that had driven by slow several times while the skinny kid driver glanced up at Nudger's office window.

"Driver looked about seventeen," Danny said, wiping his hands on the grayish towel tucked in his belt. "Wish I was that young again."

"He's eighteen," Nudger said.

Danny said, "Gee, time starting to fly for him."

While Nudger was thinking about that one, Danny offered him a Dunker Delite. "Left over from yesterday," he said. "Already been microwaved, so go ahead and have a couple; I'll just have to pitch 'em in the trash otherwise."

Nudger disguised his grimace as a smile and politely declined.

He dodged raindrops, went upstairs, and slumped in his squealing swivel chair behind his desk. The light playing through the rain that was streaming down the window shimmered and did tricks on the opposite wall. Prismlike, it cast wavering colors. Blue, yellow. Red—disturbingly like blood—up near the bullet hole.

Nudger looked away from the wall, then used the eraser tip of a pencil to peck out Bonnie's number on the phone.

She answered on the second ring, sounding out of breath. She'd just gotten home after a hard day of delivering Nora Dove. But she was dying to see him, she said, and invited him to come right over.

He went. Time to be quick and decisive. To act out of necessity. To be cruel to be kind. Wasn't that the rationale behind the guillotine? Behind most cruelty?

Bonnie was wearing a white terrycloth robe when she came to the door. She rose on her open-toe slippers and kissed Nudger on the mouth before he knew what was going on, tugged him inside by the sleeve of his brown corduroy sport coat.

He said, "Possessive vixen." Wisecracking even when he had something soul-wrenching to do. Especially then. Papering over pain.

"I just took a shower," she said. "Back in a minute."

She left him sitting on the sofa and disappeared down the hall.

The living room was a mess. A toy tank was parked on the coffee table, colored plastic blocks were scattered over the floor, and a chair was leaning with its back against the wall as if someone invisible were sitting in it with his feet propped up. The place was clean, though. Smelled of a combination of Pine-sol and perfume that made Nudger's stomach growl to him that it was wise to have skipped lunch.

There was a piercing scream from behind the sofa. He actually felt his buttocks rise from the cushions.

In full battle gear—camouflage, backpack, and carbine—James charged around the end of the couch and came at Nudger.

James had obtained a bayonet. Nasty pointed thing that extended twelve inches beyond the barrel of the realistic plastic carbine he was expertly wielding.

Startled, Nudger said, "Uh!" and watched in horror as the bayonet arced toward his stomach. He didn't have time to move. Felt the point make contact.

Saw the bayonet disappear as James screamed again and lunged.

Realized with a rush of relief that the bayonet blade had bent. Was rubber. Said, "Holy Christ, James!"

"Dead!" James proclaimed with satisfaction. He danced backward, grinning. There were dark streaks beneath his eyes, commando fashion. It was easy to imagine him creeping through the jungle, seeking action. Search-and-destroy was his meat.

"James, calm down!" Bonnie yelled.

A moment later she appeared in the doorway, still wearing the white robe but with her hair carefully engineered and her makeup on. She caught sight of the dark streaks on James's cheeks and said, "Dammit, James, I told you to stay away from my mascara!" She shook her head and muttered, "God, I don't know!"

James brandished the bayonet, screamed again, and charged past her into the kitchen, barely brushing the robe and causing it to swing and reveal a shapely pale ankle. In the back of the house, Belinda began to wail.

Bonnie was adjusting her robe, seemed not to hear the air-raid siren sound.

Nudger said, "Maybe she's hungry."

Bonnie smiled serenely, as if her world were in perfect order. "No, she's supposed to be taking a short nap. The babysitter's coming any minute to drive Belinda and James to her place. The other kids are in school."

Nudger sensed the trap easing shut. He started to say that he had something to tell Bonnie. Actually had his lips parted to speak. But just then a horn blasted three times in the driveway.

Bonnie shouted, "Get your stuff, James!"

Then she flounced to the front door and opened it. Signaled with a raised forefinger—one minute—to whoever was waiting in the driveway. She turned to Nudger and explained, "There are other kids in the car, so she can't come in."

"She watch the kids often?"

"Nyla? Yeah, she's my regular. My safety valve. Expensive, but she's worth it for the peace of mind. I don't worry when she's in charge."

Bonnie bustled to the back of the house and James reappeared in the living room. He sneered at Nudger and made a few menacing swipes in the air with the bayonet. Tomorrow's Rambo staying in the mood. Nudger wished he could give him a real bayonet, sic him on Jack Palp.

"Gonna be a soldier when you grow up?" he asked.

James said, "Die!" and plunged the bayonet into the leaves of an artificial potted plant.

Nudger thought, Kids. Someday they'd take over the world.

James might by then be in a position of influence and authority. Scary.

Bonnie returned carrying Belinda, who was quiet now. She walked directly out the open front door and in passing used her free hand to shove the back of James's helmeted head in a signal to follow.

James narrowed his eyes like a silent film star at Nudger, took a quick shot at him with the carbine, then crouched and ran outside. He was swinging the barrel of the gun so its field of fire would cover any hidden enemy. Vicious. Aggressive. Shrewd. What would James actually be when he grew up? A divorce lawyer?

Nudger admonished himself for being too rough on lawyers. There were some good ones. Like Benedict and Schill, who occasionally gave him work.

He heard female voices, hurried instructions about a bottle. Children's voices, arguing. Car doors slamming. Last-minute instructions through a rolled-down window. The engine of the car in the driveway got louder and then faded as the babysitter backed into the street.

Bonnie came back in and said, "Whew!" She wiped her forehead with the back of her hand, even though she wasn't perspiring. Nudger got the impression it was an unconscious gesture she often made when dealing with her kids. She looked fresh-skinned and beautiful standing in the light from the living room window. Tiny yet voluptuous. Nora Dove cosmetics couldn't account for it all.

In the absence of James and Belinda, the house throbbed with silence.

Nudger averted his eyes from the gap in the white terrycloth across Bonnie's centerfold breasts. None of that. Not this trip. He mustered his courage and said, "I've got something important to tell you." There. Done. And he was glad. Knew it was time to take charge of his life.

She let the white robe drop and was wearing nothing but the open-toed slippers. "Can it wait till later?"

He decided it could.

Half an hour later, he said that the something important he had to tell her was that Tad had been skipping school and following him. She whispered she'd have a talk with Tad, though she doubted it would do any good. Kissed Nudger. Slid a warm thigh over his bare stomach.

He knew his life was in charge of him.

When he returned to his office at 4:30 there was a message on his answering machine from Claudia. She needed to see him as soon as possible. Sounded upset.

He splashed a few handfuls of cold water over his face. Combed his hair. Then he put on the spare fresh shirt he kept in the office and got out of there, thinking, busy day.

It wasn't until he was halfway down the stairs that the fear cut through him.

27

Claudia and Jack Palp. Jack Palp and Claudia. That was all
Nudger could think of as he drove toward Claudia's. He'd
brought danger and pain to her before through his half-ass occupation. Some of the people he had to deal with, and who
were looking for an edge with him, naturally saw her as one
of his weaknesses. Get to Claudia, get to Nudger. The primi-
tive, direct logic of a vicious animal. Cruel but effective. Not
surprising that Kyle would think that way; he was a denizen
of the jungle. One of the serpents that sent jackals like Palp.

But when Nudger used his key and barged into Claudia's
apartment, he found her seated alone on the sofa.

She was wearing stone-washed jeans and a white cotton
blouse. Her right fist was clenching blue denim, wrinkling the
jeans. The redness around her dark eyes told him she'd been
crying, but she seemed to have control of herself now. On the
outside, anyway. The fingers of her clenched fist remained rigid
and bloodless. She had long fingernails; they must be digging
like claws into her palms.

Nudger glanced around. The apartment was neat, quiet. *Felt* empty except for him and Claudia.

Claudia bowed her head, maybe because she wanted to hide the puffiness around her eyes. Didn't want him to know she'd been crying. That she was still tightly strung.

He sat down next to her. His weight made the sofa creak and sag, and her body shifted closer to him. He touched her shoulder lightly and picked up a faint trembling in his fingertips. Had Palp done something after all? Been here and gone?

Nudger said, "What's wrong, Claudia?"

She sniffled. Touched but didn't wipe the tip of her long, straight nose. This wasn't like her, to be crushed this way. Scared. Even the old, suicidal Claudia was more a victim of despair than of fear.

"My Pap smear."

That one was unexpected. At first Nudger didn't understand what she meant. Then the weight of her words fell on him, and his insides turned to ice. The air in the apartment became hard to breathe.

He said, "The other day at the doctor's?"

She nodded. "My test came back a three. It's my third positive test, each one the same."

"A three?" Nudger said. He was confused.

"The results are on a sliding scale of one to five. One being normal, five being most serious."

"So what's a three mean?"

"Normally it'd mean they'd do a regular biopsy to test for cancer. But they tried that, and whatever's wrong is too far up in the cervical canal."

So what did *that* mean? Nudger wasn't a doctor. Knew nothing about a cervical canal. Where was it, in Panama? He wiped his sweaty palms on his pants legs.

"The doctor told me I needed a conization right away," Claudia said. "In the hospital."

Nudger said, "Wait up here . . . What the hell's a conization? And how serious is all of this?"

"A conization is when the surgeon removes a cone-shaped portion of the cervix for diagnosis. The idea's to find out how serious it is."

"*It* being . . . ?"

"Cervical cancer."

Nudger felt the air go out of him. Cancer. Maybe the most terrifying word in the English language. He said, "Oh, Jesus!"

She loosened her grip on her jeans and touched the back of his hand, comforting *him* now. "Hey, remember, they don't know for sure. That's the idea of the conization, to find out."

"You said as soon as possible."

She took a deep breath and nodded. "I go in for surgery day after tomorrow at Deaconess hospital."

"How soon after the operation will they know?"

"Sometime that day."

"Do you . . . feel okay?"

"Yeah. Depressed, is all."

"My God, no wonder. What can I do?"

"Hold my hand. Stay all night. Drive me to the hospital. Care."

He kissed her forehead. Her flesh was cool. "You know I care." She'd asked him, not Archway, to stay with her. *Not Archway.* "Archway know about this?"

"Yes."

Nudger had to ask. "What did he say when you told him?"

"Doesn't matter."

"Doesn't it?"

She almost began crying again. Tremors in the lower lip. Not for long. Strong Claudia. Class. "He didn't come to see me. He apologized for it and explained that a lot of his family died of cancer. Since then, he's had a deep-seated and irrational fear of the disease. He doesn't even like to talk about it, much less be around it." She raised her head and looked hurt and resigned. "You're right, his reaction does matter. He offered me no comfort, unless you count sympathy by phone."

Nudger said, "I don't."

Obviously, neither did Claudia.

Nudger had never hated Archway more. He, Nudger, would stick by Claudia. Would hold her close. Would draw the cancer through his fingertips to himself if it were possible. Die so that she might live. He meant it. He was surprised by the fact that he meant it.

Claudia sighed and leaned back. A looseness came over her lean body, as if for the first time in hours she was relaxing. "The best thing now is to forget about all this as much as possible until it's time to go into the hospital. Carry on normally."

"How long will you be in?" This wasn't forgetting and carrying on, but Nudger had to know.

"Overnight. The procedure's pretty simple, really. Sometimes it's even possible to go home the same day."

He noticed he was breathing all right again. His world had changed and he was adapting. But he didn't feel the same as when he'd walked into the apartment. Not nearly the same.

"Want to get out of here and have some supper?" he asked. There—that was a normal thing to suggest.

"No. I mean, yes, I wouldn't mind getting out for a while, but I'm not really very hungry."

He wasn't either, but he needed something for them to do. "Want to watch me eat? Might give you an appetite."

"I can fix you something here if you'd rather."

"Naw, let's drive up to White Castle, get me some miniature hamburgers and a milkshake." He knew she was addicted to the peculiar White Castle fare. "You'll smell the food and change your mind, have something to eat."

She fought to create a smile. It reached her face and lasted half a second, not with much wattage. "Maybe." She stood up and left the room.

He heard water running in the bathroom. She was working on her eyes so she wouldn't look as if she'd been crying.

Nudger sat in the quiet apartment, listening to the street noises filtering in. Claudia's fear was his own. He felt older, vulnerable. Cancer. Nothing definite, but more tests were warranted. Cancer. He couldn't shake the thought, the terrible word, from his mind. A car passed outside, going too fast, its tires swishing on the wet pavement. Cancer.

After a while Claudia came back into the living room. She looked better. As if nothing were wrong. But she shivered. She said, "The sooner this is over and I know, the better. Even if it is cancer."

"And if the conization result is positive, then what?"

"At the least, it means a hysterectomy. At the most, who knows?"

Nudger knew. Didn't say it. For the moment, the dread *C* word was enough to have hanging heavy in the air. It would follow both of them everywhere, grant them no peace. Part of them now. He stood up and tucked in his shirt, ready to leave.

Claudia said, "You'll stay with me?"

"Through supper at least."

He'd been joking, his way of holding back the darkness, but his heart lurched when he saw the flare of fear in her eyes. Hurriedly he said, "I'll stay."

He didn't mean only tonight, or until the results of the conization were known.

In the past few minutes he'd made up his mind to see Bonnie only once more, to tell her that what was between them couldn't work.

That it was ended. Over. Forever.

Claudia said, "Let's *not* go out. I'll fix some supper here, if you can put up with a microwaved frozen dinner."

"You're a fickle woman."

"Sometimes."

"Here sounds fine, if that's what you want to do."

"It is. Stay in with you."

The sky had cleared, then become cloudy again, though it wasn't raining. The dusty evening light lay like gently swirling gas over the floor near the window.

Nudger kissed Claudia. Switched on a lamp and chased the gloom. Illuminated the apartment and made it the entire world.

Nothing outside its walls existed. Not cancer, not wayward politicians and secretaries and stolen money, not Jack Palp. Not a waiting cold hospital operating room.

Nothing.

It would work for a while.

He awoke lying on his stomach with the warmth of her nestled against his side. Thought immediately how Claudia felt so familiar, and how she'd feel that way even if they were apart for decades. Her distinct way of draping an arm lightly over him, and of barely touching his leg with her knee, as if to maintain tenuous contact even in sleep.

Nudger had a terrible taste in his mouth, and his tongue seemed to have grown fungus. His head was turned sideways at a sharp angle, his face mashed into the pillow.

He opened his exposed eye, which seemed to have grit beneath its lid, and let its hazy gaze roam until it found the clock near the bed and focused on it. Seven-thirty. Early. But he'd crossed the line into wakefulness and knew he might as well force himself to get up, take a shower, and get dressed. A hot shower didn't sound so bad, did it? Loosen up the oil between the joints.

He tried to ease his body out from beneath Claudia's arm without waking her. He failed, but she merely opened her eyes, smiled at him, and then made a sort of cooing sound and appeared to fall back asleep.

In the old tiled bathroom, he stood in the claw-footed tub and rotated the hot water tap handle, then gave the porcelain cold handle a squeaking half-twist so he wouldn't be boiled when he turned on the shower.

The bathroom was chilled and drafty, but that soon changed. He stood inside the shower curtain, beneath the beating hot needles of water, while steam rose and the kinks left his back and shoulders. What would it be like, he wondered, to follow the swirling water down the drain and be free of all his problems, like death in a Hitchcock movie?

But he knew that death, like life, wasn't the way it was portrayed in the movies. He'd seen death. It was painful, distressingly banal, and final. There were few if any bizarre reprieves.

He turned off the water, swept the plastic curtain aside and admitted cool air, then stepped out of the tub.

After toweling dry, he located a disposable razor (Archway's?) and shaved. He nicked himself a couple of times with the dull blade, once wickedly just beneath his nose. Took him a few minutes to stem the flow of blood with toilet paper. He combed back his wet hair with his fingertips. Reasonably neat. It would have to do until he got his comb from his pants pocket.

When he went back into the cool bedroom Claudia was awake. She got out of bed quickly, gracefully, as if she hadn't a care, and touched him on his damp shoulder as she walked past on her way to the warm bathroom. Her bare feet made soft, padded sounds on the floor.

He found his underwear and socks and started to get dressed. Pipes clattered in the old walls and the shower began to roar. Sometimes Claudia sang in the shower, but not this morning.

When he was dressed, he sat on the edge of the bed until she emerged from the bathroom with a towel wrapped around her. Steam from the shower swirled in the doorway behind her like show-biz manufactured fog, the kind rock singers cavorted through.

He said, "You could've slept in this morning."

She shook her head, not violently, but hard enough to send glistening drops of water flying, fragmenting the morning light. "I'm going to work." She gave him a don't-question-me look.

He didn't say anything. Understood that this was her way of maintaining normalcy and sanity until her precariously balanced fate tilted one way or the other with the weight of the medical report.

She got dressed methodically, putting on panties and bra, a dark skirt. She blow-dried her hair and combed it before slipping into a pale green blouse and buttoning it deftly with her odd elegance. A touch of makeup and she was beautiful—ready to have a go at life. She looked so healthy that a lump formed in Nudger's throat. He wasn't fooled; cancer was a wily saboteur.

He helped her prepare eggs, toast, and coffee for breakfast. She'd had only a roll and a glass of red wine last night, and she was hungry.

"I better fill up now," she said. "I'm not supposed to eat anything after six this evening. Because of the surgery."

"What time you scheduled for tomorrow morning?"

"S'pose to be at the hospital at seven-thirty," she said around a mouthful of toast.

"Early."

"Fine with me. Get it done."

"Sure you wanna go to work today?"

"I'm sure. I overreacted last night."

"You did great."

"You're prejudiced."

"Damned right."

When they were finished eating he told her he'd take care of the dishes or she'd be late. She didn't argue. Kissed him good-bye and left.

He looked down at her from the window as her foreshortened figure crossed the street and climbed into her car. The Chevette started immediately this morning and she drove away.

How many more times would he be able to say good-bye to her?

Or hello!

After rinsing the breakfast dishes and wedging them into the dishwasher, he left the apartment and drove toward Bonnie's house.

He wanted to resolve things between them while he still carried the emotion and determination to get it done as cleanly as possible. He suspected that Bonnie had sensed why he'd come to see her yesterday, and had used sex to fend off the moment. She'd be expecting what he had to say. The end of their affair had lain sad and mocking like a foregone conclusion between them in Bonnie's bed, but in their passion they'd refused to acknowledge it.

When he steered the Granada into her driveway, he realized he should have phoned to make sure she was home. The garage's overhead door was open to reveal nothing but assorted junk, a lawn mower, and bright plastic toys. The Nora Dove station wagon was gone.

His hopes rose, however, when he straightened up out of the car. The high-pitched whooping that was seeping from the closed-up house was unmistakable: James at war.

Nudger's knock on the door was answered by a short, heavyset woman with graying brown hair worn in bangs that almost totally concealed her narrow dark eyes. She was wearing red slacks and a tentlike blouse that was stained down the front and gave off an odor of sour milk.

"I'm looking for Bonnie," he said.

The woman smiled and shook her head. The smile made her nose turn up something like Bonnie's. "Not home. I'm the babysitter."

"You a relative?"

"Nope."

Maybe being around the kids somehow did that to noses. "You're Nyla?"

She looked closely at him through her bangs. "How'd you know?"

"I was here yesterday afternoon when you came by to pick up James and Belinda."

Something struck Nyla from behind, causing her to grunt and move forward a few inches. She didn't change expression, however, as if she were used to being buffetted around. James peered from behind the tail of her baggy blouse. He was wearing his helmet with camouflage netting and had his commando black streaks beneath his eyes. Nudger could hear Belinda crying in the depths of the house.

Nyla turned her head and glanced down at James. "You wake up your sister?"

James said, "Shot her."

"Shouldn't shoot people," Nyla told him sensibly.

Nudger said, "When will Bonnie be home?"

"She told me she couldn't be sure," Nyla said. "She's out delivering Nora Dove, so it's kinda hard for her to know when she'll be done. You know, gossip's part of the game. Customers wanna sit and talk forever. Try out the new stuff and see how it smells. You can leave a message for her if you want."

"Just tell her Nudger was by."

"Okay. Nudger." Nyla's eyes widened beneath the bangs. "Hey, wait a minute. Something here for you. Bonnie said if you was to come by I should give it to you."

She disappeared into the house.

James stood his ground in the doorway and assumed a stolid martial arts fighting stance. Horatius at the bridge.

A plump arm knocked him aside and Nyla was back. She handed Nudger a small white paper sack.

He thanked her, opened the sack, and pulled out a black glass bottle with a label that resembled a silver hawk in flight. Very dramatic. Large black letters on the label said FOR THE BOLD. Nudger read the small letters molded on the glass beneath the label aloud: "Max Hawk cologne. Wild Brawn."

"That's right," Nyla said. "New stuff on the market, she told me. For men only. Nora Dove and Max Hawk—could be birdshit." She grinned, then looked a bit worried. "Hey, don't mention to Bonnie I said that. Didn't mean anything, but she might not understand."

"My beak is sealed," Nudger assured her.

He slid the bottle of Max Hawk, still in its sack, into a side pocket of his sportcoat and stepped down off the porch. He felt slightly guilty accepting it. A going-away present, even if Bonnie didn't know it. Wild Brawn. He guessed she thought that was exactly the scent for him; must have understood him a little, anyway.

He drove away from the house and made a left turn off Pleasant Lane, intending to go to his office. Then it occurred to him that he'd be spending the next several nights at Claudia's apartment, and the breakfast they'd had this morning had about depleted the refrigerator.

Claudia was in no condition to cope with supermarkets, so Nudger decided to stop and pick up some groceries, maybe even surprise her and thaw out something for an early supper, since she couldn't have anything to eat after six o'clock. Or maybe she'd rather go out to eat. Whatever she decided for tonight, she'd need food supplies over the next week.

He drove east on Manchester and stopped at a Schnuck's supermarket. It was one of those newer stores that sold everything from apples to motor oil and did a thriving side business renting home videos.

The place didn't seem to be crowded, judging by the relatively few cars in the lot. He latched onto a wire shopping cart near the door and pushed it inside. It had a flat spot on one wheel that ticked rhythmically. Every grocery cart he'd ever pushed had a flat spot on a wheel. Maybe they were manufactured that way so other shoppers could hear them coming and get out of the way; some Ralph Nader edict.

He rolled the cart parallel to the line of checkout counters, then made a ninety-degree turn, wound through the produce section, and began selecting items from the shelves.

In the frozen food department, he met the last person he expected to see, standing with arms crossed next to the brussels sprouts.

Jack Palp.

29

Palp said, "Stocking up on greens?"

Nudger stopped so his shopping cart was a barrier between him and Palp. A woman at the far end of the aisle tossed a frozen dinner into her cart and then wheeled it around the corner, leaving them alone. Nudger noticed it was cool here in the frozen food section.

Palp uncrossed his arms and assumed a loose, relaxed position with his hands dangling at his sides. The big man could move fast in any direction from such a stance.

"Us running into each other here by the stiff veggies has to be more than coincidence," Nudger said.

"Sure. I saw you over in jams and jellies."

Nudger was glad to notice a large black woman in a flower-print dress roll her cart into the aisle and stand studying the fish section. A witness who might keep Palp from trying anything fishy. Stay around, lady; don't make up your mind between salmon and flounder too soon.

Palp paid no attention to the woman and said, "Mr. Kyle wants to know if you plan on accepting his offer."

"Offer?"

"You know. Sun, sandy beaches, luaus." Palp seemed to come nearer without actually moving his feet. How'd he do that?

Nudger's stomach did some intricate gymnastics. "I need more time to think about it."

Palp gave his undertaker's smile and shook his head. "Sorry, time's up."

"Why's there have to be such a rush to decide?"

"'Cause Mr. Kyle says so, jerkoff. That bother you?"

"Somewhat. Like it bothers me that Skip Monohan was found dead in my car's trunk."

"This bothers you, that bothers you. Maybe you should read *Dianetics*. Now, I wouldn't know a thing about this Monohan fella, having been out of town."

"Are you forgetting our conversation at Scullin Steel?"

"The important thing is for you *not* to forget it, Nudger. Which brings us back around to whether you're going to accept Mr. Kyle's generous offer. You go to Hawaii, who knows, you might stumble across Hiller and his secretary frolicking on the beach. Get a paid vacation, solve a mystery, make your pretty client happy."

The thought of Adelaide Lacy made Nudger wonder if Kyle and Palp had leaned on her in an attempt to get her to drop the search for Mary. He decided probably not. She might report it, and that would tie them in too closely to the Hiller disappearance for even the police to ignore. Besides, Nudger was sure Adelaide would have told him about any further contact with Kyle, or any conversation with Palp. Anyone would think a conversation with Palp worth mentioning.

"Gonna be yes or no?" Palp asked impatiently. "Tell me so I can buy a dozen eggs and get outta here. They're on sale, you know."

"I didn't know."

Two more women pushing shopping carts rounded the corner into the aisle. One of the carts contained a small child waving a celery stalk as if it were a Fourth of July sparkler.

Encouraged by the sudden company, Nudger said, "Tell Arnie Kyle I said no thanks."

"I got instructions to see you're absolutely sure," Palp said. "Think about it, asshole. You're turning down Hawaii. Not to mention fifty thousand dollars. That's a lotta dead presidents."

Something deep in Nudger's mind sparked to life, stirred.

"You listening?" Palp asked.

Nudger said, "Reagan."

"Reagan who?"

"You said I was turning down a lot of dead presidents."

Palp said, "I meant folding money, bills with their pictures on them."

"I know, but I thought of Ronald Reagan."

"Reagan's not dead. Not president anymore, either. Enough about politics. This isn't Meet the fuckin' Press. You taking up Mr. Kyle's offer, or you standing by your decision to turn it down? Last chance, sweetheart."

Nudger glanced up the aisle to make sure he wasn't alone with Palp. Good. He was still in the reassuring presence of other shoppers.

He said, "I'm sure. My answer's still no."

The large black woman decided against buying frozen fish and abruptly rolled her cart around the corner and out of sight. The two other women each hurriedly reached into the freezer, plunked containers of frozen strawberries into their carts, then followed her. The child in the cart dropped his celery stalk and waved to Nudger before disappearing around the corner. So much for safety in numbers. Nudger and Palp were by themselves in the cold aisle.

Palp's face eased into its toothy, grim reaper grin. "Your mistake is my treat."

He started to move toward Nudger, but Nudger kept his shopping cart between them, raising it in front and swiveling it on its rear wheels. Palp moved sideways to get around the cart, and Nudger shoved it hard into his stomach.

Palp said, "Oof!" and angrily shoved the cart back. It struck Nudger in the hip and pinned him against a freezer case. He felt cold air creep up his back. Something wet on his hip and thigh. The Max Hawk bottle had broken in his pocket.

Palp stopped, sniffed. Said, "Something stinks."

"Wild Brawn."

"Huh?"

Taking advantage of the momentary distraction, Nudger wedged out from behind the cart and ran to the end of the aisle, lifting his knees high. He skidded around the corner.

Palp had moved like a jungle cat going for the kill and was right behind him. Nudger felt a hand clutch at his shoulder and put on another burst of speed.

Broke free.

Then he was in the cereal aisle. There were at least a dozen shoppers here, including the three who'd just left Frozen Foods. One of the shoppers, a huge man with a ponytail and a walrus mustache, stared at Nudger and Palp. A display of blue and yellow cereal boxes, upset by the action in the adjacent Frozen Foods aisle, had collapsed and partially blocked the aisle.

Nudger bounded away from Palp, over and through the scattered boxes. The cereal was one of those sugary candied brands and contained a free squeeze-toy replica of a cuddly cartoon character pictured on the front of the box. As Nudger tromped over the boxes, some of them squealed as if in pain.

"I'm gonna fetch the manager," the large black woman said. "Put us an end to this shit."

Nudger said, "That's him back there. Tall man in a black suit."

The woman kicked aside a box of the squealing cereal and swaggered menacingly toward Palp. He started to move away, but several other shoppers had rounded the corner and their carts blocked his path. Palp shoved the woman aside and began barging through the spilled boxes. The woman almost fell, then scrambled and regained her balance and shouted, "You gonna *pay* for that, you bastard! I'll have your job!"

The big guy with the walrus mustache said, "Easy, bub," and grabbed Palp's arm. "Better calm down and apologize to the lady."

Palp put some kind of martial arts move on him and the guy went flailing into the shelves and knocked down more cereal. The big woman had caught up with Palp again. Several other shoppers had joined her. The woman with the child in the cart stayed back and contributed by screaming. The kid puckered up and began a duet with Mom. Had stronger lungs.

Nudger bolted toward the front of the store, saw the doors, and made for them. The cashiers, the people in the checkout lines all had stopped what they were doing and were staring at him, not quite believing what was happening. Nudger knew the feeling.

Someone clutched his sleeve. A squat little muscular man with bristly black hair and a forest of pens and pencils protruding from a plastic liner in his shirt pocket. The man said, "I'm the manager. What's going on back there?"

"Fella causing trouble. Big guy in a black suit. Says *he's* the manager."

"Oh, he *does*, does he?"

Somebody said, "What's that smell?"

Nudger pulled his sleeve free. "You better call the police. Take care of the matter. I'm getting outta here. Won't shop here again."

He ran, not breaking stride as he neared the exit. The pneumatic door barely opened in time and he was out in the parking lot, beating feet for the Granada.

He knocked over an empty cart, bounced off another and sent it careening into a blue Oldsmobile, chipping paint. Sorry.

Then he was in the Granada. Bumped his head getting in but barely felt it. He didn't remember digging into his pocket for his keys, but they were in his hand. He fumbled with them and somehow got the engine started.

Thought he saw Palp jogging across the lot, as he yanked the steering wheel left and screeched into the street. A brown delivery van braked so hard the driver laid a palm flat against the windshield to keep from flying through it. Opened his eyes wide in fear, his mouth wider as he screamed curses. Nudger got the Granada straightened out and kept his foot to the floor, wondering what the van driver had said to him. Better not to know, he decided.

He made a fast right turn off of Manchester, slowed down, and wound through side streets lined with similar brick and frame ranch houses. Peaceful residential avenues, not unlike Bonnie's street. Peaceful if you only drove through and didn't go inside any of the houses.

He picked the pieces of the broken Max Hawk bottle and what was left of the sodden bag from his pocket without cutting his fingers, then he zigzagged east until he found himself on Big Bend, finally satisfied that he'd shaken Palp.

Still trembling from his encounter with Kyle's eerie enforcer, he thought, Maybe I'm crazy. Maybe I'm remembering it wrong.

A lot of dead presidents . . .

After another ten minutes of aimless driving, he decided to go to Mary Lacy's apartment.

30

Nudger was unlocking Mary's apartment, using the key Adelaide had given him, when the door of 1W, across the hall, eased open like the heavy entrance to a vault.

A tall, gray-haired woman in slacks and a threadbare red sweater with reindeer on the front stepped halfway out and said, "You a relative?"

"Almost everybody's somebody's relative."

"I mean, of Mary Lacy."

"Nope. Friend."

"Sorry. I thought, since you had a key . . ." She moved all the way out into the hall. Shut the door all but a crack. She was about fifty, with a sallow face that might once have been breathtakingly beautiful, but now wore frown lines and crow's feet and an I've-been-hurt expression that probably endured even in sleep. "I'm Grace Knowland, the building manager. The owner read about Mary disappearing and all, and he's wondering about the apartment. I mean, whether somebody's gonna pay the month's rent."

"I wouldn't know about that," Nudger said. He flashed her

a smile to soften the words. "I'm not that close a friend." So full of bullshit he was. "In fact, I'm acting more in my professional capacity than as a family friend."

Grace raised a penciled, arched eyebrow almost to her hairline. "What *is* your profession?"

"I'm a private investigator, looking into Mary's disappearance."

"You mean trying to find her and that politician?"

"If they're together."

"Wouldn't they be? The papers and TV news seem to think so."

"What do you think?"

Grace crossed her lean arms. She had long, tapered fingers with red-painted nails, wore a total of five rings, all of them cheap, some of them gaudy. A bulky silver bracelet on each bony wrist. She was the kind of big woman who could drape herself with jewelry and get by with it. She took a long time thinking about Nudger's question. Finally she said, "I can't see Mary running away with her boss."

"You're not the only one who can't. She and you friends?"

"Oh, no. Mary's the type that keeps to herself. Tell you the truth, so'm I. Around here, anyway. That's the way I have to be 'cause I'm the one that collects the rent, if you know what I mean."

"Sure. Mary usually on time with her rent?"

"Always."

"She on a lease?"

"Yeah. Signed her fourth one-year lease just before she disappeared."

"So she lived here three years."

"Three years and a week."

"Good tenant?"

"One of my all-time best."

"What kinda social life she lead?"

"Now you sound like a cop."

"Well, I am a cop. Sort of."

Grace seemed skeptical even of that. Nudger thought she

might ask to see his identification, but he was wrong. Didn't really matter to her who he was. The shrill cries of neighborhood kids playing sifted in from outside. Too far away to understand what they were shouting. Other than that, it was quiet in the hall.

She said, "Mary was almost reclusive, I'd say. Now and then somebody'd come by to see her, but she hardly ever went out. Never caused a bit of trouble. Like I said, she was a dandy tenant and I wish she'd come back. God knows what'll rent the place if she doesn't."

Nudger told her he hoped Mary came back soon, too. Then he stepped inside the apartment and closed the door.

He was met by dusty silence and stale air. A reminder of death.

Oh, God, cancer!

Then he noticed that the refrigerator was humming a tenor monotone in the kitchen. But that only made the silence, the emptiness, seem all the more forlorn.

Everything was still neatly in place. The low green sofa squarely faced the console TV, the remote control lying on the coffee table and waiting patiently for a finger to punch the power button. The museum prints were still precisely aligned on the walls; they had the patience of ages. The venetian blind slats were still slanted upward, casting light off the ceiling and lending the apartment a soft, unreal illumination. Discernible under the scent of the Max Hawk soaked into his pants was a faint, unpleasant smell, like that of brackish water.

Nudger said, "Hello, Mary!" just to hear his own voice. Then he walked down the hall to the bedroom with its black-lacquered furniture. Its mood of desolation.

He knew what he was looking for, and went directly to Mary's dresser. After making neat piles of lingerie, sweaters, pantyhose on the bed, he carefully removed the newspaper lining the bottoms of the drawers. It was the St. Louis *Globe-Democrat* for March 31, 1981, covering Hinckley's attempt to assassinate President Reagan, more than eight years ago.

But Mary Lacy had lived in the apartment only three years.

The newspaper sections were separated but hardly crinkled. They hadn't been read before being placed in the drawers three years ago. Or more recently. Of course, there was always the possibility that Mary had the newspaper lining in the drawers at her previous address, and moved the dresser here papers and all. Not likely, though, knowing Mary's compulsive neatness. In fact, it was unlikely she'd use newspapers rather than shelf paper to line her dresser drawers. Newsprint rubbed off and stained.

But she might have used the newspaper this way as a means of hiding it, and also of leaving a message that wouldn't be removed, in case harm came to her. Left this edition, containing sensational news, as a signal to someone close enough to her to realize she'd only been in the apartment three years. Someone who knew it was out of character for her to use newspaper for drawer lining.

But what was there about *this* newspaper? The attempt on Reagan's life? Was that why she'd saved this edition, and had it to use in the drawers?

Nudger arranged the paper's sections more or less in order, the front page on top. There was Reagan ducking into the limo, there in the foreground Hinckley's arm and hand holding the gun, in midrange the Secret Service men still looking around, startled and angry. The bodies on the pavement. Paul Dobbs would probably have killed for a photo like that.

Nudger sat down on the floor cross-legged and read the front page. Then he turned pages, scanning each slowly before going on to the next.

Hinckley's try for Reagan's life had pushed what Nudger was looking for all the way back to page six.

On the same day as the presidential assassination attempt, the city comptroller, Marvin Nolander, who was planning to run for reelection, died with his wife and son in the crash of his small private plane.

Nolander had been succeeded in office by the present comptroller, Dan Gray, who had as his assistant comptroller Virgil Hiller.

Who disappeared with Mary Lacy.

None of it meant much to Nudger now, but he knew it would soon. The thread had become a string had become a rope, and would form a tenuous bridge to the truth. But the crossing would be dangerous.

He painstakingly replaced the newspapers and the rest of the drawers' contents the way he'd found them. Then he left the apartment, careful not to draw Grace Knowland's attention on his way out.

He was climbing into his car when he thought he caught a glimpse of Tad's old Plymouth turning the corner off of Hoover two blocks down. A flash of primered gray metal and dark exhaust fumes. The sun was in his eyes. He might have been mistaken.

But probably not.

Teenagers, he thought. They shouldn't be allowed to own a car until they were much older and their glands were less of a factor in their driving. It would make for safer streets. Fewer jackrabbit starts, screaming rubber, and heart-stopping near collisions.

Excited by what he'd found in Mary's apartment, he pulled away from the curb faster than he should have, tires squealing, almost rammed a parked car, and drove toward the county library on Lindbergh.

3

As he pushed through the library turnstile, Nudger saw Adelaide standing behind the long counter, using the electronic scanner to record the card number of an elderly woman checking out a tall stack of books.

Adelaide was wearing a gray skirt, a high-collared blouse, and a nubby white cardigan sweater. Her hair was pulled back more severely than before, and a pen dangled from a thin silver chain around her neck. Today her fire was banked; she was everyone's idea of a librarian.

He waited until the elderly woman had left, lugging her books with the top one tucked beneath her pointed chin, before approaching the desk. It was especially quiet in the library; the only people there other than Nudger and Adelaide were a fidgety, birdlike employee and two browsers over in the periodical section. It felt cool and spacious.

Adelaide folded her hands on top of the checkout counter, smiled at Nudger, and said, "You look tired."

"Didn't get much sleep."

"You look excited, too. Kind of odd. As if you just had a nifty dream."

"My dreams haven't been nifty lately."

She raised her head, sniffed. "That your cologne I smell?"

"Not exactly. Some was spilled on me."

"It's a little much, but actually not bad."

"You have copies of the St. Louis newspapers from nineteen eighty-one?" He realized he was speaking with unnecessary softness. In his library mode.

Adelaide didn't answer. She moved to the side to receive books being returned by an obese blond man in a blue windbreaker. Nudger sidled over to stand near her, and when the man had paid a small overdue fine and wandered off toward the mystery section, she said, "We'd have the papers on microfilm. Any particular month or day?"

"Around when Hinckley shot Reagan."

She looked at him. Blinked. "Hinckley? Reagan? This have something to do with my sister and Virgil Hiller?"

"Not the Reagan thing—something else. You recall seeing Mary's dresser drawers lined with newspaper?"

"Sure. Like Mary to cover shelves and drawers. She wouldn't put her clothes on bare wood. Might pick up a splinter. Snag something."

"The paper she used was from nineteen eighty-one, all about when Hinckley shot Reagan."

"Mary wouldn't have left newspaper in the bottom of her drawers that long without putting in fresh. She was a compulsive neatnik; she equated dirt with sin and disease. My God, she used to clean around her kitchen baseboard with a rag stretched over a knife point."

"Which means that the newspaper might have some significance. That she wanted somebody to notice it and look at the date. Realize what it meant."

Adelaide cocked her head to the side, puzzled.

"She'd only lived in the apartment three years," Nudger pointed out, "which makes the date wrong. And the newspaper looked fresh enough to have been bought yesterday."

"Maybe she'd saved it as a souvenir. Or bought it at one of those specialty shops that re-create old and memorable newspaper editions. You know, stories on Pearl Harbor or the John Kennedy assassination."

"Either way, she wouldn't have used it to line drawers. Unless she had a reason."

Adelaide placed her elbows on the counter and leaned forward, so close he could see his twin reflections in her blue eyes. For an instant it took him outside himself. Two Nudgers looking out from another's skull, reassessing the world from a different point of view.

She said, "You have some idea as to the reason?"

Nudger nodded. "On page six, taking a backseat to all the ink about the Reagan shooting, is a news item about the accidental death of the city comptroller, a man named Nolander."

Adelaide sighed and stood up straight, gazing off across the library at Biography, poking her tongue against the inside of her cheek. Considering. "And you think that's more than coincidence?"

"I think we need to find out. I want to look at the newspapers for the rest of that time period. I think Mary saved or obtained that paper because of the Nolander piece. In case something happened to her, she wanted to leave it in her apartment in such a way that it might be overlooked and not removed. People searching apartments, rummaging through drawers, don't generally pay much attention to what's used to line the drawers. Especially when they're in a hurry. She hoped that eventually somebody else, somebody who knew her or was suspicious and worried about her, would pick up on what she'd done. Have their attention drawn to the date."

Adelaide smiled. Beautiful. "And now somebody has."

"If I'm right," Nudger said.

She was already moving out from behind the desk. "C'mon." She waved an arm for Nudger to follow, like a cavalry officer summoning troops for a charge. He spurred his mount.

There was no one else in the microfilm room. Adelaide stooped gracefully in front of a bank of small wooden file drawers marked with dates and the names of newspapers, pressing her knees together and swinging them wide to one side. She pulled out one of the drawers and removed several small boxes containing plastic reels of microfilm.

"These cover the weeks just before and after the Reagan assassination attempt," she told him, handing him the boxes. "Know how to work the machines?"

He told her he did, then sat down before one of the viewers lined along the wall. He switched the machine on, clicked the reel into place, and fed the end of the microfilm into the mechanism. After turning the oversized knob on the side of the machine, playing the microfilm so it showed on a backlighted screen, he watched the front page of the March 15, 1981, edition of the St. Louis *Globe-Democrat* slide into view.

Nudger adjusted angle and focus, then settled back to scan as he ran the microfilm slowly through the machine. He said, "This figures to take a while."

Adelaide rested an encouraging hand on his shoulder for a second, then left the room. Through the door, he could see her busying herself behind the checkout counter, stacking returned books on a small wooden cart to be reshelved. Her heart didn't seem to be in her work. *Murder on the Orient Express* might wind up in Travel.

The only news about Nolander in the weeks before the accident was his announcement that he intended to run again for the office of city comptroller. It wasn't a glamour office. Most people in the city probably didn't know the name of the comptroller. Didn't *care* who he was, as long as he stayed honest. So there was no more news of Nolander until the report of the plane crash.

He and his wife and three-year-old son had been flying back to St. Louis from Jefferson City, the state capital, and hadn't landed at Lambert Airport as scheduled. People there to meet him had become alarmed, and their worst fears were realized when a farmer in Forestel notified authorities that a plane had skimmed the trees behind his house and crashed in his cornfield.

The plane turned out to be Nolander's single-engine Cessna 170. It had flipped upside down and caught fire on impact. The pilot—Nolander—and his two passengers hadn't had a chance. They were found still strapped in their seats, burned to death.

Nudger fed another reel of microfilm into the viewer. He read through the flowery and genuinely sad Nolander eulogies. Studied the grainy newspaper photographs of Nolander, a big blond man, and his pretty, dark-haired wife and towheaded lookalike son. Smiling in the photos, no premonition of death haunting their eyes. A family, alive and presumably happy one second, and dead and on fire the next. Nudger knew that the world could do that to anyone; it was a distressing thought.

He was getting dizzy watching the sideways motion of the microfilm, and his stomach was starting to feel as if he were seasick.

But he forgot how he felt, suddenly leaning forward, as if shoved from behind, when he saw the photograph of Nolander's funeral.

He immediately recognized one of the mourners. A bereaved-looking man in an unbuttoned dark overcoat, his hat held before him at crotch level with both hands on the brim, as if his pants might be unzipped, his head slightly bowed.

A younger Virgil Hiller.

So much for coincidence. Mary Lacy had been afraid. That was why she'd left the newspaper lining her dresser drawers. And why, earlier, she'd left the envelope with Adelaide.

And what was in the missing envelope, and what the missing Mary Lacy had been afraid of, concerned Virgil Hiller.

The missing Virgil Hiller.

32

Before leaving the library, Nudger used one of the pay phones just inside the door to call Claudia at Stowe High School. A bored-sounding secretary told him Claudia was teaching her freshman English class at the moment, and offered to take a message.

Nudger couldn't think of a message. There was too much he wanted to say for it to be condensed to a few notes on a secretary's memo pad. So much he wanted to convey that he doubted it could be condensed into mere, inadequate words. This was about Death—the forever thing. The true and irrevocable finish of it all. Message indeed.

He said, "No, thanks," and hung up.

He stuffed another quarter into the phone and punched out the number of Don Crinklaw, a friend and local free-lance journalist who sometimes did feature stories for the *Post-Dispatch* and various St. Louis weeklies.

Crinklaw was home. Nudger told him what he needed, and they agreed to meet later and talk at the Matrix Lounge on Grand Avenue, near Crinklaw's home and office.

The Matrix was a working-man's hangout with a long polished bar, a few tables and booths, and arrangements of sports photographs on the pine-paneled walls. Near the table where Nudger sat with Crinklaw was a shot of Stan Musial in his prime, grinning and demonstrating how to hold a bat, squinting against the brilliance of a long-ago sun. There was an autographed photo of Ken Reitz, who in the seventies had been a dandy defensive third baseman for the Cardinals. A photo of a soccer player Nudger didn't recognize, standing hipshot and grinning aggressively, with a ball tucked beneath his right arm. Who knew soccer players?

Crinklaw said, "Everybody's on the walls here except Joaquin Andujar. The owner hates Andujar."

"I thought he was a helluva pitcher," Nudger said. "Got a bum deal."

Crinklaw shrugged. Sports were another world. Andujar's problems were his own.

Crinklaw was a big man with a graying beard. He admired everything British; even drove a Jaguar. An Anglophile, Nudger thought people like that were called. Though Crinklaw was from Iowa, he spoke with what many thought was a British accent. It wasn't a put-on—he simply spoke that way. Often wore a blue blazer and turtleneck, too, so that with his beard and English bearing he looked as if he belonged on an ale label. He wrote straight stuff, was married to Elaine Viets, a beautiful and talented woman who had a syndicated column in the *Post-Dispatch*, and often helped Nudger by exhuming information in the newspaper's morgue. He'd even loaned Nudger money from time to time, and been paid back on schedule. That put him in a special category.

Nudger told him what he'd learned about the Hiller disappearance, and watched his calm but alert gray eyes brighten behind his glasses.

Crinklaw said, "Gad, now I see why you wanted the information you asked about." Nudger envisioned him riding to hounds on a fox hunt through the cornfields.

The blond barmaid walked over with an inquiring expression, and Nudger told her to bring a draught beer and a gin and tonic.

He filled in details for Crinklaw until she returned. She left the drinks and went back to her station near the end of the bar. She knew where to place the gin and tonic, knew by looking who was beer and who was mixed drink. That was okay by Nudger. If she was that shrewd an observer, she'd probably leave the check with Crinklaw.

He waited till Crinklaw was finished with his first gentlemanly sip, then he said, "So what did you find out?"

Crinklaw's smile was so wide it made him appear to have a handlebar mustache. "Virgil Hiller was the last important holdover from the old city administration." He tapped the side of his glass sharply with his forefinger and sat back with a satisfied expression, as if he'd scored a point. Smug Monty Python fan.

"Why's that significant?" Nudger asked. He didn't really understand politics, but politics were Crinklaw's specialty. Especially local politics.

"Because *assistant* comptroller is an appointed post, not elected. That means the present comptroller, Dan Gray, had to have wanted Hiller to stay on."

"That unusual?"

"It is in my estimation. Usually a bureaucrat likes to wipe the slate clean and bring in his own cronies. The political spoils and patronage system. Sweep clean with a new broom. That was how Gray worked it—except for Virgil Hiller. Which is odd, because Gray's a hard charger, eaten up by ambition, and Hiller's long had a reputation for being less than alert in his work. Also, the word is that his longtime drinking problem got much worse in the past couple of years."

"You mean he was a secret alcoholic?"

"Not so secret for years. Even less secret lately."

That was something Gina Hiller would hardly have confided to Bonnie during Nora Dove chitchat. "What about women? Was he a skirt chaser?"

"No. He talked a good game, but he seldom scored that anyone knew about. And they'd have known. Hiller was definitely a kiss-and-tell sort of player. He was also quite devoted to his children. Family man with an itch, I suppose you'd call him."

Nudger said, "What did you find on the Nolander plane crash?"

"Ah, here's where it gets even curiouser. The weather was clear, little wind, and Nolander and his family set off toward St. Louis from Jeff City after a fund-raiser. He was an experienced pilot, ex-military. The cause of the crash was never determined, mainly because the mechanic who'd done preflight work on the aircraft shortly before it took off disappeared and was unable to testify at the ensuing FAA investigation."

Nudger almost coughed in his beer. Set down the glass hurriedly and accidentally sloshed some of the icy liquid over his hand. "Disappeared how?"

"Simply didn't return to the furnished room where he'd lived in Jeff City for the last two years. None of his clothes seemed to be missing, but who knows? He was a kind of drifter. From California, originally. Name was Del Westerson. Does that strike a chord?"

Nudger remembered reading Westerson's name, briefly mentioned in the newspaper accounts just after the crash, but the microfilm copies Nudger had scanned at the library hadn't quite reached the date of the FAA investigation.

"Not much of a chord," he said. "What was the theory at the time?"

"Officially or otherwise?"

Nudger said, "Both ways."

"The official line was that there was no connection between the plane crash and Westerson's disappearance, merely coincidence. Unofficially, the feeling was that Westerson had gotten scared after the crash. Knew how the FAA would dig into it and knew how intensely he'd be grilled. So he decided to cut and run. He was the type."

"How come he was working on Nolander's plane in the first place?"

"He was an employee at the airport. Doing regular fueling and maintenance for the pilots who frequented the place. I know what you're thinking, and there was never anything but mild speculation that he'd sabotaged the plane." Crinklaw made a wry face and raised his shoulders so turtleneck sweater met beard. "Private planes do fall from the sky, Nudge. People die."

"Secretaries run away with their bosses, too."

"Gad, yes. Every day, somewhere. Maybe every hour. How the business world often works, I'm afraid; people aren't computers, thank God. Listen, Nudge, you didn't give me much time on this. I'll keep looking, and I'll call you if I find anything else, okay?"

"Fine. Thanks, Don."

Crinklaw glanced at his watch. "One o'clock. They serve sandwiches here. What say to a spot of lunch?"

Nudger agreed. He had to eat to energize the old machine, keep flailing away at the world. Got tougher every year. Time working away, being persistent. It was showing in the mirror lately, hairline a bit more receded, glimmer in the eyes slightly dimmed, another seam here, deeper one there; Dorian Gray bullshit.

"How's Claudia?" Crinklaw asked.

Nudger mumbled that she was fine. Possibly she was. He'd give anything to make her fine. Anything.

"Good." Crinklaw raised a forefinger and his bearded chin to signal the barmaid, maybe pretending he was in a London pub. He smiled at Nudger and said, "There's no menu, but everything's quite tasty here."

They had open-faced beef sandwiches and another round of drinks. It was a waste of good food. Nudger hardly knew what he was eating. He wasn't the best company. Through most of lunch he sat silently, absently chewing. Reminding himself now and then to swallow.

Thinking.

After lunch he went back to his office, refused free pastry from Danny, and thought some more. Tried to add what he knew and get a sum of at least partial understanding. He had no success.

At three o'clock Crinklaw, British bulldog with a bone to worry, phoned him with more odds-and-ends information about the Nolander plane crash.

When Nudger was about to leave to meet Claudia at her apartment as she came home from work, the penny dropped, the doors in his mind opened, and suddenly he knew how it must have been.

He called Adelaide at the library and asked her if she could get away early and meet him as soon as possible at her apartment. She caught the anticipation in his voice and agreed at once.

Nudger could get there before she did, so he had about fifteen minutes before it was time to leave. He made a few more phone calls, then held the cradle button down for a second with his thumb, let it snap up, and pecked out Claudia's number with a pencil.

He was surprised when she answered.

"Home early?" he asked.

"They insisted I leave. Thought they were doing me a favor." She paused. "Maybe they are."

Her voice sounded normal enough, he thought. "You okay?"

"We'll find out tomorrow, won't we?"

He said, "I'll come over later tonight, all right?"

"Not all right if you don't. What time?"

"Can't be sure, but I'll be there."

"Something happening on the missing secretary case?"

"I think so."

She said, "Do your job before you come here. I mean that. I'll see you afterward, whatever time it is."

"Claudia—"

"I mean it, Nudger."

"I love you," Nudger said. "You're what they call class."

"I guess a lot depends on who 'they' are."

— 225 —

"I'm they."

"If you love me, be careful."

"You betcha." He meant *that*.

But he wasn't careful enough to realize he was being followed when he left his office.

33

Low lead-colored clouds were spitting rain when Nudger parked on Oleatha Avenue across from Adelaide's apartment. She lived in a large brick building with green-striped metal awnings. Ornate concrete urns, containing a few scraggly geraniums and a lot of something green and viny, flanked the steps off the sidewalk. The pavement was multishaded from the beginning rain, patterned wildly like modern art in mottled shades of gray.

Nudger jogged through the rain and entered the vestibule. Brushing water off his corduroy sportcoat, he pushed the intercom button for Adelaide's apartment.

A metallic voice said something unintelligible.

Nudger leaned close to the intercom. "It's Nudger!"

"'M'on up."

He began climbing the stairs. He felt the strain in his thighs and realized he was tired; his night had been restless and his day had started early and been a rough one. But he was sure that at the top of the stairs, in Adelaide's apartment, was the answer to the disappearance of Hiller and Mary Lacy.

Adelaide was standing waiting for him with the door open. She couldn't have been home long. She was still wearing the gray skirt and white cardigan sweater she'd had on at the library, but she'd unpinned her blond hair and let it tumble down over her shoulders. Her hair picked up the rose in the hall carpet, the bounce of light off the pale blue walls. Nudger thought, the beautiful sister.

She smiled nervously at him and stood back, moving her high heels on the carpet in a precise pattern like a dance step. "You've found out something about Mary?"

"Maybe."

He brushed past her and went into the apartment. He noticed for the first time that, though the furniture seemed to have been chosen and placed randomly, there was a subtle order to the place; it didn't reek of decorator, but there was a distinct scent. Though most of the furnishings were traditional, the sofa appeared to be a genuine antique, a reupholstered creation with what Nudger thought were Queen Anne legs. Queen Anne must have been some number.

The dining room was adjacent to the living room, separated only by a wooden arch. It contained a dark drop-leaf table and a tall china cabinet lined with blue dishes behind glass doors. The kitchen, he recalled, was beyond a door at the other end of the dining room, out of sight. There was a hall off the living room, leading to dimness and a closed door Nudger assumed would open to the bedroom.

Adelaide said, "Sit down, please—tell me about it."

"Tell all of us about it," a voice said.

Adelaide hadn't locked her door. Arnie Kyle had walked right in. Jack Palp stood beside and slightly behind him, kept his eerie smile and his dark eyes aimed at Nudger as he twisted his body slightly and closed the door. *He* thought to lock it. Kyle was wearing a well-cut gray suit with light pinstripes and dark rain spots. Palp had on a long black plastic raincoat, probably the kind that folded into a small package and could be kept in a suitcase or glove compartment.

Adelaide's blue eyes widened as if she didn't know whether to be scared or angry. "Mr. Kyle!"

He nodded, as if politely acknowledging her greeting at a social event, and said, "Miss Lacy."

"You and your friend can't just barge in this way!"

Kyle said, "Shut up, Miss Lacy," in the same courteous tone. Maybe next he'd inquire about her health.

Adelaide stuck out her chin and stepped toward him. Her fists were clenched.

Nudger said, "Adelaide, better sit here with me." He lowered himself to sit on the antique sofa.

She paused, though it was obvious that she didn't like it. Her lower lip trembled, jaw still jutting. Feisty as well as beautiful. Then she backed to the sofa, glaring at Kyle and Palp, and sat down alongside Nudger.

Kyle looked mildly concerned. Palp wore a lazy, watchful expression. Like something sunning itself after a meal of flies and spiders.

Kyle gave Nudger his attention and said, "We had a talk with a Mr. Crinklaw, then drove over to your office to chat with you. When we saw you driving away, we followed, even though there was no need. I worked it out the same as you did, Nudger."

"Worked what out?"

"Play dumb some more," Palp said. "You're the best at it."

Kyle shot him a cautioning glance, said, "Jack." Palp seemed not to notice.

"What's happening here?" Adelaide asked in a squeaking voice. "Worked what out?"

"Nudger was about to tell us," Kyle said. "What say we let him talk?"

Nudger sat silently. His stomach had become a nasty, clawed thing stirring around restlessly, starting to cause pain.

Kyle looked at Palp, who drew a small, dark revolver from the pocket of his plastic raincoat and aimed it at Nudger. This one wasn't the scare-tactic cannon Palp had used to threaten him at Scullin Steel. It was a pro's gun, very businesslike. Small caliber and with a soft enough report not to attract much attention, but lethal enough in capable hands; dead was dead.

Palp said, "If you're shy, here's a little conversational aid that'll break the ice."

At the sight of the gun, fear won out over anger in Adelaide. Sensible woman. She said, "Better go ahead and tell them. Please!" Nudger thought inanely that she didn't want blood on her carpet. Well, he didn't, either.

He said, "Virgil Hiller is dead. He knew too much, and he drank too much, and it killed him."

"Because he talked too much," Palp said.

Again Kyle flicked his eyes to Palp, signaling him to be quiet, let Nudger roll.

"Talked about what?" Adelaide asked.

"In nineteen eighty-one," Nudger said, "Kyle decided he wanted more control over the city government he'd corrupted. He wanted his own comptroller in office, cooking the books, diverting tax money. The advantages for somebody in Kyle's business could be enormous. But the problem was that the office of comptroller is elective. And the comptroller was planning on running again and, since he hadn't committed rape, murder, or general mayhem, was a shoo-in; it's that kind of office. His name was Marvin Nolander, and he and his family died in a plane crash that conveniently left the office open. The election was near, so a political hack interim comptroller was appointed to take over Nolander's duties. Until Kyle's man could be elected."

"How did they know he *would* be elected?" Adelaide asked.

Kyle chuckled at her naïveté.

"It's pretty much a one-party city," Nudger said, "but Kyle didn't take any chances. He intimidated the opposing candidate and saw that his man ran unopposed."

"Won in a landslide," Kyle said, smiling. He and Palp were both smiling. The catbird seat was big enough for two.

"At the time," Nudger said, "Virgil Hiller was assistant comptroller. When Kyle's man, Dan Gray, took over the office after the election, he appointed his own staff members. All except Hiller, who stayed on even though he was an inept product of cronyism who, under normal circumstances, would have been first out the door after the election."

Kyle chuckled again and said, "The strange bedfellows of politics."

"And of murder," Nudger said. "A mechanic name of Del Westerson, who'd worked on Nolander's plane before it took off from Jefferson City, conveniently dropped from sight and didn't testify at the FAA hearing to determine the cause of the crash. That was because *he* was the cause. And Westerson was what Hiller had on Kyle and his clique that had gained political power. It was the only way an obnoxious incompetent like Hiller could hang onto his job while Kyle controlled his boss, the new comptroller, Dan Gray. Hiller knew Westerson had been paid to sabotage Nolander's plane. He also knew that after the crash Kyle had Westerson killed to ensure his silence.

"Hiller could have revealed the entire mess, but he decided to use his knowledge to his advantage. Kyle couldn't risk murdering him to shut him up. Hiller's death might serve to draw more suspicion to the circumstances of the Nolander plane crash. No one wanted the ashes stirred, so accommodations were made, and Hiller stayed in the comptroller's office."

"That was all long before Mary became his secretary," Adelaide said.

Nudger said, "She was drawn into this, had no choice. During the last few years, Hiller's drinking problem got worse, and his tongue got loose. Kyle realized he might slip and tell someone how he'd been able to stay in office and collect blackmail money the last eight years. Hiller was no longer an acceptable risk. He was also no fool, and Kyle knew it. Knew Hiller had stashed proof of the Nolander and Westerson murders somewhere, and in such a way that it would surface if he met a premature death."

Palp moved a step to the side, his plastic raincoat rustling. "You got this pretty well puzzled out, Nudger. You're not such a lunkhead detective after all."

Nudger ignored him; he was talking to Adelaide. "They solved their problem by murdering Hiller and making it appear that he'd absconded with city money—money Kyle now has. But before killing him, they tortured him. Thinking he was bargaining for his life, his mind clouded by pain, Hiller gave up his proof of the murders."

"Gave it up rather easily," Kyle said. "Makes me wonder why we endured him all these years."

"What about Mary?" Adelaide asked, scooting forward to sit on the edge of the sofa.

"Hiller must have confessed he'd given a copy of his proof to his secretary for added insurance."

"Exactly," Kyle said.

Adelaide said, "The brown envelope."

Nudger gripped the cool flesh of her arm. "They must have tortured Mary until she told them she'd left the envelope with you."

"You mean she's . . ."

A boiling rage tore at Nudger's stomach. He glared at Kyle and Palp. Said, "Ask them."

Palp said, "'Fraid so, sweets. I'll tell you, though, she lasted longer than Hiller before she emptied out. Long as some of the slants I interrogated in 'Nam. You oughta be proud of little Mary."

Adelaide expelled more air than Nudger would have thought possible. She turned white and slumped back into the sofa. He squeezed her arm, which had become even colder and oddly limp, almost like the arm of a corpse.

Kyle gazed remotely at her while Palp seemed amused.

Nudger swallowed and said, "What did you do to Crinklaw?"

Palp laughed his girlish giggle. "Scared him, is all. Made some imaginative threats regarding his wife. Man loves his wife more than he loves you, Nudger, so it had to work. He mentioned Dobbs's second visit, and we reasoned the thing out same as you."

Nudger thought of Claudia and couldn't blame Crinklaw.

John Wayne was dead and in the ground and had never been real anyway. Name was actually Marion something.

Adelaide was staring at Nudger, her eyes wide and without depth. "What's he mean, Nudger?"

"Kyle had you look for the envelope on his first visit, which was when Dobbs was here. But Kyle didn't know it was Dobbs's *second* visit. After seeing the photograph he'd taken of Hiller dead, Dobbs searched Mary's apartment and learned she'd left the envelope with you. You must have told her where you'd put it and she'd made a note of it, or left some indication that could be figured out, because he even knew that."

Adelaide nodded, remembering.

"Dobbs's first visit here was actually to sneak the envelope away, which he managed. But after seeing what was inside, he realized he was a small-timer onto something big-time and dangerous. He also knew that if Kyle followed in his footsteps and the envelope was missing, he'd be suspected; he'd already told too many people about the Hiller photo. So he photographed the envelope's contents, and his second visit—when Kyle was here—was to secretly return the envelope to the closet shelf. Only he hadn't had an opportunity to do it before Kyle arrived. That's why the envelope was gone when you went to get it from the closet. After Kyle left, Dobbs stayed a while. Did he have a chance to sneak into the bedroom and replace the envelope?"

"He told me he was thirsty," Adelaide said. "I went to the kitchen and made coffee. But when I got back, he was sitting right where he'd been when I left the room."

"How long were you gone?"

"Five minutes or so. Enough time for him to do what you described."

Nudger looked at Kyle and said, "Then you caught up with Dobbs and killed him, too."

"Not yet," Kyle said. "But we will. If he's ever dumb enough to return to the Western Hemisphere."

Adelaide started to stand, but Kyle held up a hand palm out in a signal for her to stay seated, and she settled back down.

Her body was tense and trembling; Nudger could feel the vibration through the sofa. He felt like Dobbs—a small-timer in over his head. Kyle had warned him about deep water, but he hadn't listened; he'd swum too far out to sea, and now here he was drowning. Maybe some of the trembling was his own.

Kyle raised an eyebrow and glanced at Palp.

Said, "Pop these two, Jack, while I go get the envelope."

34

Palp smiled and leveled the wicked little revolver.

Nudger's stomach twisted, turned, knotted. Staring into the implacable eye of the gun's black bore, he said, "I wouldn't just yet."

"Bet not," Palp said.

"I mean, we got some things to talk about." Nudger's voice whined with desperation. He wasn't embarrassed. Beside him, Adelaide was gripping her knees with whitened knuckles, her breathing harsh and irregular. She couldn't agree more with Nudger that it wasn't time for them to die; the door couldn't slam so abruptly on the years, the minutes they'd assumed lay ahead.

Palp gave his brittle, broken-crystal chuckle. He was getting his jollies, all right. "Things to talk about, huh? Believe me, Nudger, everybody feels that way. Fact is, your time for talking's all over. You just don't like believing it. Rather think you'll live a hundred years."

"I'd settle for making octogenarian."

"Octogenarian, sagittarian, vegetarian, preacher, or sinner.

It doesn't matter; eventually we all sleep forever. It's time to tuck you in."

Kyle had paused in the hall, not liking the way the sadistic Palp was stringing this out. "Dammit, Jack! Do what you got to!"

Something made the hair on the back of Nudger's neck stir. Something only he was aware of. A feeling that became faint sound. It was almost as if he possessed an animal's keen hearing and could pick it up before mere humans.

The distant baying of sirens.

"You oughta know I called the police before I came here," he stammered. "I mean, I wasn't dumb enough not to cover myself. You *do* know that. *Don't* you?"

Not listening, Palp said, "Ladies first," and raised the revolver with both hands, aimed at Adelaide.

Adelaide sucked in what she thought was her last breath, a frantic, rasping shriek.

The sirens meant nothing. Death was too close.

"Hold up, Jack!"

Kyle's voice.

He paced back into the living room. "Listen!"

Palp reluctantly lowered the gun.

"Sirens," Kyle said. "Maybe he's *not* bluffing."

"He's trying to talk himself alive," Palp said. "That's all this is about. Every word's another second he exists. It's a natural reaction to the gun. I've seen it happen lots of times."

But Kyle slowly raised a manicured hand and let it float before him, as if he were a monarch waiting for his ring to be kissed, and both men stood quietly for a moment, their heads cocked to the side, listening.

There wasn't any doubt—the sirens were getting closer, their baying now a distinct, impatient yodeling as the vehicles wended their way through obstructing traffic.

Palp stared intently at Nudger with bleak dark eyes as human as a reptile's. Eyes that had seen so much death they'd become death. Then he seemed to reach a conclusion.

"He's bluffing," he said. "Those are probably fire engines.

Maybe an ambulance; they can raise a helluva racket some-times, like they got a dozen sirens."

Kyle said, "I'm not so sure."

Nudger, forcing breath and words, caught Kyle's eye. "You haven't personally murdered anyone yet," he said.

Palp said, "Shut your face, Nudger."

Nudger figured he had everything to gain by continuing talking. As Palp had pointed out, every word was another sec-ond of existence, another pearl in the string. And he had Kyle's attention; he could feel it. Had him where it counted. "After Palp does us with that gun, if you're stopped in or around this building with that envelope you can be thinking about life in prison and maybe the gas chamber. And the envelope'll do something else—it'll nail you for the Nolander murder. Even your high-powered attorneys won't be able to help you. They'll go through the motions and collect their fee, then they'll write you off and won't even be there to hold your hand when the pellet drops."

Palp knew Nudger was playing on Kyle's nerves and was getting irritated, not having nerves himself. The aim of the revolver had remained steady. Palp's torso and extended arms might as well have been sculptured steel. "Don't listen to his bullshit, Arnie. Let's do it to these two, then grab the envelope and get outta here."

But Kyle was wavering. The sirens were getting louder, closer, their shrillness boring deep into his courage. He glared at Palp. Said, "So it's 'Arnie,' is it?"

"Okay, it's 'Mr. Kyle.' But there's no reason to believe this asshole. He doesn't want to die, that's all."

"No reason? Listen to the fuckin' reason! He says he called the cops, and we can hear mother-lovin' sirens!"

"Said he called the cops *after* we heard the sirens," Palp noted.

Kyle couldn't stand still. He slid his hands in his pants pockets, then immediately pulled them out. Ran his fingers through his hair, wiped his hands on his thighs. Paced to the window and looked outside.

His body stiffened and he leaned on the sill, supporting himself with both hands and peering between the blind slats. "Jesus! There's a car parked across the street, and the driver's sitting there staring up at this window!"

Palp glanced his way, then back to sight along the gun barrel. "Police car?"

"An old Plymouth. Guy in it's not in uniform. Dressed like a regular street turkey. Undercover shit, Jack. You can spot it a mile off."

"Maybe he's not a cop."

"C'mon now, Jack."

"Maybe it's got nothing to do with us."

Nudger said, "Don't be silly. What are the odds?"

Palp said, "Shut up, goddamn you!"

Kyle drew back from the window as if the sill had suddenly gotten too hot for his hands. The sirens continued to yowl like hounds on the hunt. "We're getting out, Jack. Now!"

Palp licked his lips, his dark eyes glowing. He was set to kill, having a hard time deprogramming himself. "Listen, Mr, Kyle—"

"Let's move, Jack!"

Kyle bolted for the door.

Not at all spooked, Palp held his breath for a long moment, as if to steady himself to squeeze off a shot.

Then he exhaled, lowering the revolver. He smiled resignedly and shook his head, disappointed, then followed Kyle. Nudger listened to the clamor of their footsteps as they ran down the stairs toward the vestibule and street door.

He stood up on shaky legs and made his way to the window. Behind him Adelaide said, "Thank God you weren't bluffing. You really *did* call the police."

Nudger looked out the window. Tad's old Plymouth was parked across the street. Tad himself—skinny kid in faded jeans, oversized boots, and a flappy red T-shirt—had climbed out of the car and was crossing the street toward the apartment building. Figuring Nudger was two-timing his mom, probably, and wanting to make sure.

Loping straight toward the door Kyle and Palp would burst out of any second.

"Christ!" Nudger moaned, and raced for the door to the hall.

"Nudger!" Adelaide yelled.

She shouted something else, but Nudger was already half-running, half-falling down the stairs, and he didn't understand her.

On the second-floor landing, Palp looked up and saw him. Couldn't believe it at first. Then said almost happily, "Here comes a dead man."

"No, Jack!" Kyle yelled. "We're outta here! And now!"

Palp was still holding the revolver. But he was a good soldier and couldn't disobey a command from his superior.

He waved the gun helplessly at Nudger, then spun on his heel and ran after Kyle.

Nudger had barely paused. He was on the second-floor landing, bouncing off the wall like a two-cushion billiard shot, throwing himself at Palp and Kyle before they could reach the bottom of the stairs.

Landed on Palp's back. Knocked both of them into Kyle and sent him crashing against a closed door. All three men went sprawling. Somebody said, "Uumph!" Nudger wasn't sure who. Might have been him.

Palp sprang upright with panther grace and swept the gun across Nudger's head, grazing him behind the ear.

Nudger was slumped where they'd have to climb over him, his head pulsing with pain. A glossy black shoe mashed down on one of his fingers. He grabbed at Palp's leg, gripped a pants cuff, and tried desperately to hang on.

The door Kyle had landed against swung open. "Through here!" he gasped. "We'll get out through the goddamn basement."

The pants cuff was yanked painfully from Nudger's grasp as Kyle and Palp struggled through the narrow doorway. There was cleaning paraphernalia—mops, brooms, bottles, and some square metal cans—on the landing just inside the door. His balance upset by Nudger's grip on his leg, Palp caught his foot on something, and mops and cans and bottles and Palp tumbled down the stairs, knocking Kyle over.

Both men scrambled to their feet at the base of the steps. Nudger wasn't thinking now. Only reacting. He was a lot of things, and stubborn was one of them. His eyes watering from the stench and fumes of spilled cleaning fluid, he hurled himself down the stairs after Kyle and Palp, into the dim basement.

His fingers closed on the back of Palp's plastic raincoat, but he couldn't hold onto the slick surface. He slid down Palp's body to the concrete floor. There was broken glass around him. A piece bit into the heel of his hand. Palp and Kyle backed several steps away, out of his reach.

Palp said, "Fucker's game. He won't quit," and raised the revolver.

Kyle's shadowed face was contorted, his mouth twisted and open wide. "Jack, don't!"

The muzzle flashed brilliant orange in the dimness.

An iron fist slammed into Nudger's shoulder, throwing him backward. He was on the floor, aware that the back of his head had struck hard. The shoulder was numb but his head hurt terribly. He knew he'd been shot, though he hadn't heard the gun's report. It had all been too sudden and mind-boggling.

It did seem, he realized in his cocoon of shock and silence, that the muzzle flare had been out of proportion to the size of the gun. Like a blossoming orange flower.

Someone was screaming. He craned his neck so he could see beyond his awkwardly twisted legs.

Palp was dancing in a circle, his right hand and arm on fire. The gunshot had ignited the cleaning fluid he'd slopped through on his tumble down the stairs. He'd dropped the gun and was struggling with the plastic raincoat's buttons, waving the blazing arm as if the movement of air might put out the flames. But it was no use; the coat was melting, sticking to his clothing and skin, and the flames were spreading. Palp's right side was on fire now. His back. His mad dance became more frantic.

The basement was filled with a nauseating, acrid-sweet smell of burning plastic and flesh.

Kyle was yelling, "Roll on the floor, Jack! Roll on the floor!" Paralyzed by what he was seeing, he stood rigidly, leaning toward Palp but unable to budge, unable to help. The glow of the spectacle flickered across his horrified features.

Finally he moaned, "Oh, shit!" and turned and sprinted for the dusty rectangle of light that was the window in the basement door.

A blue uniform barged in through the door, framed for an instant by the angular glare of outside light. Gathered the fleeing Kyle into his arms like a possessive lover.

Then spurned him by shoving him hard against the concrete wall. Dug a gun barrel into the small of his back and yelled something at him.

More blue uniforms. Leather soles scraping concrete. Low curses. Scuffling and loud, rapid breathing.

Nudger tried to move but couldn't. He was aware of someone choking, someone beating at Palp with a uniform jacket. The jacket threw madly waltzing shadows on the walls and sounded like a flag flapping in the wind. A voice yelled, "Fire extinguisher! Fast, dammit!"

More shadowed movement. Lights winking on, but not bright. The gurgling hiss of a fire extinguisher.

Another voice. Nearby. "Hey, this one's hurt!"

God, the stench!

Then Hammersmith was there, but not smoking a cigar; couldn't blame *him* for what had happened to the air in the basement. He was blocking the light, his bulk looming mountainous over Nudger. Bending down close.

Chanting in a chiding but genuinely concerned voice, "Nudge, Nudge, Nudge . . ."

Nudger rolled his eyes and saw the foam-coated, smoldering thing that had been Jack Palp. Thought about a long-ago campfire and toasted, burst marshmallows.

He wondered if Palp had lived long enough to realize the phone call to the law hadn't been a bluff.

35

When Nudger floated to consciousness, Hammersmith was still standing over him. The reason eluded Nudger. His mouth was dry and tasted like cotton—no, there actually *was* a shred of cotton stuck to his upper gum, above his front teeth. Yuk! He peeled most of it away from the gum with the tip of his tongue. Pain. Not just his mouth. His body was stiff and his shoulder ached. Throbbed in time with his heartbeat.

Suddenly he remembered. *He'd been shot!*

He spat cotton and tried to sit up, but a jolt of *real* pain knocked him back down and his head sank into his pillow.

Which is when he realized he was in a bed. A minty, medicinal scent floated in the air; nothing like Max Hawk. His eyes darted around. Hospital room. A glucose bottle hung suspended like a bulbous spider alongside the bed, its clear plastic tube coiling down to a needle inserted into a vein in the back of his right hand. Patch of white tape there. Mottled purple bruise.

His abrupt movement had caused his head to explode in

agony. The pain gradually lessened as he lay perfectly motionless.

Hammersmith leaned closer and said, "Ah, you're awake!"

Nudger looked up into his smooth, broad face. Hammersmith appeared immensely pleased, his sharp blue eyes glinting in their pads of flesh. Were those tears? No, couldn't be.

It was obvious to Nudger that he'd passed out in the basement of Adelaide Lacy's apartment building and that he'd been rushed here and undergone an operation to have Palp's bullet removed from his shoulder. But he was still groggy, his mind functioning in a haze. Anesthetic hangover, probably. With a pang of dread, he wondered how badly he was injured.

His disorientation and fear must have registered on his face, because Hammersmith said, "Don't worry, Nudge, your shoulder's gonna be okay. There can be bowling in your future. And Palp's dead and Arnie Kyle's in custody without bond."

Palp and Kyle.

Nudger said, "What was in the envelope?"

Hammersmith grinned. "A detailed explanation of Nolander's murder. Along with blueprints for the downtown Adamson Hotel, built shortly thereafter, with the spot marked where Del Westerson's corpse was encased in concrete. A traditional way to get rid of a body, eh?" He shook his head as if disappointed by the lack of imagination in big-time crime. "What's left of Westerson was recovered this morning, even though Kyle's lawyers delayed things by claiming the hotel might collapse if a crew broke into the concrete at that point with jackhammers."

Nudger managed a smile. Lawyers were some pumpkins. He'd split his upper lip. Tasted the salt of blood. He said, "Then I was right."

"Sure. All the way down the line. You're slicker'n okra, Nudge."

"Charges gonna stick?"

Hammersmith nodded firmly, his smooth jowls jiggling and spilling over his blue collar. "They'll stick, all right. We'll see indictments for Kyle, Gray, and just about everybody else we find in the net. Maybe even hizzoner the mayor. The corruption spread, like it always does, just like Kyle planned. You've stirred up enough of the past to bring down most of the city government. Make it crash and burn like Nolander's plane. The news media and Board of Aldermen are going nuts. Lots of clamor for a special general election. My guess is it'll come to pass. Change politics in this city forever."

Hammersmith was as ebullient as Nudger had ever seen him. Some of the police department higher-ups had to know they'd be implicated in the cover-up if not the crime, and right now they were sweating blood; Hammersmith was an honest cop and enjoyed that. He absently pulled a cigar from his shirt pocket, then remembered where he was and slid it back in, still in its cellophane wrapper. The crinkling of the wrapper reminded Nudger of Palp and his plastic raincoat. His stomach lurched and bile rose like acid in his throat.

"You all right, Nudge?"

Nudger swallowed. Coughed. His throat still burned. "Sure."

Hammersmith gently patted Nudger's good shoulder. "You did one helluva job. Got the bad guys falling all over themselves trying to cover their asses."

Something Hammersmith had said echoed in Nudger's mind. "You mentioned Kyle's lawyers delayed you, but that Westerson's body was recovered this morning."

"Sure. 'Bout two hours ago."

"But I was at Adelaide Lacy's—got shot—just yesterday evening."

"Two evenings ago, to be exact," Hammersmith said. "You were zonked out all day yesterday and last night, Nudge."

Yesterday and last night!

Nudger ignored the pain and sat up straight.

Said, "Claudia!"

36

She said, "I still can't get over it. You were in the hospital longer than I was."

Nudger watched Claudia walk across her living room toward the kitchen. His favorite walk to watch. She was wearing her blue robe and slippers but still had on her pantyhose from work. Even in floppy slippers, the line of her ankles was exquisite; every part of her seemed to move with the rhythm of the universe. Maybe, to Nudger, she was indeed the universe. The deep emerald mystery of life.

The conization tissue sample taken from her cervix had tested benign. A noncancerous infection only, which had been easily removed during a D and C after her operation. She'd come home from Deaconess Hospital that same day, while Nudger still lay unconscious at Incarnate Word after the operation on his shoulder.

Claudia—young and healthy Claudia—sauntered back into the living room, carrying a whiskey sour for her and a glass of beer for Nudger. He was slouched on her sofa, watching the second inning of a scoreless Cardinals ball game with the despised New York Mets on television. The Cards were driving for the Eastern Division championship, but they had to play consistently well. Better than well. The pressure was on them. Nudger thought it was a nice change to witness someone else under pressure.

Claudia handed him his beer and settled down beside him. Close to him. Sipped her drink and sighed. He caught the fresh scent of her perfumed shampoo, felt the warmth of her hip and thigh. God, it was good to have her alive and near him!

Ozzie Smith, the Cards acrobatic shortstop, made a diving catch of a Mets line drive. Pressure didn't bother *him*. Nudger slopped beer onto his chin and said, "The guy has no equal!"

Claudia said, "Neither do you."

Her interest in baseball was minimal. And it had been a long time since Nudger had played a tentative center field in a kids league in Forest Park. No equal. She couldn't be talking about baseball.

He wiped his chin with the palm of his hand and wriggled his fingers as the dampness evaporated. Then he leaned back into the soft cushions and considered recent events and where they had left the people involved. Took one of those infrequent time-outs from life and assessed the game from the bench.

Most important: Claudia was healthy.

Mary Lacy was dead. Had been dead when her sister, Adelaide, hired him to find her. She'd been found, all right, and Adelaide's nightmare had proved true. As in most of Nudger's cases, he'd merely confirmed his client's despair; that was the nature of his business.

Virgil Hiller was dead. His and Mary's bodies had been recovered at the same construction site.

Jack Palp was dead.

Arnie Kyle, Mayor Faherty, and at least a dozen lesser local politicians, police brass, and crime figures were on the conveyer belt to prison. The city would never be the same, even if the world hadn't changed.

Paul Dobbs had read the papers and ventured back home.

Bonnie and her brood had adjusted with apparent ease to life without Nudger. Especially Tad.

Nudger was alive, a condition that, for a while, had been in serious doubt. He'd almost recovered the full range of motion in his right shoulder. The doctors had told him it would ache on damp days but would otherwise not inhibit him, and that was pretty much how it had shaped up.

Claudia rested her head on his uninjured shoulder. The Cards were taking their turn at bat.

With a warm rush of contentment, Nudger sipped his beer and waited for the next pitch. All in all, his life was approximately as it had been before Adelaide Lacy jogged across the street toward the doughnut shop and hired him.

Could be worse. For the first time in a while, the future seemed manageable.

The next pitch was a curve.